internal 1 JUL 2016
fifteen million
has achieved the
bestseller in all five Nord

She has been awarded numero
the inaugural Petrona award for b
crime novel of the year 2013 for *Last Will*,
nomination for the Glass Key for best Scandi
crime novel.

Visit her website at www.lizamarklund.com

Neil Smith studied Scandinavian Studies at University
College London, and lived in Stockholm for several
years. He now lives in Norfolk.

THE FINAL WORD

Liza Marklund

Translated from the Swedish by Neil Smith

CORGI BOOKS

TRANSWORLD PUBLISHERS
61–63 Uxbridge Road, London W5 5SA
www.transworldbooks.co.uk

Transworld is part of the Penguin Random House group of companies
whose addresses can be found at global.penguinrandomhouse.com

Penguin
Random House
UK

Originally published in Swedish by Piratförlaget in 2015
as *Järnblod*

First published in Great Britain in 2016 by Corgi
an imprint of Transworld Publishers

A CIP catalogue record for this book
is available from the British Library.

ISBN
9780552170970

Typeset in 11/14.5 pt Sabon by Jouve (UK), Milton Keynes

Printed and bound in Great Britain by Clays Ltd, Bungay, Suffolk.

Pengu
future for
made

THE FINAL WORD

MONDAY, 1 JUNE

This was the last body.

It was a powerful feeling, a sort of farewell. The setting was beautiful, in its barren, unassuming way, and over the course of time it had become almost sacred: the rough moraine, the shimmering trunks of the dry pines, the birch with its mouse-ear leaves.

Already eight had ended up here, and this was the ninth. He remembered them all, not so much their faces as their tones, their frequencies, the vibration that had been their lifeline. No more now.

He looked down at the last body. Jeans and trainers, a shirt, belt, brown jacket. A perfect example of *Homo sapiens*. He'd had the chance to get to know this one: they'd spent some time together. Nice clothes. Every now and then he felt sad that he'd had to eliminate them, all their lovely belongings, given that he had been brought up to be thrifty, to look after the Earth's resources in a humble and responsible way.

He glanced up at the sky. It was so low here, near

to the Arctic Circle, the clouds skimming just above people's heads, combing their eyebrows. Soon the sun wouldn't be going down, not until autumn when the cold bit the leaves off the trees and the Russian winter rolled in from the east.

He missed his brother. All their lives they had been mirror images of each other, sharing thoughts and feelings, but now he sensed the abyss. He kept himself updated about developments in the high-security courtroom, but the loneliness tormented him, and he was no good at dealing with pain.

He wiped the slaughter mask on the moss.

He would have to share the pain.

'You had a breakdown,' the psychologist said. 'That's what happened, isn't it?'

Annika Bengtzon squirmed in the armchair. She felt too skinny and sharp for the clumsy piece of furniture. She was holding on to its arms to stop herself drowning, could feel that her palms were sticky. How many others had sat there in a cold sweat, leaving their angst-ridden excretions in the rough fabric? She snatched her hands away from the armrests and clasped them tightly in her lap. 'I've been to the health centre, and occupational health,' she said, 'and they examined me all over. There's nothing physically wrong with me, so . . . Jimmy, my partner, suggested I come here.'

'It wasn't your decision?'

Annika glanced at the woman on the other side of the wooden table, her face as neutral as her voice and haircut. What was she really thinking? That Annika was ridiculous for making an appointment to see her? That she was using up time that could have been spent with someone who really needed it? Or was she just interested in the fee?

Annika reached for the glass of water on the table between them and drank some. There was a box of tissues beside it. Was she supposed to cry? 'I've got to do something because I frighten the children. Or I did, that one time.'

'When they found you having a panic attack?'

Annika shifted in the chair again. She couldn't find a comfortable position, so she gave up and tried to relax.

'Can you tell me what happened?'

The ceiling light reflected off the psychologist's glasses. This was just an ordinary day at work for her – maybe she'd have lasagne for lunch, go for a walk and pick up her dry-cleaning.

'I . . . It was in the hall. I collapsed, couldn't breathe. Everything went black . . . It was just as Serena and Jacob got home from school – they're Jimmy's children. They called an ambulance.' She drank some more water. 'When it arrived I sent it away again.'

'You knew what had happened to you?'

The darkness, shadows swirling, snatching the air . . . Her hands were burning, her eyes stung, her legs had given way and the oxygen had run out. Then the darkness had swallowed her. But she hadn't died. She cleared her throat. 'There's nothing wrong with me.'

'Do you know what panic disorder is?'

Oh, yes. She'd googled it secretly. Normal, healthy

people weren't tormented by darkness and ghosts. 'My life's all sorted now. I don't feel bad. I'm not depressed, really not.'

'People can be depressed without being aware of it,' the psychologist said. 'A lot of people who have a panic attack think it's their heart and end up in A and E.'

'But why has it got worse?' Annika looked out of the window. It had been raining all morning, and water was still trickling down the pane. 'My life has never been so good. Jimmy and I have a great relationship, we have the kids, I'm happy at work, my ex-husband is behaving himself. I've even become friendly with Sophia, the woman he had an affair with . . .'

'So what do you think is going on?'

Anger flared. Was she supposed to come up with all the answers? What was she paying the woman for? Her jaw tensed.

'Your father died when you were a teenager,' the psychologist went on, leafing through her notes. 'Were you close to him?'

Annika rubbed her hands on her jeans. 'That was such a long time ago, more than twenty years now.'

The room fell silent. The traffic in the street outside roared. The tissue sticking out of the box trembled in an almost imperceptible draught. The cover of the armchair was scratching her back.

'But your mother's still alive? How is your relationship with her?'

Annika looked at her watch. 'When can I leave?'

The psychologist leaned back in her chair. 'We can stop now, if you like.'

Annika stayed where she was. Was she being thrown out? Even though she was paying eleven hundred kronor for an hour? 'Do you want me to go?'

The psychologist glanced at the clock on the wall. 'We still have some time. It's up to you whether you choose to stay or leave.'

The room shrank.

The woman smiled at her. 'I'd like you to stay.'

The sound of the traffic faded.

Annika steeled herself. 'She . . . my mother doesn't like me.'

'Why do you think that?'

'She and my father had to get married because of me. She couldn't go to art school and she's never forgiven me.'

The psychologist looked at her for a few moments, then at her notes. 'You have a sister – Birgitta? Do you get on well?'

Annika tried to smile. 'When she gave birth, I found out about it on Facebook. I didn't even know she was pregnant.'

'Has it always been like that?'

'We shared a room when we were growing up, but now I don't even know where she lives.'

The psychologist jotted something on her little pad. 'When you filled in the form, under "Additional Information" you wrote that you were convicted of a criminal

14

offence fifteen years ago. Do you want to say any more about that?'

The room shrank even further.

'Causing another person's death. Two years' probation. My boyfriend, Sven. It was . . . well, it was an accident, you could say.'

The words bounced around the little room.

The psychologist didn't react. 'How does it make you feel when you talk about it?'

A siren went off inside Annika's head, a loud, persistent sound. 'Nothing much. Fifteen years is a long time.'

If she could only switch off the noise she'd be able to speak. If she could make her inner self more compact than the darkness outside, she'd be able to breathe.

The *Evening Post*'s main newsroom was bathed in its usual bluish light. Annika could see Berit Hamrin sitting at her computer, and the tension evaporated, leaving her with just a trace of a headache. She had spent most of her waking hours over the past fifteen years in this room, on an endless hunt for what had happened or might happen, and for most of that time her colleague Berit had occupied the chair next to hers.

She dropped her bag next to the desk she and Berit shared, pulled off her jacket and tossed it over the arm of her chair. Berit was older, had grown-up children and lived on a farm in the country with her husband.

'How's the Twitter row going?' Annika asked.

Berit let out a deep sigh. 'The TV woman has apologized

for her attack on the soap star in the latest tweet, and the soap star has accepted the apology in a new post on Facebook.'

The psychologist's room slid away and dissolved. The darkness around her, the darkness that swallowed and suffocated her, withdrew to the corners. In the newsroom it almost always stayed in its place. Here, her world was clear and comprehensible. She was part of the life of the newspaper, a functioning, integrated part. The early edition, the first deadline, the first run, which was printed by contractors all around the country or distributed by plane at dawn, the second deadline, the updated suburban edition that was taken around the Mälar Valley by road, and then the final deadline, the inner-city edition that was only printed in times of crisis or when a princess got engaged: reality, structured and made manageable. And then there was the preliminary edition, which Annika loathed. It existed only on the newspaper's internal network.

Annika unpacked her laptop and fetched some coffee while the programs loaded. She sat down, cup in hand, and steeled herself. The preliminary edition contained what Patrik Nilsson, the head of news, thought the following day's paper should contain: the future as it ought to be, with headlines and often pictures. All the reporters had to do was to make reality fit his vision.

Tomorrow's hypothetical paper was topped by Berit's story: the TV pundit, a leader writer from a provincial paper who guested on breakfast television every third

16

Wednesday, had posted a bitchy tweet about a former soap star who had put on weight. Patrik Nilsson liked to sift out the most pointless squabbles on the internet and recast them as massive rows in the paper. This time he had excelled himself:

TV PUNDIT BULLIES ROSA ABOUT HER WEIGHT

ran the suggested headline. There was a picture of a painfully thin blonde, with the caption: 'Rosa: deeply upset that her weight has been criticized'.

'Sadly the planned storm of outrage on social media has failed to materialize,' Berit said.

The paper had been planning to base its coverage on the furore, but there was virtually nothing. A few 'Why must people judge women on how they look?' comments would have helped, but there weren't even many of those. Rosa's story would end up on the mass-media scrapheap.

'I reckon she could do with putting *on* a few kilos,' Berit said. 'I'm sure it would make her feel better. What are you doing today?'

'Josefin's murder,' Annika said.

Berit took off her glasses. 'That summer when Sweden was a banana republic? Hot as a furnace, inflation through the roof, and we were brilliant at football?'

'Fifteen years ago,' Annika said. 'My first by-line.'

Berit returned to Rosa while Annika got out her background material.

During the spring the paper's readers had been invited

17

to vote on which historical crimes they wanted to read more about (it was called *interactivity*, the watchword of the new age). Annika had produced articles and videos about several of the most popular criminal cases, and most had received an impressive number of hits online. The Sunday supplements had also sold well. She was surprised by the popularity of old stories, which seemed to be everywhere in all manner of guises. Television kept showing reconstructions of and documentaries on crime scenes, all the papers were producing supplements, and established authors were writing about historical cases.

She looked through the summary of the case entitled 'The Sex Killing in the Cemetery'. Nineteen-year-old Josefin Liljeberg had been found dead behind a headstone one boiling-hot Saturday morning, naked and strangled. The murder remained unsolved. She clicked to bring up the girl's photograph, taken at her high-school graduation, with a white cap on her blonde hair, her eyes radiant. She had worked as a stripper at Studio Six. Annika thought she knew who had killed her: her boyfriend, Joachim, who owned the club. The club was long since gone, but Joachim was out there somewhere, presumably still in the shadowy world where he belonged.

Berit sighed and looked at her watch. 'I'm going to leave poor Rosa to fend for herself,' she said, closing her laptop.

'Are you heading back to the high-security courtroom?'

Berit was covering the trial of Ivar Berglund: he owned a company that sold wood and wood products, and had been nicknamed 'The Timberman' in the tabloids. The case had just entered its second week at the Stockholm District Court. 'The police officer who arrested him is due to give evidence. Do you know what the connection is between Berglund and that politician who was assaulted in Solsidan?'

Annika pulled her hair into a knot on top of her head. It wasn't easy to keep track of the case. The unmarried fifty-five-year-old from Vidsel in Norrbotten was accused of murdering a homeless man in Nacka, and Annika had written the articles that had led to his arrest, then broken the news of it, which meant that the *Evening Post* had won the circulation war that day. Afterwards she had produced a long article about Berglund's background, filmed his home and workshop, looked through the annual accounts of his business and talked to his customers and neighbours.

'Nina Hoffman arrested him,' Annika said. 'We've talked about it a lot, and we can't publish this, but she's sure that the murder of the homeless man and the assault on Ingemar Lerberg were carried out by the same person. They were only a few days apart, and there are other connections too.'

'There's been nothing in the trial to suggest that,' Berit said.

'True,' Annika said. 'But the homeless man was acting as a front for Nora Lerberg's Spanish businesses. The police found a child's drawing at the murder scene in Nacka, and similar crayons were found in the Lerberg

19

children's bedroom. The level of brutality in both cases was almost identical. There's no proof, but that can't all be coincidence. The two crimes are definitely linked.'

'The case against Berglund is extremely thin,' Berit said. 'It'll be interesting to see if they get a conviction.'

'You saw Patrik's dream scenario in the preliminary edition?' Annika said.

The anticipated headline on the paper's internal network read:

TIMBERMAN'S DOUBLE LIFE:
Freelanced as an executioner

Berit picked up her bag and headed for the office manager's desk.

Annika went back to the outline of the following day's paper. There were optimistic predictions about other developments. Sweden's National Day was approaching, and there was speculation that Princess Madeleine might drag herself across the Atlantic to take part in the celebrations at Skansen with the rest of the royal family. The prospective headline was 'MADDE LETS SWEDEN DOWN', as if the entire nation had been holding its breath in anticipation of the King's youngest child leaving her Manhattan apartment to put on a badly fitting folk costume. A sports star was expected to speak out about a possible doping scandal, a heatwave was on its way, and the latest opinion poll was expected to show that the government would lose that autumn's election.

'Annika, can you do something on the heatwave?'

Patrik was hovering above her, and she glanced at the screen of her phone. 'I'm really sorry,' she said. 'I'm meeting a prosecutor in a little while.'

He groaned theatrically and turned on his heel. He knew full well that she had been taken off regular news coverage but she couldn't blame him for trying.

She shut down her laptop and gathered her things together.

Anders Schyman looked out across the newsroom with a sensation of vertigo. Through the glass wall he could see the newsdesk and Patrik Nilsson talking into two mobile phones at the same time, Sjölander hammering away at the next article about Princess Madeleine, and Annika Bengtzon on her way out with her bag slung over her shoulder. The scene was so painfully familiar, yet simultaneously so indescribably alien, and soon it would all be over.

He sank back heavily in his chair, and reached for the sheet of paper at the top of the pile closest to him: the minutes of the management committee meeting, held on Friday, 29 May. It was a date that would go down in history, because it marked the indisputable beginning of the end. The age of Gutenberg was over; the printed word had played out its role.

He got up and stood so close to the window that his breath misted the glass. Could he have done anything differently? Swedish journalism had developed hand in hand with the welfare state, the 'People's Home', for almost a century, the connection between power and the people. When one was falling apart, the other was bound to go the same way. Media researchers were claiming twenty years ago that 'The 1990s could be seen as the end of an era: the era of the national welfare state and journalism.'

For a quarter of a century, the majority of his career, he had worked on borrowed time. It was no good crying over it: he could hardly rebuild the People's Home single-handedly.

On impulse, he took a book off the shelf, Jan Ekecrantz and Tom Olsson's *The Edited Society*, and read an underlined passage in the introduction, even though he knew it by heart:

Journalism based on substantiated evidence and serious reporting has increasingly been replaced by abstract descriptions of the state of affairs, in which those involved often feature as invisible sources. Modern journalism is characterized by an informed common sense that tends to change societal problems into informational problems, and the public arena into talk shows and infotainment. Openly commercial and biased journalism is gaining more and more ground. The traditional journalistic ideal (reflect what is actually happening, examine and criticize power, act as a channel between government and governed) has become counterproductive . . .

He shut the book.

We live our lives as we live our days, it had said on his

breakfast bill at the hotel in Oslo, where he had been at a seminar with the family who owned the paper. The words had hit him like a punch in the gut. A cold sweat had broken on his palms. How did he live his days? How had he lived his life? That day in Norway, in a windowless conference room, they had discussed the digitalization of the media; today, their hopes for tomorrow's front page rested upon two women exchanging barely literate insults on social media that no one in their right mind would read.

He sat down again, his knees aching, and ran his fingers over the stacks of papers on his desk. Maybe he should have started his own business, built a house, had children, done something of lasting value. But he had done nothing like that: he had built for today, not the future; he had spent his entire working life defining and trying to explain the society he lived in, trying to make it better, fairer. He had his reputation, his role in media history. He was hardly likely to leave anything else behind.

He looked out at the newsroom. How was he going to do this? Throughout all his years at the paper he had worked ceaselessly on development, nurturing colleagues to fill the posts that were required to keep finances and headlines alike in the black. But the industry wasn't the only thing that kept changing: time itself kept being redrawn, and there were no maps. He was navigating the jungle on adrenalin and instinct, doing his best to avoid chasms and landmines. He had managed to fashion a number of colleagues into key figures within the organization, in news, sport, entertainment, online, arts and television. They had all had to define their own roles in the new, uncharted media landscape, and he was proud of them, of himself, and his capacity to see what was coming.

But there was one overriding role that he had not managed to reconstruct: his own, model 2.0. A publisher with freedom of speech in his very marrow, lack of respect in his heart, technology at the forefront of his mind. He hadn't had time to do it: the days were too short, passed too quickly, and now it was too late.

There was so much time, until it was suddenly too late.

Objective, critical, informative journalism, the way everyone knew it, everyone active today, would be no more than a short parenthesis in the history of humankind, and he was at the helm while they headed straight for Hell.

The morning's heavy rain had eased, leaving the streets dank and dark. The cold front was on its way north, and Mediterranean heat was due to reach central Sweden that afternoon. Annika could already feel the humidity on her skin. The traffic was moving like treacle so she ignored the buses and walked fast along the pavement.

She cut through Rålambshovsparken and into the labyrinth of streets and alleys that made up Kungsholmen. She could find her way without thinking: she would walk and walk and suddenly find herself somewhere without being aware of how she had got there. The buildings leaned conspiratorially towards her, whispering a welcome. She had ended up among these streets when she had first arrived in Stockholm, in an unmodernized flat tucked away in a courtyard on Agnegatan, with just a cold tap and a bathroom in the basement of the adjacent building. And that building over there was where she had lived, in a magnificent apartment looking out on to Hantverkargatan, with Thomas when the children were young – they had held their wedding reception there. And Kungsholmen was where she had lived in a three-room flat after her divorce from Thomas.

And this was where Josefin Liljeberg had worked, and where she had died.

Annika crossed Hantverkargatan and saw Kronoberget rise behind the fire station, with its paths and lawns. The trees hadn't yet developed the same shade of chlorophyll-heavy green that they'd had back then. The playground on Kronobergsgatan was full of people, mothers and children, a few fathers, the laughter and shouting triggering inside her a sadness for what had once been. She walked past the sandpits, climbing-frames and slides, and made her way up to the crown of the hill.

'The Sex Killing in the Cemetery' was how Josefin's murder had been described, but that wasn't really accurate.

She had been found in an old Jewish cemetery, located on the outskirts of the city in the eighteenth century but now incorporated into one of the largest parks in inner

Stockholm. And it wasn't a sexually motivated killing: she had been strangled by her boyfriend.

Annika walked slowly to the cast-iron railings. The area had been restored in recent years. The abundant vegetation was gone, the toppled headstones raised. Two hundred and nine people lay there, she knew, the last buried in 1857. There was something magical about the place. The noise of the city faded away – it was like a hole through time. She put her hand on the railing, her fingers tracing the circles and curls, the stylized stars of David.

During that hot summer, Annika's first on the paper as a temp, she had been manning the telephone tip-off line and this was her big break. She had insisted on being allowed to write about Josefin, her first articles under her own by-line. This was where the girl had been lying, just on the other side of the railings. *The barren greyness of the rocks in the background, the silent greenery, the shadow-play of the leaves, the humidity and heat.* Annika had looked into her eyes, clouded and grey, listened to her soundless scream.

'He got away with it,' Annika whispered to Josefin. 'He was sent to prison, but not for what he did to you. Maybe it's too late now.' Tears welled in her eyes. That had been the first truth she never wrote about, and there had been more over the years. So long ago, yet still so close. Sven had been alive that summer. She could feel his anger in the darkness around her, how upset he had been that she had taken a job in Stockholm, consciously seeking to get away from him. *Don't you love me?*

26

Insecurity and fear had gone hand in hand: how would her life turn out? she had wondered.

It had turned out like this, she thought, wiping her tears. I stayed here. This was where I was meant to be.

She let go of the railings, took out her little video-camera, and filmed the cemetery freehand (she hadn't felt like lugging the tripod with her). She zoomed into the place where Josefin had been lying, then focused on the trees above. If necessary, she could always come back and do a piece to camera in front of the murder scene, but for the time being she couldn't judge what to say. First she had to edit and structure her material. She turned her back on the cemetery, suddenly eager to get away.

She made her way down towards the Public Prosecution Authority on Kungsbron. The temperature was rising. The road smelt of tar.

Preliminary investigations were, in principle, always regarded as confidential, and this was true of Josefin's murder, even if Annika had a good idea of what the file contained. It showed that Joachim, Josefin's boyfriend, was probably guilty of her murder. Annika had requested to see the material, either in full or in part: information deemed unlikely to damage the investigation could, in exceptional cases, be released, even if no prosecution had ever been brought.

The wind was getting stronger and the clouds were breaking up. She quickened her pace.

Fifteen years had passed, but after the murder of Olof Palme the law had been changed so that murders never fell under the statute of limitations. There was still time for justice to be done if new evidence emerged, if a witness suddenly decided to talk.

Her mobile rang, deep in her bag. She stopped and dug it out from among the ballpoint pens at the bottom. She glanced at the screen: Barbro, her mother. She took the call, a little warily.

'Where are you?' Barbro asked.

Annika looked around. The corner of Bergsgatan and Agnegatan, right next to Police Headquarters. 'I'm at work – or, rather, I'm about to interview a prosecutor about a murder case.'

'Is it that Timberman?'

'No, this is different.'

'Do you know where Birgitta is?'

Clouds were scudding across the sky. Darkness was curling in from the background. 'I haven't a clue. Why?' Annika heard the anxiety in her own voice. What had she done wrong now?

'When did you last hear from her?'

God, when could it have been? Annika brushed the hair from her forehead. 'About a year ago, I think. She needed a babysitter for the weekend. She and Steven were going to look for work in Norway.'

'What about after that?'

Annika felt a degree of stubbornness alongside her insecurity, and her jaw tightened. 'Birgitta and I don't talk often.'

Why had she said that? Why not tell the truth? *My*

sister and I have no contact at all. I don't even know where she lives.

She heard her mother sniff.

'What's happened?' Annika asked, making an effort to sound friendly (not scared, not angry, not nonchalant).

'She didn't come home from work yesterday.'

'Work?'

'She was doing a day-shift in MatExtra, the supermarket. Steven and I are really worried.'

Yes, they must be, if Barbro had taken the trouble to phone. Annika shifted position. 'Have you called her work? Her friends? Have you tried Sara?'

'Steven talked to her boss, and I've spoken to Sara.'

Annika was anxious now. 'What about her old art teacher, Margareta? They used to stay in touch.'

'We've called everyone.'

Of course Annika had been last on the list.

'Have you any idea how worried we are?' Barbro said, her voice rising.

Annika closed her eyes. It made no difference what she said or did. She could see her mother before her, rubbing her hands, fumbling with her wine glass, trying to find someone to blame. She might as well say what was on her mind. 'Mum,' she said slowly, 'are you sure Steven's telling the truth?'

A moment's silence. 'What do you mean?'

'I'm not always sure that Steven is . . . well, very nice to Birgitta. I got the impression he was taking advantage of her, and she almost seemed a bit scared of him.'

29

'Why would you say that? There's nothing wrong with Steven.'

'Are you sure he doesn't hit her?'

Another pause. Her mother's voice was sharp when she eventually replied, 'Don't mix yourself up with Birgitta.' Then she hung up.

Annika brushed the hair from her face. She peered at the buildings. Up there was her old flat, where her former husband still lived. God, these streets were full of ghosts.

A police car passed and turned into Kronoberg Prison a little way along the street. She glimpsed a young man with matted hair in the back seat. Perhaps he was going to be arrested and remanded in custody, or possibly just questioned. He must have done something: if he wasn't a criminal, then he had been in the wrong place at the wrong time. Unless he knew something he probably shouldn't know.

She had found herself in the back of a police car once, on that summer's day out at the old ironworks in Hälleforsnäs when Sven died. She had been clutching her dead cat in her arms, refusing to let go of him, little Whiskas, her lovely, sandy-coloured cat, and in the end they had let her take his body into the car with her, and she had spent the journey crying into his fur.

Birgitta had never forgiven her for Sven. Her sister had been crazy about him, in an irritating little-sister way. He used to grab Birgitta and tickle her until she screamed. There had been something uncomfortably intimate about it – Birgitta was only two years younger than her, blonde and pretty. Annika hunched her shoulders and took a firmer grip of her bag, then looked up 'Birgitta Bengtzon' on the phone-directory app on her mobile. (She hadn't taken Steven's surname, Andersson, when they married.)

One result: Branteviksgatan 5F in Malmö.

Malmö? Hadn't she been going to move to Oslo?

Thomas watched Annika put her mobile into that hideous bag of hers and hurry off towards Scheelegatan, a tiny bobbing head four floors below, dark hair flying. He watched her until she disappeared, just a few seconds later, swallowed by cars and treetops. His heart sank, his pulse slowed. He had caught sight of her by chance: she was standing on the pavement, her face turned up towards his bedroom window, and he'd assumed she was on her way to see him. He had made up his mind not to let her in: he had nothing to say to her.

Then she had turned away and walked off.

His disappointment turned to prickling rage.

He was *no one* to her, the sort of no one whose windows you walked past or stopped directly below to talk on your mobile for a while, maybe to your new man. He hoped she'd been talking to him because she had looked uncomfortable. Trouble in Paradise? Already?

The thought made him feel a bit better. He realized he was hungry, and he had some gourmet food in the fridge, ready to heat up. He was the sort of man who ate and drank well, who put a bit of effort into making sure everyday life had a bit of style to it. He had been brought up to recognize the importance and advantages of a well-groomed exterior, correct behaviour, and an engaging, articulate manner. And that was why he was so ill-suited to this terrible flat, a mere three rooms on the top floor of a building in an old working-class district. He opened the fridge with the hook, got out the sole fillets with his hand – his only hand – and put the dish into the microwave. It was so fucking unfair that he of all people should have suffered such an affliction.

The microwave whirred. A light fish lunch because he would be having a substantial dinner, an official dinner, in the dining room on the ground floor of the government Chancellery. At least his job suited him. He had a high-profile role as a civil servant in the Ministry of Justice: he was secretary to a large inquiry with its own parliamentary committee, a prestigious assignment.

He was looking into online anonymity (a superannuated former minister was the official investigator, but Thomas was doing all the work). Online bullying was a growing problem. Society needed sharper tools to find people who insulted others on the internet, but who should be allowed to identify their IP-addresses, when, and in what ways? The police, prosecutors, or should it require a court order? How should international cooperation be coordinated, and what were the complications if the servers were in other countries? As usual, technology and criminality were several steps ahead of the authorities and the police, and the law was without doubt lagging well behind.

The directives governing the inquiry had been worked out by the under-secretary of state, Jimmy Halenius, with the minister and the director general for legal affairs. It was an open investigation, rather than one with specific goals. Occasionally the government instigated an inquiry simply to confirm something that had already been decided, but that wasn't the case this time. The result of the inquiry wasn't predetermined, and therefore lay entirely in his hands. He was in charge of his own time, could come and go as he pleased, and now the report was practically finished, ready to be discussed at the next cabinet meeting, then sent out for consultation. Thomas was, in short, a representative of power, a man of responsibility, someone who was shaping the future.

The microwave pinged. The sole fillets were ready, but they would have to wait. Instead he made his way to his computer and logged in via a site whose IP-address could never be traced. He went on to the discussion forum where he had created an alternative identity for himself some time ago. He had called himself Gregorius (after Hjalmar Söderberg's antihero in the novel *Doctor Glas*: betrayed by his wife, murdered by his doctor). He had started by posting something there, just to see what happened. The text had been about Annika's boss, a pretentious bastard. To this day, people were still contributing to the thread he had started, and he found it interesting to see how the debate had developed.

GREGORIUS
Anders Schyman should be fucked up the arse with a baseball bat. Hope the splinters form a bleeding wreath around his anus.

His palms always felt a bit clammy when he read those lines. His pulse increased and he felt his top lip start to sweat. No further comments had been added since he had last checked, he noted, with a degree of disappointment. He scrolled down the existing comments. The first, 'Hahaha, way to go man! U buttfuck him real good', was representative of those that followed. The level of debate wasn't particularly high, he had to admit. A number of contributors had questioned his choice of language, calling him a *vulgar idiot* and a *brain-dead amoeba*, but how tasteful was it of them to express themselves like that? He couldn't claim to be particularly proud of it, but who hadn't made mistakes along the way?

Besides, it was both interesting and justified, a way of gaining knowledge of the issue he was investigating. A democracy is based upon the fact that unpleasant things must be allowed to exist. As Voltaire said, 'I disapprove of what you say, but I will defend to the death your right to say it' (well, he hadn't actually used those words, but that was the meaning of a letter he wrote to Abbot le Riche on 6 February 1770).

Thomas looked back at his post once more.

> Anders Schyman should be fucked up the arse with
> a baseball bat . . .

The words were there, expressed and eternal, commented upon and affirmed.

He took a deep breath and closed the site. A sense of calm spread through him. Annika was welcome to stand down there in the street with her mobile phone and her ugly bag.

He was properly hungry now, and the sole fillets were just the right temperature.

Admired, respected, feared.

Someone.

Annika announced her arrival at the reception desk of the Public Prosecution Authority and was asked to take a seat in a waiting room that might have belonged to a dentist. It smelt of disinfectant and unspecified discomfort. She was alone, and for that she was grateful.

The man who had been in charge of the preliminary investigation into Josefin's murder, Chief Prosecutor Kjell Lindström, had retired, and the matter was now in the hands of Deputy Prosecutor Sanna Andersson. Discreetly, she took out her camera. She filmed the room and the signs on the walls for a minute or so: they might be good as inserts. She put the camera away and started to read a two-year-old issue of *Illustrated Science*, which featured an article about how fish had crawled up on to land 150 million years ago, developed legs and turned into reptiles, carnivores and humans.

'Annika Bengtzon? Deputy Prosecutor Andersson can see you now.'

She put down the magazine, picked up her bag, and was shown along a corridor to a cramped office. The woman who met her, hand outstretched, was barely thirty. 'Welcome,' she said, in a thin, high voice.

Fifteen years had passed, so obviously Josefin had sunk like a stone down the list of the justice system's priorities.

'Sorry you had to wait,' Sanna Andersson said. 'I've got a case in court in forty-five minutes. It was Liljeberg you wanted help with, wasn't it?'

Annika sat down on a chair and waited until Sanna Andersson had gone back round her desk and taken her seat. 'I've put in a request to see the preliminary investigation into the murder. She was found in Kronoberg Park on Kungsholmen on the morning of the twenty-eighth of July, fifteen years ago.'

'Of course,' the deputy prosecutor said, opening a drawer and taking out a thick file. 'It was looked into again last year. A man confessed to the murder.'

Annika nodded. 'Gustaf Holmerud,' she said. 'The serial killer. He confessed to the murders of a number of other women as well.'

Sanna glanced at her, then went back to the file. 'Yes, he confessed to pretty much all the murders we've got, and was actually found guilty of five before someone

36

pulled the emergency brake. I know that the prosecutor general is looking into several of those convictions, to see if he can order a retrial. Here it is.' She ran her hand over one page in the folder. 'Josefin Liljeberg. Death by strangulation. I went through this last night. It wasn't a particularly complicated case.' She turned the first page and looked at the headings. 'You've asked to see the whole file?'

'I covered the case at the time and followed all the developments.'

Sanna Andersson leaned over the documents. 'There are some pretty sensational ingredients here: a notorious porn club, a government minister brought in for questioning. Is that why you're interested in the case?'

She shot Annika a neutral, expressionless look, and Annika opened her mouth but found herself unable to reply. *No, that's not why. Josefin got too close to me. I became her, she became me. I took a job in the club where she worked. I wore her bikini, her underwear.* 'As I understand it, the police regard the case as cleared up,' she said eventually. 'Joachim, her boyfriend, killed her. The reason he was never prosecuted was that six people gave him an alibi.'

Sanna Andersson closed the file. 'Correct,' she said. 'Violence within relationships ought to be classed as a public-health problem.' She checked the screen of her mobile phone.

'Can I quote you on that?' Annika asked.

The woman smiled. 'Sure,' she said, standing up. 'I've

decided you can have the names of the six witnesses who gave Josefin's boyfriend his alibi.'

Annika, too, got to her feet, astonished at the young woman's authority and efficiency.

'They lied to the police,' the deputy prosecutor said, 'which could well mean they were guilty of protecting a criminal. That passed the statute of limitations a long time ago now, so they're not risking prosecution if they change their minds. Maybe they feel like talking now – if not to us, then perhaps to you.' She held out a document as she reached for a brown briefcase that looked extremely heavy.

'Can I quote you on what you said about the prosecutor general as well?' Annika asked. 'That they're looking into the possibility of asking for a retrial of Gustaf Holmerud's cases?'

Sanna laughed. 'Nice try! If you'll excuse me, I've got to run.'

Annika hurried after her, jogging to keep up.

Maybe Josefin wasn't at the bottom of the priority list after all.

The small high-security courtroom of Stockholm District Court was located on the top floor of the Stockholm City Law Courts, a strategic choice to make escapes and rescues more difficult. Nina Hoffman strode breathlessly up the last flight of steps. Defendants would have a long labyrinth of corridors and floors to negotiate on the way out, if they tried to escape. She looked towards the entrance to the secure chamber.

The media were out in force again that afternoon. Most of the nationals were in place: she could see Berit Hamrin of the *Evening Post* in the queue for security clearance to sit on the public benches. Nina showed her ID and was let into the cramped, windowless anteroom. The prosecutor and his legal assistant were already there. A low-energy lamp in the ceiling cast a subdued bluish-white light that seemed unable to reach the corners of the room.

'Ready, Hoffman?' Svante Crispinsson said, greeting her warmly. 'His lawyer's likely to go for you hard. Don't take it personally.'

Nina gave a curt nod. She hadn't been expecting anything else.

'Just keep a clear head.'

Svante Crispinsson was one of the northern district's youngest prosecutors, and Nina had had dealings with him before. He was regarded as a little disorganized, as far as investigative work was concerned, but in court he was a great asset, unafraid and combative.

'Let's see if we can keep the members of the jury awake,' the prosecutor said. 'The old boy at the far left has a tendency to doze off.'

Nina got herself a cup of coffee and sat on a chair close to the door. Crispinsson leafed through his papers, muttering inaudibly to himself. His suit was slightly too large and his hair too long; he gave the impression of being confused and artless, which made him seem honest and likeable.

She straightened her back and stared at the wall in front of her. Ivar Berglund was guilty. She was certain of it. His timid appearance was an act. There was something extremely disturbing just beneath that unassuming exterior, something impervious and untouchable that only deeply criminal people possessed. She had felt it before, had lived close to it, far too close, when she was far too young.

The coffee was insipid.

Giving evidence in court was the part of her job she liked least. The public hearing was a performance in the service of justice. The judge and jury needed to be convinced that the chain of evidence was strong enough for a guilty verdict. But she preferred the darkness behind the scenes, complex investigations, getting closer and closer, tightening the noose.

A bell rang and the parties were called for the continuation of the main hearing into the case of murder or assisted murder. The prosecutor and his assistant went into the courtroom. Nina sat in the anteroom and waited, motionless. Usual practice was for the accused to be questioned first, followed by the witnesses, but Berglund had asked to be questioned last. That was unusual, but the judge had upheld his request when Crispinsson was given an assurance that he could recall certain witnesses afterwards.

Control, Nina thought. He doesn't want to speak until he's heard what everyone else has to say.

The door to the courtroom opened. She stood up,

stepped into the dazzling daylight and walked straight to the witness stand without looking left or right. Everyone was staring at her as she crossed the floor: the spectators on the other side of the reinforced glass, Berglund, showing no emotion, his lawyer, openly provocative, and Svante Crispinsson, with the trace of a smile.

She raised her hand to take the oath, and her jacket strained across her back. She had put on a bit of muscle since she'd last worn the outfit, whenever that had been. The last time she'd given evidence, presumably. She, Nina Victoria Hoffman, promised and swore on her honour and conscience to tell the truth, and nothing but the truth, with no embellishments or amendments.

Crispinsson coughed into his hand before he began to speak, and tugged at his hair. 'Nina Hoffman, what is your job?'

She was standing absolutely straight. She didn't really need her suit to make her look like a plain-clothes police officer: she knew she looked like one, restrained and correct, unambiguous but lacking colour. 'I'm a trained police officer, criminologist and behavioural scientist. I currently work as an operational analyst for the National Crime Unit in Stockholm.'

The clerk typed, the sunlight reflecting off the strengthened glass. One of the peculiarities of the high-security court was the barrier that separated the public from those involved in the case. She was aware that the reporters behind her were hearing her words through a loudspeaker, with a tiny delay.

'Can you give us a bit of background to your work last spring?'

She stretched her shoulders, and felt Berglund's eyes on her. It was hugely important that he was convicted. He was dangerous, unpredictable; his impervious core meant that he lacked the usual human inhibitions. She could sense his inner self behind those blank eyes, like oil on a stretch of water.

'New information came to light that led us to take another look at a twenty-year-old case, the disappearance of Viola Söderland, and examine all the evidence once more.'

Crispinsson nodded almost imperceptibly but encouragingly. 'And what happened on Saturday, the seventeenth of May last year?'

'A DNA sample was taken from the accused's home in Täby.' *The house at the end of the cul-de-sac, a one-storey villa from the 1960s, red brick, closed shutters over the windows.*

He had been there, surprised but amiable and accommodating. His eyes had been the same then as they were now, heavy and dark, untarnished by more than a year in custody. No normal person would react in that way. Isolation, twenty-three hours at a stretch, and with maximum restrictions at first: no newspapers, no television, no contact with the outside world. An hour of fresh air each day in the exercise yard on the roof of the prison, in a space the shape of a slice of cake, blocked off by wire netting. She knew he hadn't received a single visitor, not even after the restrictions were relaxed. She was aware of his hands from the corner of her eye, resting on the table, his watchful pose.

He was made of iron, bog ore from the marshlands where he had grown up.

'Can you give us a brief summary of the main aspects of the Viola Söderland case?' Crispinsson said.

'Is this really relevant?' Martha Genzélius, Berglund's lawyer, interrupted. 'My client is not accused of anything to do with Viola Söderland.'

'The prosecution is based upon a chain of evidence,' the prosecutor said. 'We need to explain the nature of each link or the case will be incomprehensible.'

'That won't help. The entire case is incomprehensible, no matter how the prosecutor presents it.'

The judge struck his gavel. The lawyer, Martha Genzélius, fidgeted on her chair, the picture of frustration. Nina raised her chin and waited.

'Viola Söderland, if you don't mind,' Crispinsson said, nodding towards Nina.

She made an effort to reply in a calm and factual way. 'Viola Söderland disappeared from her villa in Djursholm on the night of the twenty-third of September almost twenty-one years ago. Her body has never been found. There was one witness, a neighbour who was walking his dog on the night in question, who saw a man get out of a car outside Söderland's home. The neighbour made a note of the car's number plate, but the owner had an alibi.'

43

'Who was the owner?' Crispinsson interrupted.

She swallowed what she was about to say and lost her flow. 'The car was registered to Ivar Berglund.'

'And there were signs of a struggle in the villa in Djursholm?'

She had spent hours studying the photographs, grainy and poorly lit, taken during the last shaky days of colour film, just before everything had gone digital, infinitely sharper and easier to work with. She had examined countless pictures of that sort, from hundreds of different crime scenes, and 'struggle' wasn't the word she would have used, but this wasn't the time or place to make pedantic points about the prosecutor's choice of vocabulary.

'There was a smashed vase on the hall floor, and strands of hair that didn't belong to Viola, her children, or any of the staff in the house. That was as far as the original investigation got. DNA technology was in its infancy and it wasn't possible to get a result from a few strands of hair – they would have needed a sackful to identify the entire sequence.'

'But that is possible today?'

It seemed almost incredible that there had been a time before DNA. How had any crimes ever been solved twenty years ago?

'It's possible to extract so-called mitochondrial DNA from strands of hair now. That's an alternative form of analysis that doesn't give quite as much information as a complete DNA sequence, but it's very reliable.'

'So once you had the new information, you requested

a DNA sample from the car-owner under suspicion, a saliva sample. What happened?'

'It was a perfect match.'

She couldn't help looking at Ivar Berglund, and was aware of everyone around her doing the same thing, both inside the court and on the public benches. All eyes landed on the accused, who sat there, still as a statue, his hands resting heavily one on top of the other. He was looking straight at her and their eyes met. His were narrow and dark. She tried to see any depth in them, but failed.

'Did you take the man in for further questioning?'

'A colleague and I interviewed him at his home in Täby.'

'What did he have to say for himself?' *A heaviness to his movements, superficial politeness and surprise, but she could sense hidden depths, the snakes within.*

'He stuck to his alibi, that he had been giving a lecture on the genetic modification of aspen trees up in Sandviken on the night in question.'

'Were you able to confirm what he told you?'

'There were about seventy people in the audience, but no one knows exactly when Viola Söderland went missing.'

'Could he have been in both places? On the same night?'

'The distance between Sandviken and Stockholm is a hundred and ninety-one kilometres, so, yes. It's theoretically possible for him to have been in both places on the same night.'

Berglund's lawyer seemed amused, and whispered

something in her client's ear. Nina clenched her teeth. She wouldn't let herself be provoked.

'But Ivar Berglund is facing charges regarding an entirely separate allegation, not Viola Söderland's disappearance,' the defence lawyer said, looking through her papers.

Nina reached for the glass of water on the table in front of her. It was refreshing, tasted earthy.

'Can you tell the court how you and your colleagues at National Crime proceeded with the case?'

'We compared Berglund's DNA profile with every ongoing criminal investigation in Sweden.'

'And what happened?'

'We found another match.'

'To an ongoing criminal investigation?'

'Yes.'

'Which one?'

'The murder of Karl Gustaf Evert Ekblad in Nacka last year.'

It was as if a sudden wind had passed through the spectators' benches on the other side of the glass, a soundless storm, rising and falling, hair fluttering, arms moving, lips talking, pens scribbling. The facts in the case were already public knowledge, but up to now they had been one-dimensional, words on a page. Now they came to life. The man was revealed as the monster he was.

The prosecutor looked at his notes. 'You were coordinating that investigation at National Crime. Can you tell us in more detail about the case?'

Her first week in her new job. She hadn't even had time to attend the induction course before real life got in the way.

'Karl Gustaf Evert Ekblad, known as Kag, used to spend a lot of time sitting on the benches in Orminge shopping centre. He was tortured and killed in May last year.'

'Tortured?'

Nina took her eyes off the prosecutor and looked directly at Ivar Berglund. She wasn't scared of him: she knew what he was. 'The victim was found hanging by his knees from a tree, above an anthill, naked and smeared with honey. His ankles and wrists were tied with duct-tape. His nails had been pulled out, his rectum had been severely damaged, and his nose broken. He had died from lack of oxygen, asphyxiated by a plastic bag.'

Ivar Berglund leaned back in his chair, as though he needed to distance himself from what was being said. He whispered something to his representative, who gave a quick nod.

The prosecutor held up a sheet of paper towards the judge. 'The details of the forensic pathology report on the murder victim, Karl Gustaf Evert Ekblad, are in Appendix Fifty-three B.'

The judge made a note. Crispinsson turned back to Nina. 'Did you visit the scene of the crime?'

The pine tree on a rocky outcrop, with a thick trunk and stubby crown. The lower branches were thick as a man's thighs, long dead, and the wood had taken on the colour and structure of driftwood, grey and silky smooth.

'Yes, I did.'

'While the victim was still . . . hanging there?'

The harsh white light of the forensics team's lamps, police officers like shadows.

'Yes.'

'What did the crime scene tell you?'

'It was carefully chosen. Isolated, relatively close to a built-up area, but out of earshot.'

'And the victim?'

Nina looked at Berglund again. He gazed back at her as she answered, evaluating her certainty. 'Hanging people from their knees like that is an established method of torture, known as *La Barra*, 'the Parrot's Perch'. It's extremely painful, because the flow of blood to the legs is cut off. If the victim survives, the injuries often lead to gangrene and amputation. Smearing victims with honey and putting them on top of anthills is a tried-and-tested method in Africa, particularly Angola.'

'Where at the crime scene was the perpetrator's DNA found?'

She turned to Crispinsson. 'A fragment of skin was found under the nail of the victim's right index finger, and the DNA matched Ivar Berglund's.'

'Was that match confirmed?'

She replied in a forceful tone to camouflage the deficiency of her answer. 'That was the information we received from the National Forensics Laboratory.'

The prosecutor looked down at his papers. The air in the court was quite still. She glanced at the jury. They were alert and wide-eyed. Even the man on the far left was awake.

'The victim, Karl Gustaf Ekblad, where was he living?' Crispinsson asked.

Dark wooden panelling that needed varnishing. The crooked letterbox, no flowerbeds. A pair of greyish-white curtains in the big picture window.

'He rented a room in a villa in Orminge, but he was registered as living in Marbella in the south of Spain.'

'What was the next step in your investigation?'

'Considering the victim's international connections, we asked for the assistance of the Spanish police. This cooperation was formalized via Europol, but I was in direct contact with the Spanish National Police about the case.'

'Spanish is your mother tongue?'

'I grew up on the Canary Islands.'

The prosecutor smiled at her, then looked at the judge and gathered his papers together. 'Thank you. No further questions.'

Nina turned towards Martha Genzélius, Ivar Berglund's lawyer. She was a slim woman, in her forties, wearing an expensive suit and high heels, with medium-length, shiny blonde hair that had been straightened. It was evidently important to her that she personify the Swedish Career Woman: she would doubtless have looked the same if she'd been a boutique-owner or a bank manager, a fashion designer or a television presenter. She was leafing through her papers, her acrylic nails slipping over the interview transcripts.

Then she looked up, straight at Nina, without smiling. 'Nina Hoffman, why did you stop working as a police officer?'

Just keep a cool head.

'I haven't stopped working as a police officer.'

The woman picked up a sheet of paper with exaggerated slowness and studied it for a moment. 'You told us a little while ago that you work as an operational analyst.'

Nina made her voice as friendly as she could when she replied. 'Because I'm a trained police officer and work for the Police Authority, I still have police powers. That means I can arrest and release people, question them, or use force if that should be necessary.'

The lawyer looked at her patiently. 'Let me rephrase the question. Why did you resign from your job as a police officer in the Södermalm police district?'

'I requested a leave of absence so that I could study Criminology and Behavioural Science at Stockholm University.'

Crispinsson leaned forward across his desk, his hair on end. 'What does this have to do with the matter at hand?' he asked.

'Did you enjoy working on Södermalm?'

Nina fought to suppress the sense that she was being insulted: did this lawyer really think she was so easily fooled?

'Where is this line of questioning going?' the judge asked.

Martha Genzélius tapped her fountain pen with her varnished thumbnail. 'That will become apparent later in my questioning,' she said.

Nina made an effort not to show any sign of irritation: the woman's response was a typical lawyer's manoeuvre, designed to unsettle the judge and worry the witness.

'Ask the witness a question, or move on,' the judge said.

The lawyer turned towards Nina. 'How did you come to re-examine the Viola Söderland case after twenty years?'

'Her disappearance was still an open case. We received fresh information that justified a re-examination of the evidence.'

'Information from a reporter at the *Evening Post* newspaper?'

'That's correct.'

Behind the reflection of the toughened glass, Nina could see the journalists, focused and straining to hear, a united group defending freedom of expression, but also bitter rivals. She knew that a number of them were reporting live from the trial, sending her words out into the world the moment she said them, interpreting and occasionally misrepresenting them. She had no control over her words: they had a life of their own.

'Why did the investigation become active again?' Martha Genzélius asked.

'As I said, we received new information that led to the case becoming active again,' Nina said.

'Was it not the case that a newspaper wrote about the investigation, and that this so-called "new information" came from the media?'

Easy, now, Nina thought. 'That's right.'

'Do you think that's a serious way of conducting a police investigation, letting it be governed by a sensationalist tabloid?'

The question came like the crack of a whip, and Crispinsson stood up. 'This is harassment!'

Nina raised her chin and looked at him, signalling that the question was okay. Then she caught the defence lawyer's gaze and held it firmly. 'Information from the general public, including all forms of media, constitutes a significant contribution to our ability to solve crimes.' She managed to sound smooth as silk, a professional who was gently explaining how the police worked to an ignorant outsider.

The lawyer adopted a triumphant smile, as though she had just won a great victory, then picked up a different document from the table in front of her. 'You claim that my client's DNA was found at a crime scene in Orminge in May last year. Is that right?'

'According to the National Forensics Laboratory, yes.'

The lawyer raised her voice. 'Is that really correct?'

Nina took a shallow breath. This was the cornerstone of the prosecution's case, its foundation. She opened her mouth to reply, but Martha Genzélius cut her off. 'Please bear in mind that you're under oath!'

Her hostility hit Nina like a sledgehammer. Genzélius was pulling out all the tricks of her trade, interrupting and confusing, changing the tempo of her questions, and then that particular remark, so absurdly insulting, yet so horribly effective. She had been saving it specifically for that moment, because that was what the defence was based on: that the DNA match hadn't been utterly perfect.

Nina took pains not to change her expression, not to blink, not to seem bothered. Summoning all of her authority, she replied, 'It was so close a match that only a vanishingly small number of people on the entire planet could have been considered alternative perpetrators.'

Martha Genzélius threw out her hands. 'Thank you! "Alternative perpetrators"! And have you made any genuine attempts to look for them?'

'This is a disgrace!' Crispinsson cried. 'Is the defendant's lawyer calling the witness's professional honour into question? Is she trying to imply that the National Criminal Police did not keep an open mind in this investigation?'

The judge struck his gavel. 'That's enough! Let the defence lawyer proceed.'

Nina let her shoulders sink. Calling her evidence into question was the point of this cross-examination, but she couldn't help being grateful to Crispinsson.

Martha Genzélius turned back towards her. 'So, what

have you all been doing during the protracted period of time that my client has been in custody?'

The lawyer obviously knew the answer to her question: she was trying to provoke a response.

Nina's unit at National Crime had searched through practically the whole of criminal history in Sweden, and she herself had spoken to police forces right across Europe, in every language imaginable, persuading and pleading, instructing and cajoling: look, check, compare! 'The victim was of Finnish extraction, grew up in Sweden, and had just become a Spanish citizen when he was murdered,' Nina replied calmly. 'We required the assistance of our Spanish colleagues, and several other police forces, in order to coordinate the investigation.'

' "Several other police forces", you say. Which might those be?'

'After we contacted the Spanish police,' Nina said, 'and then Europol, it turned out that there were a number of other unsolved murders in different countries, which show similarities to the case in Orminge. In the past year, Ivar Berglund's DNA profile has been compared against other open investigations both in the Nordic countries and elsewhere in Europe. That isn't the reason for the long period the accused spent in custody, but work on the investigation has been extensive, and has made significant progress throughout that period.'

'And what was the result?'

'The work of comparing samples is ongoing, so I am unable to answer that question.'

'You haven't found a single match, have you?'

Nina managed not to let her sense of bitter disappointment show. There hadn't been any DNA to make comparisons with: the crime scenes that had been checked so far had been clean, at least where comparable forensic evidence was concerned. 'Not so far.'

'So the only thing you've got is one poor match in Orminge. Tell me, exactly where was this supposed DNA found?'

Back to hard facts: excellent.

'Under the victim's fingernail.'

'Which was found where?'

Nina looked at her. That question could be a mistake: it could leave the lawyer floundering.

'The victim's fingernails were pulled out while he was still alive. He tried to resist, and managed to scratch his killer before the nail was removed.'

Martha Genzélius appeared unconcerned by the uncomfortable answer. 'This alleged piece of evidence was found in an anthill, wasn't it?'

'Karl Gustaf Ekblad was naked and smeared with honey. He was little more than an anthill when he was found.'

Using the victim's name was an obvious move, making him a human being. Had she succeeded in building a bit of empathy, some identification with him among the jury?

The lawyer jotted some notes, then looked up. 'Tell me, what exactly does an anthill consist of, apart from ants? Mould? Spores of fungus? Formic acid? How can you be sure that the microscopic trace of skin that was found down in the anthill wasn't contaminated?'

Crispinsson raised his hand. 'The witness is not a forensic crime-scene investigator.'

The defence lawyer looked at Crispinsson in surprise. 'But the prosecution called this witness. Aren't I allowed to question her?'

The judge nodded to Genzélius. 'Go on.'

The lawyer turned to Nina. 'No, you're not a forensic crime-scene investigator. Your task is merely to analyse material and write reports, isn't it?'

Nina straightened her back again. She had no intention of allowing herself to be belittled.

Martha Genzélius picked up a bundle of papers and flipped through them. She read, then leafed back a few pages. A wave of unease ran down Nina's spine. 'If we could return briefly to the case of Viola Söderland,' the lawyer eventually said, putting her papers down. 'The witness with the dog, who made a note of the number plate of the car parked outside his neighbour's house on the twenty-third of September, twenty-one years ago, did he give any specific time for his observation?'

'It was around midnight.'

'Exactly. And how reliable is that recollection, twenty-one years on?'

'The witness can't know that,' Crispinsson said.

'Let the defence lawyer finish,' the judge said.

Nina waited while the defence lawyer tilted her head.

'The lecture in Sandviken,' she went on, 'didn't finish

until just after ten p.m. My client stayed behind to sort out the hall with the organizers, had a cup of coffee and refuelled his car. Do we agree on that?'

'That's correct.'

'Which means that he is supposed to have driven from Sandviken to Stockholm in less than forty-five minutes, which in turn implies an average speed of approximately two hundred and fifty kilometres per hour.'

Nina was about to reply when she was cut off again. Martha Genzélius was addressing the judge: 'I would like to remind the court that there wasn't even a motorway between Gävle and Uppsala in those days. The E4 ran through the centre of various built-up areas with speed limits of both seventy and fifty kilometres per hour.' She looked at Nina again. 'Do you think that sounds plausible?'

There was nothing she could do, except get it over with as smoothly and quickly as possible. 'No,' Nina said.

The lawyer looked directly at her, in complete silence, for a long time. Then she very slowly put her pen down on the table. 'Thank you. No further questions.'

Elegant.

The judge turned towards Nina and asked if she had incurred any expenses as a result of her attendance in court. Nina said she hadn't, then got to her feet and left the courtroom through a tunnel that led to the prosecution's windowless anteroom. An intangible feeling of anxiety and powerlessness went with her as she left the court.

*

Because a heatwave was supposedly on its way, the air-conditioning in the newsroom had been switched on. Evidently it only had one setting, somewhere just below freezing, and Annika had to put her jacket on before she switched on her laptop.

In spite of the cold, her fingers were burning as she looked through the notes and list of witnesses. Here they were, the liars who'd seen to it that Josefin had never got any justice. She recognized some of the men's names, but others were new to her. Ludvig Emmanuel Eriksson must be Ludde, who used to work behind the bar at the club, and Robin Oscar Bertelsson was presumably the Robin responsible for security there, but who had left shortly after Josefin was murdered. Annika had never met him, but Joachim had mentioned him several times. She had always suspected he was one of the witnesses, and now she knew.

She remembered Ludvig Emmanuel Eriksson as a fairly quiet, sullen guy. He had thin blond hair and pale eyes, and used to stare at her breasts shamelessly. She looked him up on Google and found him at once. Cancer Research, donation via debit card or PayPal. A picture showed him already marked by the disease, his hair cropped and his eyes exhausted. He had lived to be just thirty-two, horribly sad.

Berit put her bag down on the desk. 'Why's it so cold in here?'

Annika looked away from poor dead Ludde, and gestured towards the ventilation unit in the corner. 'Did Nina have anything interesting to contribute?'

'She did, actually. There are similar cases in other countries. The investigations are being coordinated.'

'And she said that in the witness stand? Brilliant. Do you think he'll be found guilty?'

Berit settled on her chair. 'The entire case rests on one DNA result,' she said. 'It might not be enough.'

'Berglund's never been linked to any other violent crime,' Annika said.

'And now there's actually reasonable doubt,' Berit said.

'Has he talked?' Patrik Nilsson asked, materializing next to them.

'He used to pan-fry his victims' livers and eat them with capers and garlic,' Annika said.

Patrik looked as irritated as she had hoped.

'There's one new piece of evidence,' Berit said. 'National Crime and Europol are sharing the investigation with police forces in other countries. That's why it's taken so long to come to trial.'

Red circles appeared on Patrik's cheeks. 'SUSPECTED OF SERIAL KILLINGS ALL OVER EUROPE!' he said, in capital letters.

'I don't know,' Berit said. 'He hasn't been convicted yet.'

'That's just a matter of how you phrase it,' Patrik said, and bounced off towards the newsdesk.

'Did you get anything from your prosecutor?' Berit asked.

Annika handed her the list of witnesses as her intercom crackled into life.

'Can you come into my office for a moment?' editor-in-chief Anders Schyman asked, through the tinny speaker.

'Now?' Annika said. 'Right away?'

'Preferably.'

The intercom crackled and died.

'Great news,' Berit said, passing the list back. 'Imagine if you could get them to talk.'

Annika stood up and went over to Schyman's glass box. He was sitting there looking at her so she didn't bother to knock, just walked in and closed the door firmly behind her. It was never left open, these days.

'What did the prosecutor say?' her boss asked. He was seated behind his desk, looking heavier than ever.

'I got the list of witnesses. Why do we have to have the air-conditioning set to below freezing?'

He looked at her quizzically. On the desk in front of him lay bundles of notes, printouts, Post-its and something Annika thought might, with a bit of imagination, be a flowchart.

'What witnesses? There were witnesses to the murder?'

'The ones who gave the killer his alibi. Did you want anything in particular?'

The editor-in-chief scratched his beard. 'Sit down,' he said, pointing at the chair on the other side of the desk.

Without knowing why, she felt suddenly unsettled. Something in his tone, perhaps, or the greyness of his skin. The chair wobbled as she sat.

'Have you got much left to do on the stripper's murder?'

'The stripper's name was Josefin. She dreamed of becoming a reporter, and she liked cats. Yes, I've got a bit to do – I've only just started. Why?'

'What do you think are the chances of one of these cases being solved? Or getting to trial?'

'Are we in a hurry?'

Schyman sat motionless, his arms resting on the desk.

'Has your successor been appointed?' she asked. 'Is it going to be that bloke from the radio?'

Schyman breathed out, making a sort of bottomless sigh, then pushed his chair back and hit the bookcase. 'It's not going to be him. Why? Have you got any suggestions?'

'I have, actually,' she said. 'Berit.'

He rubbed his forehead. 'I see. Well, I already knew that.'

'I'm telling you again, because I'm right.'

'Justify it.'

'She's easily the best reporter on the *Evening Post*, with the widest range of coverage. She can do everything, and has usually already done it. She never gets stressed, she's got excellent judgement, and she'll be loyal to this paper until the day she dies.'

Schyman blinked. 'So you're saying she's got the experience, knowledge, loyalty, ability, calmness and judgement?'

'It's actually pretty disgraceful that she hasn't already been asked.'

'Let me tell you why,' the editor-in-chief said.

'This I want to hear.'

'Berit doesn't make mistakes. She's never been reported to the press ombudsman, not once. She always writes correctly, belt and braces, everything careful and considered.'

'And when did that become a handicap?'

'She doesn't take any risks.'

Annika folded her arms. 'You mean she's not courageous enough?'

'A newspaper like the *Evening Post* doesn't need a captain, to use one of your favourite metaphors, who never takes risks. The very essence of this job is precisely that, taking risks, creating disorder, then keeping things balanced when the storm breaks.'

'So why the rush with Josefin?'

'There's no rush.'

Annika looked at him without saying anything. He had been looking tired for a while, but the set of his mouth was different today.

'This isn't official yet,' he said.

'Okay,' she said. Her unease was growing.

He handed her a printout, the minutes of a committee meeting the previous week. 'Paragraph four,' he said.

She read it three times. 'In consideration of the development of the industry, it was agreed to discontinue the print edition of the *Evening Post*.'

Discontinue. Print edition.

'The print edition,' she said. 'They're closing it down.' Her voice was a little hoarse.

He nodded.

'As soon as possible.'

She sat completely motionless on the chair, paralysed.

'I've been asked to implement the closure before I leave,' Schyman said.

She cast an involuntary glance at the newsroom, at the people working and concentrating on the other side of the glass, unaware of the drop that was opening up right in front of them.

'But,' she said, 'what's going to happen to everyone who . . .?'

'We can't be selective about it,' Schyman said. 'All the reporters' posts will go.'

She stared at him, open-mouthed. The extent of this was slowly sinking into her head. *All the reporters' posts will go.* That included her, Berit, Sjölander and everyone else. Their readers would no longer be able to buy the paper and sit down to do the crossword at the coffee-table. It was a whole culture that was disappearing, a whole way of life.

'But I thought the print edition was making a profit!'

'We've kept afloat up to now with sponsored supplements and the things we've been giving away, books and music and DVDs, but digitalization is taking over in those areas too, Netflix and Spotify and Bokus. This is the only logical conclusion.'

'You can't mean that.'

'Everyone else will be forced to do the same, sooner or later. We can gain the upper hand if we take the initiative.'

'And you're going to do it? Wield the axe?'

'There will still be jobs for a few key members of staff,' he said. 'We'll be expanding our digital platform. The journalism won't just disappear simply because we're no longer using newsprint to distribute it. But I'd like to see this story about the strip— about Josefin in printed form.'

Oh, he would, would he? 'How long have I got?' She couldn't hide her sarcasm.

'The distribution contracts need to be renegotiated, all the agreements with the printers, it's going to take a while . . .'

Her mouth was dry, but she had to ask. 'And then what? What's going to happen to me?'

'Naturally there'll be a place for you in the new organization. You know I want you on the newsdesk.'

'To spend my days dreaming up imaginary newspapers?'

'Among other things.'

Tears were pricking her eyes, and she got to her feet. 'Never,' she said. 'I'd rather stack shelves in a supermarket.'

He sighed. 'Don't say anything to the others,' he said. 'We're not going public until early next week.'

She nodded and walked out of the glass box, closing the door behind her.

The Underground took her to Södermalm, the people around her jolting into her as they all swayed and rocked. Annika was trying not to cry. Obviously Schyman was right: the *Evening Post* would be the first in a long series of newspapers that would stop publishing a print edition. She looked around the carriage. A few older men were holding newspapers, but not many. The change had already happened.

She turned towards the window and caught sight of her own hollow-eyed reflection.

What would a world without newspapers be like? The streets would seem different: the bright yellow fly-sheets would disappear from outside kiosks and shops, but they would be replaced by other forms of advertising. On buses and trains people would spend even more time staring at their phones and the free papers would no longer blow about on the platforms.

How would it feel to live and work in that world?

According to a recent Norwegian study, you don't remember the things you read digitally as clearly as you would if you'd read them on paper. Fifty people had read the same story by a British crime writer, half in printed form, half as an e-book, and the people who had read the e-book had had much more trouble remembering the storyline than those who had read it on paper. The researchers weren't sure why: something to do with the weight of the paper, the act of turning the pages, the sense of forward momentum? What did it mean for her as a journalist? Would she have to simplify things even more for her readers? Make the world even more black and white?

Maybe this was her punishment, this and the panic attacks, for how she had behaved, everything she had done badly, everyone she had let down . . . Immediately she was ashamed of the thought – how could a major change in journalism have anything to do with her shortcomings? The panic attacks were founded in her personality: why shouldn't she suffer them, given the way she had behaved?

The train slowed, and she clung to a handrail to stop herself falling on to a woman with a pushchair.

A few moments later, she climbed up into the light again at Medborgarplatsen station. The yellow fly-sheets were still shrieking outside the newsagent's. Södermalm had a different rhythm from Kungsholmen, a different texture. She still felt humbled at being there – she couldn't quite believe it. She was less judgemental there, more patient, and there were no ghosts. She even felt benevolent towards the men in bright yellow helmets who had cordoned off the whole of Götgatan and were busy ripping up the tarmac, making an infernal racket.

Anyway, who was she to judge? She had betrayed her own husband when he was at his most vulnerable, tormented and mutilated, and embarked on a relationship with his boss. Why should she be shown any consideration?

The screen of her phone lit up inside her bag: the clamour of the roadworks drowned the sound but she saw it was ringing. She wiped her eyes, pressed the phone hard against one ear, stuck her finger into the other and hurried away from the noise.

'Hello, Annika,' a male voice said. 'It's Steven.'

'Hi, Steven.' She crossed the street, her bag thumping against her hip, stopped outside McDonald's and let it fall to the ground.

In spite of his Anglo-Saxon name, Steven had been born and raised in Malmköping, the neighbouring town to Hälleforsnäs. He was five years older than Birgitta, and Annika had never met him until Birgitta and he had tumbled into her flat on Kungsholmen late one night while Thomas was still with the kidnappers.

'Have you heard anything from Birgitta?' he asked.

People streamed past her along Folkungagatan.

'No. I spoke to Barbro earlier. I haven't heard anything since then. What's actually happened?' She tried to make her voice sound cheerful, keep the darkness at a distance.

'Birgitta didn't come home from work yesterday,' he said.

'So Mum said. She didn't say anything before she left? You haven't heard from her?'

'Not since . . . no.'

He fell silent. A gang of teenage girls with blue hair, their hands full of hamburgers, pushed past her on the pavement. One dropped a cup of Coca-Cola on Annika's shoes. She turned her back on them. 'Hello?' she said.

'I wondered if she'd said anything to you.'

Annika stared at the wall. 'Steven,' she said, 'why would she have done that? Birgitta and I have practically no contact with each other.'

'You didn't even come to our wedding.'

That old story. 'I thought you were going to move to Oslo,' she said.

'Oh, that . . . Well, we applied for jobs there, but it didn't work out.'

'Why not?'

He didn't reply, and she stared at the screen: no, the call hadn't been cut off. The number 71 bus rumbled past on its way to Danvikstull. She closed her eyes.

Steven cleared his throat. 'There's something about this that doesn't make any sense,' he said. 'I don't know what to do. Diny keeps asking for her. What do I say?'

All of sudden Annika felt drained. 'Steven, why did she leave? Did you have a fight?'

'No, not exactly . . .'

Not exactly.

'Did you . . . did you hit her?'

'Never.'

The answer was quick, clear. *Too* quick?

'If you manage to get hold of her, please, let me know,' he said.

Annika brushed the hair from her face. Why would Birgitta contact her, and not Steven? 'I don't think I've got her number. I've got a new phone and I couldn't transfer my old address book . . . By the way, how did you get my number?'

'From Barbro.'

Of course.

Her phone vibrated in her hand. *New contact received.*

'Promise you'll be in touch,' he said.

'Sure.'

She clicked to end the call, her heart thudding. She took several deep breaths before dropping her phone into her bag and hoisting it on to her shoulder.

She walked slowly towards Södermannagatan. She and Birgitta had nothing in common any more, except their childhood.

She went into the Co-op on Nytorgsgatan and bought some mince, cream, onions, and new potatoes from Belgium: Kalle had requested beef patties for dinner.

There was a small queue at the checkout, a line of urban middle-class people on their way home from work, just like her, wearing something a bit vintage, the odd expensive accessory, something from H&M. A young woman, who hadn't been born in Sweden and who couldn't afford to live on Södermalm, was sitting behind the counter, doing the job that Birgitta had chosen to do. It was no surprise that Birgitta had decided to work as a cashier because she loved shops. She could spend hours shopping, for food, clothes or skincare products, it didn't matter, as long as she could lose herself in products and labels. As a child, she had often spent her pocket money on a pretty jar of jam or rose-scented soap.

Annika used her Co-op member's card to pay, and noted that the woman behind the till had artistically designed acrylic nails, the sort Birgitta usually wore.

The meal with the children went well, even though Jimmy was working late. They sat round the table in the dining room and talked through the day, just as they always had. Serena had finally stopped her seemingly interminable testing and questioning, and the sense of liberation Annika felt was greater than she cared to admit. Now her stepdaughter described in great detail something they had discussed in her craft lesson. She was good at sewing and handicrafts, and very interested in techniques and materials. Ellen chattered on about a YouTube video she had watched, with some Norwegians singing a song about a fox. Jacob was quiet, but ate a lot. Kalle wouldn't drink the milk she had poured for him. He continued to refuse it, even after Annika had explained that 'best before' did not mean 'poisonous after'.

Once they had helped clear up after the meal, the children disappeared into their rooms to play with various electronic gadgets. Annika sat down at the kitchen table, the dishwasher humming in the background, and dialled Birgitta's number. She put her hand over her eyes as she waited for the call to be connected, then listened to the hissing silence. She steeled herself to be friendly and polite to her sister, but found herself listening to her voicemail message instead: *Hi, this is Birgitta, I'm afraid I can't take your call, but if you leave me a message after the tone, I'll call you back as soon as I can. Bye!*

The bleep that followed was long and piercing. Oddly Annika felt rather let down, and hesitated for a moment before she spoke. 'Yes, er, hi,' she said, into the silence. 'It's Annika. I've heard you didn't go home after work

70

yesterday, and, well, we're wondering where you are. Get in touch, okay? Bye for now.'

She clicked to end the call, relieved to have passed responsibility for any further communication to her sister. At that moment a minor tussle broke out along the corridor leading to the children's rooms. 'Time to brush your teeth!' she called.

The noise got louder, and there was shouting and crying. She made her way to the boys' room, where a catastrophe had evidently occurred. Jacob had lost his mobile phone. He didn't think anyone had taken it, just couldn't remember where he'd put it or when he'd last seen it.

Together they turned the flat upside down, to no avail. But at the bottom of an old removal box she found her own old one. It wasn't a smartphone, but it would be usable with a new battery. She explained that you couldn't expect to get a replacement smartphone straight away if you lost yours.

Through the careful use of gestures, words, hugs and a bit of rough and tumble, along with reference to the general rules, she got the situation under control, succeeded in uniting sworn enemies against a common foe (her) and, with some appreciative noises about YouTube videos of songs about foxes and a short collective reading from one of C. S. Lewis's Narnia books, she brought peace and harmony to the children's department.

Then she went and sat on the sofa in the living room and watched the evening news, which included a debate about internet privacy and who should take responsibility for it. One of the participants was a representative of Feminist Initiative, who thought everyone should be allowed to be anonymous on the internet at all times. Her adversary was a representative of the music industry, who reckoned that people sharing files ought to be traced and given the same punishment as if they had stolen a CD from a record store. Annika agreed with each of them while they were talking, which told her that she was very tired but also that they were probably both right, albeit in different ways.

That was what Jimmy was doing this evening. There was a meeting of the parliamentary committee that was looking into the issue, the inquiry that Thomas was working on. She couldn't help wondering how on earth that could happen. Thomas and Jimmy were far enough apart within the ministry that they didn't bump into each other very often, but in this instance they couldn't avoid one another.

She dozed off on the sofa and woke up to find Jimmy stroking her hair. Overjoyed, she wrapped her arms round his neck, breathing in his scent. 'How did it go?'

Jimmy pulled her upright, then sank down beside her on the sofa. She ended up on his lap, his breath in her ear. 'Semi-okay,' he said.

She looked at him over her shoulder.

'I haven't read Thomas's report properly,' he said, in response to her quizzical expression. 'There are details I missed. If his proposals go through, it would be impossible for the police and prosecutors to track down IP-addresses on the internet.' He fell silent.

'I saw a discussion about it on the news,' Annika said. 'I agreed with both sides.'

Jimmy sighed. 'This sort of stuff isn't easy,' he said, his stubble catching in her hair. 'Even the members of the parliamentary committee are having trouble getting to grips with it. Several of them think that freedom of expression means being able to say whatever you like anonymously online. And I wasn't well enough prepared. I should have kept myself better informed of how the work was going . . .'

She turned her head. 'What's Thomas done?' she asked.

He kissed her hair. 'I'll have to have a chat with him about it tomorrow. How did you get on with the psychologist?'

She sat up. 'I don't really know. She asked me a bit about my childhood, and how it *felt* to talk about it . . .'

'So how *did* it feel?'

'Unpleasant.' She looked across the room with half-closed eyes. 'Why is it so important for people to have the right to spew out hatred without anyone knowing who they are?'

'You don't want to talk about the psychologist?'

She leaned her head back, looked into his eyes, and tried to smile. There was something wrong with her. Healthy people didn't collapse on the hall floor, frightening the life out of their children. 'My mother called

73

today,' she said. 'And Steven, my brother-in-law. Birgitta's gone missing. She didn't come home from work yesterday.'

'What happened?'

Annika shut her eyes, and saw in her mind's eye the rented flat on Odendalsgatan in Hälleforsnäs, the bunks, her on top, Birgitta underneath, as close to each other as any two people could be but without having anything in common. Annika was always wanting to get away and Birgitta just wanted to stay at home.

'She was frightened of everything when we were little,' Annika said. 'Ants, wasps, ghosts, aeroplanes . . . She could never stay with Grandma in Lyckebo, because there were snakes in the grass . . .'

'Didn't she buy a place of her own out there somewhere?'

'She only rented it one summer.' She screwed her eyes shut and took a deep breath. 'The print edition of the paper is being closed down,' she said. She could feel him staring at her and opened her eyes. 'I got called in to see Schyman today. The board took the decision last Friday. It's going to be made public next week.'

'What'll happen to the staff?'

'A lot of them will have to leave, but not all. They'll need people on the newsdesk who can deal with the digital side of things.' He didn't ask the obvious question, but she answered it anyway. 'Schyman wants me to stay on, to help invent the future with wish-list layouts.'

Jimmy sighed. 'Sometimes I can't help wondering what's going to become of humanity,' he said.

'We're really nothing but a load of fish who crawled out of the sea a hundred and fifty million years ago,' Annika said.

'Come here.' He pulled her towards him.

TUESDAY, 2 JUNE

Nina walked into her office at a quarter past seven. The sun was nudging above the roof of the inner courtyard, making the stacks of paper on her desk glow. It would be very warm and muggy later in the day.

She shoved her gym bag under the bookcase and put the day's papers and a bottle of mineral water on the desk. She took a sandwich and a bottle of orange juice from the bag and put them into the top drawer – she'd need something to eat after she'd been to the gym.

She sat down at the desk and listened to the silence around her. Most of her colleagues didn't arrive until around eight o'clock, and some didn't appear until the meeting at nine. Johansson, the oversized secretary, was already there, though: she could hear him coughing further down the corridor. Fortunately the guy she shared her office with, Jesper Wou, was off on another of his long business trips. She enjoyed having the room to herself.

She logged on to her computer. Nothing much had happened overnight – no one had emailed. With a sense of relief, she pulled the newspapers towards her. She paged through them, but they contained nothing she hadn't already seen on teletext. The *Evening Post* had an article about one of the princesses on its front page, speculating about whether she would fly back to Sweden to celebrate National Day. Nina ignored the story: the royal family weren't her problem. Her colleagues in the Security Police were responsible for them. At the bottom of the page was a reference to 'the Timberman': Ivar Berglund. She turned to pages six and seven, and found herself staring into Berglund's blank eyes. The picture ran across both pages. It had been taken with a long lens through an open doorway. Berglund must have glanced in the photographer's direction for a fraction of a second, and she (according to the credit) had been ready. It must have happened very quickly, Berglund might not even have been aware of it, yet the picture had captured his cool, unruffled demeanour, his impenetrable inner life. Nina stared at it for a few seconds before she saw the headline above it:

SUSPECTED OF SERIAL KILLINGS ACROSS EUROPE

The implications of the headline struck her in an almost physical way, leaving her breathless. With her palms flat on the newspaper, Nina leaned forward and skimmed the article in the vain hope that things weren't as bad as she feared. It turned out to be a forlorn hope, of course . . .

*

According to Nina Hoffman, an operational analyst with the National Crime Unit in Stockholm, there are a number of unsolved murders in other countries that bear similarities to the case in Orminge. Ivar Berglund's DNA profile has therefore been examined in light of these other investigations, in both the Nordic countries and across the rest of Europe. This collaboration has been going on for the past year and is still not complete, although the National Crime Unit has not yet found any matches . . .

*

How could she have been so incredibly stupid? Without any reflection, she had given honest answers to the lawyer's questions. It had been a crazy thing to do. She had played right into the hands of the defence team. She had revealed that they had nothing else to offer, that they had searched and searched and searched, but hadn't found the slightest suspicion to pin on Ivar Berglund. She had revealed their fundamental failure to the court and the whole of the assembled media. She was so stupid, she ought to be locked up.

She stood up but had nowhere to go, so sat down again. In her mind she replayed the scene again, saw the smartly made-up lawyer standing there: *What have you all been doing during the protracted period of time that my client has been in custody?* And she heard herself answer, shooting herself in the foot: *Ivar Berglund's DNA profile has been compared against other open investigations both in the Nordic countries and else-where in Europe . . .*

If they lost the case, and Berglund was released, it would be her fault. She pressed her hands to her cheeks. Her fingers were icy: adrenalin had made the blood vessels in her extremities contract to prepare for a fight.

She forced her shoulders to relax: *focus!* Her eyes roamed across the table, and she saw Berglund's file. She pulled it to her and opened the section on the DNA traces. Had there really been anything wrong with the results of the DNA sample found at the crime scene in Orminge? The match was almost perfect, 99 per cent. The defence lawyer had tried to make out that it was contaminated – could that be so? Was it possible that the sample had been impure? Could something have gone wrong when it was taken, or during the analysis?

She leafed through the report from the National Forensics Laboratory, her fingers warming.

There was nothing new. She knew all the answers off by heart.

She heard Johansson cough again, hesitated, then stood up with the file in her arms.

The secretary's office was five doors away. He had a room to himself, a luxury granted to few in the department. It was possible that he had privileged status because he had once been part of the National Rapid-Response Force, but after some traumatic incident (exactly what was unclear) he had been transferred to an office job. He might have trouble dealing with the cruelty of the world, but he was a formidable administrator.

Nina knocked on his door frame and he looked up at her over his glasses. Without saying anything, he nodded to the chair on the other side of his desk.

'I've got a question,' Nina said, as she sat down. 'How many more unsolved cases are out there for us to cross-check with the Berglund case?'

Johansson took off his glasses. 'Just the bottom of the barrel,' he said. 'Our colleagues are dredging through samples taken when DNA technology was in its infancy.'

'Eighteen, twenty years ago?' Nina said.

'Something like that.'

'What are the chances of finding anything?'

Johansson looked out of the window and thought for a moment. 'Slim, but not non-existent. The technology was completely new back then, and the criminals were still making basic mistakes, hadn't learned how to get rid of DNA ...' He turned back to her. 'Something bothering you?'

She flushed. 'Have you had a chance to look at the *Evening Post*?' she asked.

He held her gaze. 'You answered the questions,' he said. 'To do anything else would have been against the law.'

Nothing but the truth, with no additions or amendments.

She straightened her back. 'I've been thinking about the DNA results from Orminge. Could something have gone wrong? Could the sample have been manipulated or contaminated?'

'If there was anything wrong with the equipment, the results wouldn't have shown a match at all,' Johansson said.

Nina opened the DNA report.

'If someone *did* manipulate the sample,' the secretary went on, 'it would have to have been someone at the National Forensics Lab, or one of the officers at the scene.'

Nina held her hand still on the folder. Planting DNA evidence at a crime scene was a fairly easy thing to do, much easier than falsifying fingerprints, she knew. Anyone could plant some saliva, or a drop of blood, a trace of semen. 'Could someone switch the DNA in a sample? Tamper with it to make it look like it came from someone else?'

Johansson took a sip of coffee and sighed. 'If you get rid of the white blood cells in a centrifuge, the DNA disappears. Then you just have to add some different DNA, from a strand of hair, for instance. Are you suggesting that someone at the lab might have . . .?'

'Is there anyone at the National Forensics Lab who has any connection with Berglund? Someone who might want to frame him? Have we checked that?'

He didn't reply.

'There are more victims out there,' Nina said quietly. 'The perpetrator in Orminge was no novice. He'd done it before. Lerberg, the assault in Solsidan, that was him as well . . .'

Johansson shook his head sadly.

'The torture methods were identical,' Nina said. 'It was the same perpetrator. I think that the first DNA we found, the mitochondrial sample in Djursholm, was Ivar Berglund's as well. No one's tampered with the tests. He abducted Viola Söderland, and he tortured Ingemar Lerberg.'

'The evidence . . .'

'He's playing with us,' Nina said in a low voice. 'And he wants us to know it.'

She thought about the drawing that the murderer had taken from the Lerberg children's room and inserted, rolled up, into the rectum of the victim in Orminge.

Tears stood in Johansson's eyes. 'I don't know,' he said. 'DNA evidence has been wrong before.'

'You mean the Phantom of Heilbronn?' Nina asked.

Johansson blew his nose.

For most of the 1990s and 2000s a female serial killer had made fools of a number of Central European police forces, mostly in south-west Germany but also in France and Austria. Her DNA was found at almost forty separate crime scenes: she committed robberies and killings. She was described by detectives as extremely brutal, probably a drug addict, and usually pretended to be male. The first DNA sample was found as early as 1993 when an elderly woman had been strangled in her home after a burglary.

In the winter of 2009 the German police devoted almost sixteen thousand hours of overtime to the search for the Phantom of Heilbronn: the investigating team was expanded, they conducted daily DNA analysis, tested seven hundred women, worked through almost three and a half thousand possible leads, and announced a €300,000 reward. All to no avail.

Then, in March 2009, the case had taken a different turn. The French police conducted a DNA test on the charred remains of a male asylum-seeker, and discovered that he was in fact a woman, and not just any woman but the Phantom of Heilbronn. Among her many other crimes, she had murdered a police officer in Heilbronn two years before. At this point it had dawned on the detectives that something was seriously wrong with the DNA evidence.

It turned out that the DNA from the forty different cases had not come from evidence gathered at the different crime scenes but from the cotton-wool swabs used to take the samples. All the swabs had come from the same factory in Eastern Europe.

'Could there be some other explanation?' Nina said. 'Could the sample be right but the match wrong? Could the DNA actually belong to someone else?'

'That's a theoretical possibility,' Johansson said.

'But who, then? As far as we know, Berglund doesn't have any sons, does he?'

'Correct,' Johansson said. 'He's never made any maintenance payments, either officially or unofficially, and he's never been the subject of any paternity claims. Mind you, that isn't proof that he doesn't have a son . . .'

Nina clasped her hands. 'It still doesn't make sense,' she said. 'Not for the Orminge case, and not for Djursholm. Even if he had a son, his DNA wouldn't be such a good match, and mitochondrial DNA is passed down the maternal line.'

They sank into silence as Nina read the report. Both of Ivar Berglund's parents were dead – they had drowned in the early 1970s. His brother, Arne Berglund, had died in a car crash in the south of Spain twenty years ago.

'Lots of accidental deaths in that family,' Johansson said gloomily. 'And it can hardly be his sister.' Ivar Berglund's younger sister, Ingela, lived in a care-home up in Luleå.

Nina stared out of the window at the far side of the room. She could almost feel the heat hitting the glass. 'Has anyone spoken to her?'

'She has learning difficulties.'

'But how bad are they? Do we know what sort of problems she's got?'

Johansson flicked through the file. 'It doesn't say. Presumably our colleagues decided it wouldn't be useful. Maybe she can't talk or perhaps they just wanted to spare her. It's possible she doesn't even know that her brother has been charged with murder.'

Nina got to her feet. 'Thanks for letting me take up your time,' she said. 'When are you next due to contact our European colleagues about the remaining cases?'

Johansson sighed again.

Nina left the room and saw Commissioner Q, head of the Criminal Intelligence Unit, disappear into his office at the end of the corridor. She hurried after him and knocked on his door. 'Sorry,' she said, 'but have you got a moment?'

Commissioner Q was holding a stained coffee mug. The buttons of his Hawaiian shirt had been done up wrongly. 'Of course I have, Nina. What can I do for you?'

Q was a very unusual sort of police chief, not just in his unorthodox style of dress and appalling taste in music (he loved the Eurovision Song Contest), but more particularly in his way of thinking, and the lack of pre-sumption with which he approached things he didn't understand. During the year she had been working for him at National Crime she had come to appreciate his acerbic way of communicating and open leadership style.

'I'd like to go up to Luleå, to talk to Ivar Berglund's sister.'

The commissioner sat down behind his chaotic desk and frowned. 'Isn't she supposed to be a bit backward? Lives in a home, or something?'

'Yes,' Nina said. 'But she might be able to communi-cate. I'd like to look into it, anyway.'

Q hesitated. 'There are probably good reasons why

she's been left alone, as a matter of respect. How old is she?'

'In her fifties,' Nina said.

He scratched his head. 'A middle-aged woman with learning difficulties? Ask to see her medical records and check what's wrong with her.' He reached for a file on his desk, indicating that the conversation was over.

Nina paused in the doorway. 'There was one other thing, about the murder of Josefin Liljeberg.'

Her boss looked up in surprise. 'Josefin?' he said. 'That was my case, once upon a time, my first when I got to Violent Crime.'

Nina straightened. 'Annika Bengtzon from the *Evening Post* got in touch yesterday. She's taking another look at the case and is wondering if she can see the preliminary investigation; unofficially, of course.'

The commissioner drank the rest of his coffee and pulled a face. 'Why didn't she call me?'

'You're the boss, so you haven't got a direct line. The prosecutor has let her have the list of witnesses, so it clearly isn't completely off-limits.'

Q put his mug down with a bang. 'Have we got the case here?'

'It's among the stack of confessions Gustaf Holmerud made.'

The commissioner groaned at the mention of Holmerud's name. He sat without speaking for a while. 'I remember Josefin,' he eventually said. 'A boiling-hot day, a Saturday. Her boyfriend did it, a nasty piece of work.

His friends gave him an alibi, or we would have got him. It might not do any harm to let Bengtzon go through the file.' He nodded to himself. 'Quite the contrary, in fact,' he went on. 'If the *Evening Post* stir things up a bit, one or two cockroaches might come to the surface. Give her a copy of the file, and remind her about the confidentiality of sources. She's not to quote from it.' He leaned over his bundle of papers.

Nina turned and headed off towards her office.

'By the way,' he called after her, 'you said the right thing in court. That bastard's guilty – let him sweat it out. He'll know we're keeping an eye on him.'

Her boss had read the *Evening Post*. That didn't improve her mood.

Anders Schyman sat back in his chair. He had adopted a neutral expression, and was trying to stop himself frowning. He could have saved himself the trouble: Albert Wennergren, the chairman of the board, was standing with his back to him, his silly ponytail swaying gently in the breeze from the air-conditioning. He was gazing out at the newsroom on the other side of the glass wall. The staff were busy absorbing news, checking it, questioning and monitoring it, a silent film in colour with no background music.

'What sort of premises do you think we'll need after the reorganization?' Wennergren asked, without turning.

Reorganization? *Reorganization?*

Schyman took a deep, soundless breath to stop himself

screaming. 'I haven't worked that out yet,' he said, in a measured tone. 'First we have to decide how many people will be needed to maintain our digital activities, and for the development of video coverage, as well as our focus on other platforms. We'll have to compare the cost of moving against scaling back our existing premises and maybe renting out . . .'

Now the chairman turned round, sat down in one of the visitors' chairs, and propped his elbows on his knees. 'And take a look at the cost of any emotional response as well,' he said.

Schyman was unsure what the man had meant.

Wennergren's gaze was fixed on him. 'Compromising and dragging the process out, that costs money. A quick strategy, without any compromises, must be cheaper. I'd like to know by how much.'

'You mean the difference?' Schyman said. 'A longer process that shields the staff versus . . .'

'Once you've taken a decision, it's best to implement it quickly and decisively. That's the most humane option,' Wennergren said.

Schyman stared at the chairman of the board. He wasn't going to be the first to look away. 'It might be a little tricky to convey the board's motives,' he said. 'Explaining and justifying this dramatic . . . change, after the newspaper has made a profit of around a billion kronor over the past twelve years.'

Wennergren nodded. 'Absolutely,' he said. 'It's important that we don't stifle debate, that people feel free to contribute to the discussion. We'll simply have to explain that we regard news and social journalism as a fundamental part of our vision of publishing. What's new about this is that we'll be where the public wants to find us, and that, of course, will cost a lot in terms of investment. The staff have to understand that.'

Schyman tried to swallow, but his mouth was bone dry. Mustn't stifle debate. Let people contribute to the discussion. 'So, in order to secure the publication of serious, considered social journalism, we have to take difficult decisions about our priorities,' he said, hoping he didn't sound too ironic.

The chairman of the board nodded excitedly. 'Exactly! We're taking this extremely difficult decision because we want to be in control of our own future. We're seizing the initiative while we still have a chance to do so!'

Schyman made a real effort to sound reasonable. 'Our competitors aren't exactly resting on their laurels, as we know.'

Wennergren leaned forward. 'Do you know,' he said, 'I was over in California last month, and met the bosses at Google. They're not worried about competition but about the consumers. Our behaviour patterns are changing so fast that even they can't keep up. The world's biggest search engine! They're worried about disappearing!'

He stood up and looked out across the newsroom again, the very embodiment of a desire for change. 'It's hard to comprehend how much the media industry is going to change in the next few years, but one thing is certain: the *Evening Post* will be part of it. We're going to be in the vanguard.'

Schyman couldn't reply. Twenty years ago there were seven thousand journalists working on daily papers in Sweden. Now there were just two thousand left. In the last year alone almost forty local papers had closed, and more than four hundred journalists had lost their jobs. The shadow hanging over the media was spreading across the country at the same pace and in the same way as neo-Fascist movements. The only roles that were gaining strength within the media were information management and PR consultancy, which existed to steer and influence.

Wennergren gestured towards the newsroom. 'Isn't that the woman who looked after Valter when he did his work-placement here last summer?'

Schyman got up and went to stand next to him, his knees aching. 'They got on pretty well,' he said.

'She made a big impression on Valter. He talks about her a lot.'

Bengtzon must have felt their eyes on her, because she turned towards them. Schyman instinctively took a step back and moved away. 'How's Valter getting on?' he asked, as he sat down again.

'Fine, thanks,' Wennergren said. 'He finished his journalism degree a few weeks ago.'

'It's a shame there are no jobs for journalists in Sweden,' Schyman said.

The chairman of the board smiled confidently. 'Valter's going to carry on with his academic career, researching media relations and press ethics.'

Schyman nodded. 'A talented lad.'

Albert Wennergren let out a contented sigh. 'I was a little sceptical when he said he wanted to do his work-placement here at the *Evening Post*, but this was actually where he worked out what he wanted to do. He had a lot of discussions about press ethics and the foundations of the tabloid press with his supervisor. What was her name? Berntson?'

'Bengtzon,' Schyman said. 'Annika.'

'I read Valter's thesis the other evening. I thought it was rather exciting. He makes a distinction between self-important media, like the morning papers and state-funded television, and tabloids like the *Evening Post*. The former are regarded as "smart" and "serious", which is partly a consequence of what they choose to cover, and how they angle their coverage. They report on the labour market and politics, sport, wars and the economy, all traditional male domains, and they do so in an official-sounding way.'

Schyman knew all of this. Hadn't he once given a speech on the subject? 'All media cover wars and politics,' he said.

'But their approaches differ. The tabloids focus on the personal and private, on people's feelings and experiences, which have traditionally been regarded as female territory. And we address the little person on the street, not the establishment. That's why the tabloids are so derided – because there's nothing as provocative as an outspoken woman on the lowest rungs of society . . . I'd like to talk to Annika Berntson,' Albert Wennergren said. 'Can you ask her to come in for a few minutes?'

Schyman experienced a sudden chill inside him: what if she shot her mouth off? What if Wennergren realized he, Schyman, had been indiscreet and had told Annika about the closure? He reached across his desk and pressed the intercom. 'Annika, can you come into my office for a moment?'

'What for?'

Why did she always have to question him?

He watched her walk towards his glass box and pull open the door without any enthusiasm.

'What is it?' she asked.

'I was just telling Anders here about Valter's doctoral thesis,' Albert Wennergren said. 'He's thinking of researching the approaches of various media towards modern journalism.'

'Exciting,' Annika Bengtzon said blankly, from the doorway.

'He often refers to conversations he had with you, about methodology and journalism and ethics. You have strong opinions on those subjects. Can you expand upon what you said about gender identification in the media?'

She glanced around in confusion, as if she were looking for a hidden camera. 'I can't really remember,' she said. 'I say so many silly things.'

'You told Valter that the *Evening Post* was a shrill working-class woman, yelling truths that no one wants to hear.'

She shifted her weight from one foot to the other, clearly uncomfortable.

'Come in and close the door,' Wennergren added. 'You know that Anders is going to be leaving – I'd like to hear your thoughts on his successor. What are the qualities we need?'

Her eyes darkened. 'An evening paper is a warship,' she said, 'in a world that is always in a state of war. And if there's no battle going on nearby, you go out and find one, or you attack someone and start one of your own. You need a captain who can steer the ship, who understands the scale of the task. Knowing how to sail and windsurf is no good.'

'Any suggestions?'

'Berit Hamrin, but apparently she won't do. She's too decent.'

'Someone from television, perhaps? Or business?'

Her eyes narrowed. 'Someone who's already a name, you mean. If you want to drive the paper on to the rocks, then get one of those self-important idiots. Was there anything else?'

'No,' Schyman said quickly. 'You can go.'

She closed the door and walked away without looking back.

Albert Wennergren watched her go. 'I'd like, as far as possible, to be sorted out before we go public with the board's decision,' he said. 'An outline of the new organization, the cost of reducing staff numbers, the question of premises, technical investment and, ideally, a new editor-in-chief as well.'

Schyman was holding on to the arms of his chair tightly. 'What about the printers and distributors? When are we going to tell them?' It wasn't just the journalists who would be losing their jobs. The printers they used had just invested in an entirely new packaging room, with all the equipment necessary for folding, trimming, stickering, inkjet address-printing and leaflet insertion. The *Evening Post* wasn't the company's only client, but it was by far the largest. Three hundred people worked there, but for how much longer?

'We'll hold back on that,' Wennergren said. 'Our contract with the printers expires this autumn, so we'll be in a damn good negotiating position then.' He reached for his briefcase. It was made of cloth, some sporting label. No traditional leather nonsense for him. 'It goes without saying that it's vitally important none of this leaks out,' he added.

A guilty shiver ran down Schyman's spine, and he saw Annika standing before him with the minutes of the board meeting in her hand. He stared at the chairman without blinking. 'Of course,' he said.

Berit put her bag on the desk and wiped the sweat from her forehead. Annika took a deep breath and switched her attention from Schyman's glass box to her colleague.

'Let me guess,' she said. 'Rosa speaks out about her weight.'

'She feels badly violated,' Berit confirmed, sinking on to her chair.

It looked like the chairman of the board was getting ready to leave: he had picked up his briefcase and he was laughing.

'I read in the preliminary edition that Rosa had spoken to her PR people and realized what a terrible ordeal she had been subjected to,' Annika said.

'She took the teasing as a general attack on her as a person,' Berit said, getting her laptop out. 'She wanted to broaden the discussion, show that she's more than good enough as she is. No one has the right to tell her how she should look.'

'You'd never guess she had PR advisers,' Annika said.

Berit switched on her computer, idly polishing her glasses while she waited for the programs to load – how many times had Annika seen her do that? How many more before it was all over?

'It's quite interesting, this business of being good enough as you are,' Berit said, inspecting her glasses. 'What it actually means is that you never need to develop, that any sort of ambition or change is negative.'

Annika raised her eyebrows. She saw Albert Wenner-gren close the door of the editor-in-chief's aquarium and head towards the exit. 'How do you mean?' she asked, following the man with her eyes.

Berit put her glasses on. 'I kept thinking about it all the way through the interview with Rosa. How angry she was at the suggestion that she might have changed somehow since that reality show. She was who she was, and she had the right to be who she was.'

'Hasn't she, then?'

Wennergren disappeared round the office manager's cubbyhole. In the glass box, Schyman was sitting motionless behind his desk, staring into space. The two men must have been discussing the details of the closure, and no one around her had any idea of what was coming. The catastrophe was approaching with full force, but here on the shop-floor everyone was still sitting at their desks, getting on with all manner of tasks. She turned to Berit and realized she hadn't been listening to her.

'Rosa,' Annika said. 'She doesn't need to change anything about herself because she's perfect.'

'It was interesting listening to her,' Berit said. 'Her whole attitude is anchored in identity politics instead of being progressive, just like the Sweden Democrats: everything new and unknown is bad and must be rejected. She has the right to demand respect in spite of her pitiful vocabulary, wasted education and stale opinions.' Berit took two apples out of her bag, passed one to Annika and took a bite out of the other.

'And that's a problem because?' Annika said.

Berit chewed and swallowed. 'In the long run, identity politics will become an ideology that produces a new underclass. It means we can never become anything other than what we are born into. Imagine how the workers' movement at the turn of the last century would have sounded if they'd acted like that. "Never mind education, carry on getting drunk! That's your identity!" '

The apple seemed to expand in Annika's mouth. Who was she? Where could she work, if not here? Was she needed anywhere, except on the ethical fringes of journalism? 'What's happening with the Timberman today?' she asked, pulling her laptop towards her.

'Technical witnesses,' Berit said. 'The mobile operator and the National Forensics Lab, then some neighbour, nothing exciting. What are you up to?'

Annika slumped and pushed her laptop away. What was the point? Should she pack up and go home, or stay and let the tidal wave hit her along with everyone else? 'Nina Hoffman's managed to get me the whole preliminary investigation into Josefin's murder, off the record, so I'm going to go through it this evening. I've tracked down all the witnesses: one's dead, four still live in Stockholm, and the most interesting one, Robin Bertelsson, has moved to Copenhagen. He works for Doomsday, one of those overhyped IT companies that doesn't have any phone lines, just an anonymous email address.' Annika looked at her watch. It was ten o'clock in the morning, a Tuesday at the start of June, the last week, the last few days. 'The prosecutor who was in charge of the case has retired. I've arranged to see him at his home in Flen.' She tossed the apple core into the paper-recycling box and walked towards the office manager's desk.

The tarmac on the motorway was steaming as Annika drove south in one of the paper's cars. The traffic was as slow and stop-start as always, which she found oddly reassuring. She was keeping an eye on her mobile, which lay silent on the passenger seat beside her. The catastrophe still hadn't broken. There were no messages, from her sister or anyone else.

There was a sort of loneliness in leaving behind everything familiar. She had moved away from Hälleforsnäs, but Birgitta had stayed, at least until she moved to Malmö. Why? And why choose to disappear now? Unless she hadn't gone of her own free will?

The turning for Skärholmen appeared ahead, one of the vast concrete housing projects from the 1960s, with a huge shopping centre that she had been to before. She pulled off the motorway and parked in a multi-storey car park the size of a small town. When she switched on the car alarm, the sound echoed off the concrete pillars.

The mall was air-conditioned, and all the discount brands in the northern hemisphere were gathered in one place. She felt an intense sense of *déjà vu*: all of these shopping centres blurred into a single amorphous mass. She had been here with Valter Wennergren, the chairman's son, when she had been supervising him on his work-placement. They had interviewed a man who sold a car to Viola Söderland. He'd had a flower stall, hadn't he? Or was it vegetables? She cruised past the clothes shops and electronics stores with growing lethargy.

People streamed past her, their voices scraping the inside of her head.

She was about to give up when she found what she was looking for: a windowless shop selling phones connected to her old mobile network. She took a numbered ticket from the machine, then stood and read about their various phones and contracts while she waited for her turn. The handsets were ridiculously cheap, almost free, but in return you had to sign up to never-ending contracts for the privilege of making calls. She had fallen for it, and was still paying for a number she hadn't used for at least six months.

There was only one customer ahead of her, a man who looked Middle Eastern. He was holding a little girl's hand, and spoke Arabic to the shop assistant. The child smiled at Annika and waved. She waved back.

'I've got a question,' Annika said, when it was her turn.

'I hope I'll be able to answer it,' said the young man behind the counter, as he crumpled her ticket and tossed it into the bin in an elegant arc.

'My phone's broken,' she said, putting her old mobile on the counter. 'It won't charge any more. Is it because of the battery or the charger?'

The young man picked it up and inspected it, then disappeared behind a curtain and came back just five seconds later. With a practised hand he removed the cover, took the battery out and inserted a new one. The screen lit up: *Searching for signal.*

'There,' he said. 'It was the battery. The new one will last until you get home. Then you must charge it for sixteen hours.'

'Is it still covered by the guarantee?' she asked.

'Are you joking?' the guy said.

She bought a new charger as well, just in case, thanked him and went back to the car. The sounds of people shopping bounced off the glass and chrome and hit her eardrums, jagged shards of light reflecting off the walls.

There was a buzzing sound from inside her bag, a sound she hadn't heard for a long time: the screen of her old mobile was glowing somewhere towards the bottom. She stopped at a café and took it out. The phone had been out of use for six months. Who was still using her old number?

Two new messages.

Her pulse-rate went up.

They were both from Birgitta.

The first had been sent on 25 May, just over a week ago, last Monday. She clicked to open the text. *Annika, please get in touch, you've got to help me! Birgitta (sent 16.25)* If her sister really wanted to get hold of her, why hadn't she mentioned what it was about?

Sent at 16.25. Wouldn't she have been at work then? Or did she work shifts?

The second had been sent on 31 May, Sunday. The text was very short, and had been sent at 04.22: *Annika, help me!*

*

103

Thomas pressed his pass card against the reader, mid-stride, then greeted the guard with a friendly nod. He received no response, which sent a little shiver of satisfaction through him: he was recognized as a regular.

Having a defined role of his own, and in such a prestigious and important inquiry, undeniably brought with it a number of advantages. The ability to organize his own time was certainly one of them: there was no one to comment on his late starts and long lunches. Because he had been at an official dinner all yesterday evening, it was only to be expected that he should balance his hectic work schedule with an hour or so of contemplation at the start of the following day.

He slowed down by the lifts, as though he were about to press the button and wait to be carried higher up the building (the office of the minister of justice was on the sixth floor, the prime minister and Cabinet Office on the seventh), then took a quick step to the left, into his own corridor on the ground floor. It didn't really matter where you were in the building: his office with its view of a brick wall on Fredsgatan was as good as any other, and plenty of civil servants were dispersed in utterly anonymous buildings all over the centre of the city, where the more peripheral departments were based.

'Good morning!' he said cheerily, to one of the older secretaries, a well-preserved woman in her early fifties who had definitely had a facelift during the Christmas holiday. He appreciated women who made a bit of an effort. The woman (was her name Majken?) lit up, and even blushed slightly. He hoped it wasn't because of the hook, that she was embarrassed by his disability. One of the younger secretaries (Marielle Simon, he knew that one) passed him in the corridor (a little too close: was she after something?), but his greeting to her was more measured: she mustn't imagine that he found her attractive.

He breezed into his room with a spring in his step, ready to tackle the day's tasks, when a voice called his name. Surprised, but careful to hide it, he leaned out into the corridor.

It was Facelift, trotting after him. 'Thomas,' she said, 'the under-secretary of state has asked for you several times this morning. He seems very keen to get hold of you.'

He adopted a concerned frown. 'Of course,' he said. 'I'll go up and see him at once.'

'No,' Facelift said. 'He said he'd come down. He just wanted to be told when you arrived. I'll let him know . . .'

Thomas felt the colour rising to his neck and cheeks, but as luck would have it the woman was already heading back to her cubbyhole. What was all this about? Had he not sacrificed an entire evening and done everything that was expected of him, entertaining the elected representatives of the people with his enthusiasm for his task?

He unpacked the contents of his briefcase and spread them across his desk, a man fully engaged in his work. One of the disadvantages of this task (well, his whole work situation, really) was, of course, that his unfaithful and treacherous wife had moved in with the under-secretary of state, his boss. Enough time had passed now for him not to devote any more thought to her betrayal. The staff (at least in his own corridor) were used to seeing him there, focused and positive, admittedly with the hook instead of a left hand, but he was respected, he could tell.

He often thought of a proverb (was it Chinese?) that Annika used to quote: *If you wait by the river long enough, the bodies of your enemies will float past.*

This was an election year, and – if the opinion polls were right – the government was going to have to pack up and move out at long last. All the political appointees in the civil service (under-secretaries of state, for instance) would be instantly dismissed and left without a job. He, on the other hand, would still be there. Who really ruled the roost in Rosenbad? he thought, settling into his ergonomically designed office chair.

He started up his old work computer (an antiquated wreck that didn't suit him at all) and went on to Facebook. He wasn't fond of social media, but his ex-girlfriend, Sophia Grenborg, had once set up an account for him. Nowadays he mostly used it to keep tabs on people, such as Annika. His former wife wasn't particularly active, he had to say. She hadn't posted anything today or yesterday. If he was honest, he found that pretty irritating. What did she have to be so secretive about?

His computer bleeped: a new Facebook message. His stomach clenched. Maybe Annika wanted something from him.

Hi, Thomas, I see you're online. It's my birthday tomorrow and I'm having a few people round to the flat for drinks. You haven't RSVP'd yet, but I was wondering if you were coming. You'd be very welcome! Seven o'clock. Big hug, Sophia.

His ex was having trouble letting go. She had even become good friends with his ex-wife: she and Annika socialized these days. The children had sleepovers at hers. He thought the whole thing showed an unpleasant degree of disloyalty.

There was a knock on his door frame and Jimmy Halenius was standing there, heavy and, actually, rather short. He couldn't imagine what Annika saw in the man. Thomas clicked to close Facebook, stood up with a smile and held out his hand. 'I heard you'd been trying to get hold of me,' he said, as they shook hands. He made sure he took a firm, tight grip.

'I'm glad you've got time to see me,' Halenius said, and Thomas wondered if the under-secretary was making fun of him – but why would he do that?

His boss sat on a chair by the door without being asked.

'What can I do for you?' Thomas asked, lifting his trousers slightly at the knees.

'I thought we could have a chat about the state of your inquiry, and go through a few things that need to be updated,' Halenius said.

Thomas tried to look as if he understood. Updated? He tried to think of a suitable question to ask. When he didn't manage to find one, the under-secretary began speaking again.

'I should have looked through your outline before you presented it to the reference group, and I accept full responsibility for the way things have turned out, but it's important that we get this right now.'

Thomas struggled to hide his surprise. 'How . . .?'

Halenius raised a hand as if to shut him up. 'The coercive measures you propose are as expected. The police have the right to search premises and trace IP-addresses once they have a court order, as they do with bugging and surveillance, but after that things get a bit tricky. What would be the effect if this change to the law were passed?'

Thomas felt his tongue swell and his mouth dried. When he didn't reply Halenius continued, 'You've suggested in the legislative proposal that coercive measures should only be used for crimes that carry a sentence of at least four years in custody.'

Thomas breathed out: this was something he had under control. He leaned back calmly in his chair and adjusted his lapels with his right hand. 'I thought we should be consistent and follow the same line as bugging. We can't have different thresholds for everything.'

Halenius scratched his eyebrow. 'If this legislation is passed, it would be utterly toothless,' he said. 'There isn't a single crime it would apply to. Almost the only offences that carry sentences of more than four years are murder and terrorism, which is why that's the threshold for bugging. Telephone interception can be applied to offences with a two-year sentence. That's a lower established threshold. You didn't consider using that one?'

Thomas took a deep breath, but couldn't think of anything to say.

'You'd only be making the work of the police harder,' Halenius went on. 'It would be practically impossible for them to function. They wouldn't be able to investigate a single case.'

A gaping hole opened in Thomas's stomach and he clung to the arm of his chair with his one hand to stop himself falling. 'But I'm giving a presentation at the cabinet meeting on Thursday. The results of the inquiry are due to be delivered then.'

'Not in this state,' Jimmy Halenius said, and stood up. 'We'd hoped to be able to send the proposal out for consultation before the summer, but now we'll have to aim at having it ready before the election instead. Can you do that?'

Thomas stared at his boss, his messy hair, the too-tight shirt. Who the hell did he think he was? 'Absolutely,' he said. 'Of course. It'll be ready before the election.'

Former Chief Prosecutor Kjell Lindström lived in an old wooden house with towers and turrets on Vegagatan in Flen. Annika parked in the neatly raked drive. A man in his seventies got up from a garden chair on the lawn and walked towards her, his gait relaxed and powerful. He had a full head of white hair, and was wearing a brown cardigan over a white T-shirt.

This is where I'd like to be when I'm seventy, Annika found herself thinking. Wooden house, cardigan, lawn.

'Editor Bengtzon, I presume?' His eyes were dark and clear.

'That's right,' Annika said, hoisting her bag higher on her shoulder and shaking his hand.

'I don't think we've met before,' Lindström said.

'No,' Annika said. 'I did try to see you at the time, but you were very busy.'

He chuckled. 'Coffee?' he asked.

'I'd love some.'

He waved towards the lawn. Carrying the tripod for the video-camera, Annika followed him to a table next to a lilac arbour. A tray with a Thermos flask, cups and buns waited on the table.

'Freshly made,' Annika said.

He laughed again. It seemed to come easily to him. 'I must admit that we tend to stick to gender stereotypes in this family. My wife is the baker. I look after the barbecue. She's at her Pilates class, by the way.'

They sat down on the garden chairs, stained blue, with thick cushions. The wind tugged at the birch leaves above them, making the sunlight flicker. Annika held up the video-camera. 'Do you mind if I use this?'

'Be my guest.'

She screwed the camera to the tripod, adjusted the

white balance, then checked that the old prosecutor was in frame. She got a pen and notepad out of her bag as he poured coffee. 'So, you're interested in Josefin Liljeberg?' he said, screwing the top back on the flask.

'Do you mind if I ask you about something entirely different before we start the interview?' she said.

The prosecutor raised his eyebrows as he dropped a sugar lump into his coffee. 'Go ahead.'

'When do you think is the right time to report someone missing?'

He looked at her in surprise. 'Missing? That depends. Are we talking about a child or an adult?'

Annika hesitated. 'My sister, actually,' she said. 'She didn't come home from work the day before yesterday.'

He stirred his coffee. 'It's not against the law to leave home. Adults can come and go as they wish without it being a criminal offence.'

'But if something really has happened?'

'If there's a risk to her life, or health, that puts matters in a very different light. Is she in a relationship?'

'She has a husband and child,' Annika said.

'Perhaps the missing person doesn't want to be found. Perhaps she just wants to be left alone for a while.'

'I thought that too. But she me sent me a text, asking me for help.'

He sipped the coffee. 'Then I think you should go to the police,' he said. 'The duty officer at the Regional Crime Unit will decide whether or not to set up an investigation.' He put the cup down. 'But I don't think you have any reason to be concerned,' he said. 'Almost everyone who disappears comes back fairly quickly.'

Annika nodded. 'I'll probably contact the police this afternoon.'

The prosecutor reached for his cup again and looked out across his garden. Annika followed his gaze. The flowerbeds in front of the fence next to the road contained a mixture of perennials and annuals, including marigolds and lobelia. A large clump of bleeding hearts swayed in the breeze in the corner beside the drive.

'I remember Josefin very well,' Kjell Lindström said. 'It was a terribly tragic story.' He turned his head to look towards his house, painted green with white detailing, and ornamental carving around the windows and front steps.

Annika waited, her notepad in her lap.

'Of course all murders are tragic,' he said slowly, 'but the young victims, the ones who never really got started in life . . . Taking someone's life from them is the very worst thing one person can do to another, and the worst form of blasphemy, pretending to be God and making decisions about life and death. No one, in any culture, has the right to take on the role of God.'

'Except for the president of the United States, perhaps,' Annika said.

Kjell Lindström chuckled. 'True enough. Our penal code is designed around that. If you kill someone by mistake, you won't necessarily be sentenced to prison, but a conviction for murder can get you a life sentence. It's the *intent* that is criminal, not necessarily the act itself.'

Annika looked at her pad. 'How does it feel, as the head of a preliminary investigation, when you think you know who the perpetrator is but can't prosecute him?'

Lindström picked up a bun and took a small bite. 'In this case we had a suspect,' he said. 'We ended up charging him with a series of financial offences instead. He received a severe custodial sentence.'

For years, Annika thought, looking towards the house. Dishonesty to creditors, false accounting, tax fraud, tax crime and obstructing tax control.

The prosecutor turned to her. 'The tip-off about his double accounting came from someone inside the club, I seem to remember.'

Annika lowered her gaze and blushed. She had taken a job at the sex club, looking after the roulette table. Joachim had given her Josefin's old work outfit, a sequined pink bikini – they had been the same size. She had found out all she could about the way the business was run, the threats, blackmail, and where Joachim hid his double-accounting records. She didn't know if the prosecutor was aware of who had phoned in with the tip-off, but she wasn't about to tell him now.

'He's been out for ten years,' Annika said. 'He's registered at his parents' address in Sollentuna. Do you know what he's doing these days?'

The prosecutor sighed. 'I know he was suspected of assaulting a seventeen-year-old girl a year or so after he

113

was released. She withdrew the allegation. The last I heard was that he was in Croatia, working as an estate agent.'

'Are you prepared to say, here and now, that Joachim killed Josefin? Can I quote you on that?'

Kjell Lindström put his cup down.

'Those men who hit women,' he said, 'they're not like people think. People are all pretty much the same, even murderers. They aren't monsters, even if their actions are monstrous.'

Annika made notes. He was answering her question, even if he wasn't.

'Most men who are convicted of murdering their wives and partners in Sweden are native Swedes,' he went on. 'The majority are sober. More than half have no previous criminal record, not even for traffic offences. Nine out of ten are mentally sound. The critical moment is when the woman says she's leaving, or when she gets custody of the children. When he loses control of her. When it's no longer possible to isolate, control, manipulate . . .' He shook his head. 'Of all the criminals I've come across, those men are the most pathetic. They're cowardly, arrogant, obsessed with power, and they accept no responsibility. They kill her because she won't obey them, only to discover that she won't obey them when she's dead either. And that's when they get really confused.'

Warming to his subject, he leaned forward across the table. 'There's an institution outside Mariestad, which houses men who have been sentenced to long stretches in prison for violence against people close to them. They are offered treatment to help them control their aggression, but half are impossible to treat. In order for them to be receptive to the treatment, they have to admit their crimes and accept responsibility for what they've done. They spend the entire duration of their sentence proclaiming their innocence. He never hit her, and if he did, it was because she deserved it.'

'Maybe they can't deal with the shame of it,' Annika said.

The prosecutor nodded. 'According to psychologists who've studied them, one shared characteristic is that they constantly expect the very worst to happen. They think they won't survive if they acknowledge what they subjected their victim to. They don't believe that people around them could cope with the truth, so they reshape reality to suit themselves. All that denial must take a phenomenal amount of effort.'

'One man's confessed to Josefin's murder, Gustaf Holmerud. What do you make of that?'

Lindström pushed his cup away. 'Attention-seeking individuals confess to crimes that they haven't committed. It's a fairly common phenomenon,' he said. 'What's most scandalous in Gustaf Holmerud's case is that he actually managed to get himself convicted of five.'

'Can I quote you on that?' Annika said.

'Absolutely.'

'And you believe that his confessions are baseless? Not

just the five cases that Holmerud was found guilty of, but all the others he's confessed to as well?'

'There's one case in which Holmerud was initially a suspect, unless I've been misinformed, and it's possible he might be guilty of that one, but I have no way of judging. But he's not guilty of Josefin's murder. I can say that with absolute certainty. We conducted a very thorough investigation into that case, and his name never cropped up once.'

'Can I quote you on that as well?'

'Why not? What are they going to do? Fire me?'

She glanced at the camera to make sure it was working. It was. 'Would you say that those five convictions constitute a miscarriage of justice?'

'Of course.'

This was great. It was the first time that a person in any position of authority, who had been actively involved in at least one of the cases, had spoken out directly.

'Have you been in contact with the prosecutor-general?'

He narrowed his eyes. 'You appear to know more than I do now,' he said.

Annika looked across the lawn. 'Josefin's murderer,' she said. 'Do you think Joachim fits the criteria you outlined earlier? Is he pathetic, cowardly, arrogant, obsessed with power, and unwilling to accept responsibility?'

'In all likelihood, yes.'

She reached for her cup. She felt his eyes on her and looked up.

'If you're done, perhaps you could switch the camera off?' he said.

She stood up and did as he asked.

'You know,' Kjell Lindström said, as she unscrewed the camera from its tripod. 'My wife comes from Flen. We've lived in this house for thirty-nine years. I used to commute from here to Stockholm, all those years.'

She felt the weight of the camera on her arm, unsure of where this was going.

'So I've paid particular attention to local stories and criminal investigations, and I remember another fatality that occurred during the summer when Josefin was killed in Hälleforsnäs. Not too far from here. Sven Matsson, the hockey player. That was you, wasn't it?'

She dropped the tripod, which fell on to the grass with a thud. She bent to pick it up.

'I don't mean to make you uncomfortable,' the prosecutor said. 'But I know you have personal experience and knowledge of issues like this.'

She stood up, her heart pounding.

'Every experience teaches you something,' he said.

She didn't feel like driving back to work straight away, didn't want to get back to the disaster that was about to hit the newsroom.

Outside the car, the countryside flew past, hills crowned with oak trees, meadows full of cows, rolling fields of ripening wheat, stretches of marshland full of nesting birds, houses that had stood there for centuries:

117

rust-red timber cottages with their double chimneys, crooked barns and haylofts. This was her patch, her land, the view from the back of the Volvo when they had gone to get the week's groceries on a Saturday from the ICA supermarket in Flen, Dad singing along to the radio, Annika arguing with Birgitta about hairgrips and sweets. The wind was making mirrors of the lakes, sending dazzling reflections into her eyes. She wished she'd brought a pair of sunglasses.

The prosecutor remembered what she had done. There weren't many people who did, these days. At the paper there had been a degree of gossip for the first few years, she was aware of that, but people gave up, things were forgotten, other things happened. Every so often a new temp would come to find her and ask breathlessly if it was true: had she really killed her boyfriend? She always replied by telling them that they shouldn't believe gossip and should go straight to the source, and they would slink off, even though they had done exactly what she was encouraging them to do. It was such a long time ago now, so many years had passed.

The bridge in Mellösa was being repaired and she turned left by the kiosk and headed slowly towards the Harpsund estate. Her grandmother had been the housekeeper at the prime minister's summer residence for several decades, and had met all the senior Swedish politicians, as well as international figures like Nikita Khrushchev and Georges Pompidou. Annika's mother and other adults would often ask about the politicians, what sort of food they liked and who drank most, but Grandma never said a word about her guests (which was how she thought of them: they were there to visit her).

The model farm appeared on the left of the car and Annika slowed. She changed into a lower gear when she came to the manor house, and crawled slowly past the entrance. There was no one from the Security Police at the gate, so the prime minister wasn't in residence.

Harpsund Lake spread out down in the valley, and she thought she could just make out the famous rowing-boat, the one in which Swedish prime ministers would row foreign statesmen around.

The forest grew thicker as she approached Granhed, and the road was narrower. The wind was no longer tugging so hard at the treetops and the sun was blazing. She wound the window down. The scent of moss and freshly cut grass found its way into the car.

Had it been a mistake to move to Stockholm?

She could have stayed here, working at Katrineholms-Kuriren. She could have had a garden of her own, joined local societies . . .

Birgitta had chosen to work as a checkout assistant in a supermarket in Flen, and never bothered to get an education. Blonde, pretty and placid, she had her place among her friends and her workmates in the shop, and Mum loved her just as she was.

Annika turned right after Granhed. The trunks of the birches shone bright white in the sunlight and the wind made the firs sigh. Some horses looked up as she drove past, an almost new-born foal among them.

Just beyond Johanneslund she slowed down once more, looking along the side of the road. There it was, overgrown with grass and almost invisible, the turning to Lyckebo, her grandmother's country cottage, right on the edge of the Harpsund estate. On the spur of the moment she turned off the road, drove a few metres over hidden roots and lumps of stone, then put the handbrake on and switched off the engine. Silence echoed through the car. She sat where she was for a few seconds, listening to the emptiness. Up ahead, half hidden between the trees, she could make out the forest track leading to the cottage. This was where she'd learned to ride a bike, and she'd learned to swim in the waters of Hosjön. This was where her childhood summers had merged together into an endless, sun-drenched rush of delight.

She got out of the car, slung her bag over her shoulder and walked towards the gap in the edge of the forest without really thinking about it. The scene was so familiar, yet still alien. She hadn't been here in more than ten years and, from the state of the track, neither had many others.

The ground was springy under her feet after the previous day's rain.

The barrier across the track was locked so she went round it instead of climbing over.

A large bird took off just beside her, making her jump. It could have been a grouse, but she didn't have time to see it properly.

The trunks of the conifers slid past her, the wind rustling their tops but not reaching all the way down. The ground was covered with bright green moss, like a carpet. She walked into a cobweb, the sticky threads clinging to her eyelashes.

The feeling of timelessness was almost overwhelming: this was how the world had been before people arrived, and this was how it would be after they had gone, if they hadn't contrived to kill every other living thing on the planet first.

She reached the place where the bedrock shot up through the vegetation, hard and naked. This was where Sven had hunted her through the forest. This was where she had run that day. She could make out the lake through the trees, sparkling, and then she reached the clearing.

The meadow of the old smallholding stretched uncut and overgrown towards the water. The grass around the cottage had grown as tall as her, and the patch of raspberries at the gable end was now an impenetrable thicket of thorns. The white birch trunks creaked. Part of the tree-house in the apple tree had collapsed – she'd helped her father to build it.

The house was smaller than she remembered. This was where she had found her grandmother on the kitchen floor after her stroke. Her bag was beginning to feel heavy on her shoulder, and she carried it in her hand the last few steps. Out of habit she put her hand on the front door, but it was locked. Cautiously she went over to the kitchen window and looked inside. The rag-rug was gone, and the ugly pine hatch leading to the cellar was visible. The gatefold table was still there, but not its waxed cloth, and someone had removed the picture of the angel watching over children standing at the edge of a cliff. She could make out a dark rectangle on the pan-elled wall where it had hung. As a child she had been fascinated by it, the children reaching down to pick a flower, and the angel with its wings spread above them. The cottage had been used as a hunting lodge for a short while, but had evidently been abandoned.

She took a deep breath. How long had Grandma rented this cottage? Forty years, almost? Where had the picture gone? She sat down on the porch steps and looked towards the lake. The whole place really did need sorting out. The wind whistled through the treetops.

She took her mobile out and tried calling Birgitta's number again, but the call went straight to voicemail.

Annika brushed the hair from her face, then rang the Regional Crime Unit in Stockholm and asked to speak to the duty officer, someone called Cecilia, apparently. She explained that her sister had disappeared, described when, where and how, and gave the woman Birgitta's name, address and mobile number. She read out the text messages she had received, and when they had been sent.

'Does she usually ask for your help?' Cecilia asked.

'Very occasionally,' Annika said.

'With what?'

'Babysitting,' Annika said. 'Or somewhere to sleep when she's missed the last train home.'

Cecilia let out a sigh. 'How was Birgitta's relationship with her husband – what was his name? Steven?'

'I don't really know,' Annika said truthfully.

'I don't think you need to be particularly worried,' Cecilia said, 'but I'll take your details and write up a report so we've got it on file. Call your sister again and ask what she wants help with.'

'Okay,' Annika said. Relieved, she put her phone away, then wondered if there were any mushrooms in the forest yet, or if it was still too early.

She went for a walk behind the barn and checked the spot where she used to pick chanterelles, but there was only moss and last year's leaves. She went on towards the jetty, which turned out to be in a surprisingly reasonable state. She sat down and gazed across the water to the road that led to Johanneslund and Old Gustav's cottage.

She wondered if there was any chance of her being able to rent Lyckebo. Maybe Jimmy knew who in the government offices was responsible for the Harpsund estate . . .

She closed her eyes: what was she thinking? In a few days' time she might well be unemployed, her workplace shut down. How on earth could she afford to rent a cottage in the country? Getting Thomas released by his kidnappers had emptied her savings account. As a reporter on the shop-floor of the newsroom, she had no financial privileges or bonuses; her salary covered her share of the bills, the rent and the children's clothes, but that was all. Jimmy was already paying more than her.

She wasn't about to ask him to provide her with a summertime refuge when he had already given her so much – he had given her himself.

He was so utterly different from Thomas.

Sometimes she wondered what it was about Thomas that had made her fall for him. He was extremely handsome, with his blond hair and broad shoulders, but mostly she had been very lonely when she met him, and he'd seemed interested and attentive, and had found her exciting and different. She ought to have known then that he was the unfaithful type (after all, he had been married to Eleonor when she'd met him). She should have been prepared when it started to happen, when he began going to 'tennis practice' or 'worked overtime', then got into the shower the moment he came home.

When she'd eventually grasped what was going on, she'd handled it badly. She had become cold, distant and stiff. How much fun could it have been to be married to a block of ice?

She had hated Sophia. She might not have posted any anonymous abuse on the internet, but what she had done was much worse. She had lied and plotted and abused her status as a journalist until she'd managed to get Thomas's lover fired from her job. Things had turned out okay for Sophia though. She had found another job, and still lived in the penthouse apartment of the building on Östermalm owned by her family.

She let herself be dazzled by the sparkling waves, then

looked at the time and pulled her bag towards her. *People are all pretty much the same, even murderers.*

Ignoring her laptop, she got out her pen and notepad. With the water lapping against the jetty, she gave herself free rein to firm up the ideas she had begun to formulate during the drive from Stockholm.

She needed to push Josefin's case up the priority list, to persuade the police to start working actively on it again, to get the prosecutor to react. Kjell Lindström had offered her two new angles: first, that the police regarded the murder as solved; and second, that the conviction of self-proclaimed serial killer Gustaf Holmerud was a miscarriage of justice.

You can't leave me like this. What am I going to do without you? Annika, for fuck's sake, I love you!

This was where Sven had chased her along the shore. She had slipped into the water, then run into the forest, her shoes squelching. All these pathetic men, obsessed with power, unable to take responsibility for anything, cowardly and arrogant. Killing because their women won't obey them. Imagining that they won't survive if they admit what they've subjected their victims to. That those around them won't be able to deal with the truth, so they reshape reality to suit themselves. So much denial . . .

Blinded by the shimmering water, she remembered that this was where she used to sit and write her diary.

I'm fumbling. The darkness is so immense.

It was thanks to her diary that she was convicted of causing another person's death rather than manslaughter. The abuse she had described had gone on for several years, almost the entire duration of their relationship. Her descriptions persuaded the judge to agree with her defence lawyer that she had acted in self-defence.

She didn't need a psychologist to understand why she was still so upset by Josefin's case. It had happened the same summer that Sven died, and now that she was being forced to think about him again, Josefin was there too, with her silent scream, the teenage girl who never got justice.

Back at the car, she was sweating and a tick was crawling over her lower arm – she flicked it away.

She wound the window down as she drove into Hälleforsnäs and let the wind pull at her hair. The surface of the road was black, freshly laid, and hissed as it stuck to the tyres.

At the turning for the beach at Tallsjön she stared straight ahead. This was where her father had fallen asleep in a snowdrift on his way home. The driver of a snowplough had found him at half past four in the morning, frozen to death.

She refused to look to the right, where he had been found beside the track leading to the lake. She hadn't swum there since, stopped cycling past with her towel, a swimsuit and a drink.

She turned left. The reclaimed industrial area ahead

126

shimmered green with plants and trees. The old ironworks spread out on one side. It had kept the town alive
for several centuries, but was now transformed into a
discount outlet for discontinued clothing ranges from
fancy labels. She could hardly object: it had to be a good
thing that the site was being used.

She slowed down as she drove up the slope behind the
blast furnace. The area where she had grown up was
known as Tattarbacken, 'Gypsy Hill', but perhaps that
name was no longer used. She hoped so. Those blocks of
flats deserved a better one – *she* deserved better than to
be Annika from Tattarbacken. Didn't she?

She couldn't avoid the peculiar feeling that the streets
had shrunk, that they were narrower than they had been
when she was a child. The roadsides, on the other hand,
felt wider, barer. Ragged tufts of grass stuck up from
the grit.

She didn't turn into Odenvägen, but stopped at the
side of the road on the next street, just behind the electricity substation. Just ahead of her was number 112, a
rust-red, two-storey house from the 1940s, built to house
men employed at the works. There were no children
playing in the gardens – probably at nursery or a holiday
club – and the afternoon was silent and deserted.

The window at the top left had been her room, the one
she'd shared with Birgitta. The curtains were closed.
They were new – she hadn't seen them before. During
her periods of sobriety her mother liked changing curtains and doing little things to the house. Next she

focused on the kitchen window, one pane open. She thought she could see something moving inside, unless it was just the reflection of the neighbouring pine. The living room and her parents' bedroom were on the north-facing side of the building.

Without taking her eyes off the kitchen window, she rang the home number. Barbro answered gruffly.

'Hi, Mum, it's Annika.'

'Have you heard from Birgitta?'

She had been drinking.

'I've had two text messages sent to my old phone.'

Her mother's voice rose: 'What does she say?'

'She wanted me to help her with something, but I don't know what.'

'Help her? Is she in danger? Why aren't you *doing* anything?'

It was stuffy inside the car and Annika was finding it hard to breathe. 'I've spoken to the police, and a prosecutor, and neither of them thinks there's anything to worry about,' she said.

'How can they know?' Barbro sounded beside herself.

'I've filed a formal report about her disappearance and—'

'Steven reported her missing, and you wouldn't believe how offhand they were!'

The kitchen window opened wider. Annika ducked instinctively. 'Did he do that in Malmö?' she asked.

'They barely even bothered to write down his details! And they didn't ask for a description.'

'Mum,' Annika said, 'perhaps Birgitta doesn't want to be found. Maybe she's gone off of her own free will. Are you sure Steven's telling the truth? That he's never been violent towards her?'

Her mother started crying. The window blew shut.

'Birgitta would have told me – she tells me everything. Why doesn't she get in touch?'

Annika's palm was so sweaty that she had to move the phone to her other hand. She was on the brink of hyperventilating, and forced herself to breathe calmly and slowly. 'Mum,' she said, 'I'll be in touch as soon as I hear anything, okay? Mum?'

But Barbro had hung up.

He liked travelling by train. His brother did too. Even if the carriages no longer rumbled along the tracks as they had when they were children and travelled between Korsträsk and Storblåliden, he felt comfortable in a way that he never was in cars or planes. The speed lulled him, and he enjoyed the irregular squeal of the rails, the smell of cleaning fluid.

He had placed his case in the rack above his seat. He left it there, out of sight, and didn't worry about it when he went to the restaurant car for coffee. The canvas was old and stained – years ago they had used it as a table and eaten soft-boiled eggs off it. He remembered the episode as if it was yesterday. They had just been to the dump and were on their way back when they stopped at a layby outside Moskosel to have their picnic lunch.

The carriage leaned as they went round a bend, and he glanced up to reassure himself that the case had not moved. He felt the absence of his brother as a physical ache, and the train could do nothing to alleviate that.

He avoided flying. Not just because of all the cameras, tickets and identity checks (occasionally it was necessary to leave a trail, and then, of course, he took a plane), but because there was something unnatural about leaving the ground. The train was better – you could pay for your ticket in cash at the counter without showing ID – although the best option was an inconspicuous car.

But he preferred train travel. You could use the internet while you journeyed, which was another bonus. He had learned to surf on his smartphones, neither of which could be traced back to him or his brother, so he could roam freely around the net, which he found interesting and occasionally rewarding.

He went on to the website of the *Evening Post* and scrolled down through the pictures and headlines. The news report about his brother's trial had already been relegated to near the tail-end of things that were happening in the world, and would soon have faded from view. But the drama documentary was still there, glowing on the screen, an intrusive description of their lives and history. He let his finger rest on it, but didn't click, and selected the news article instead.

Police officer Nina Hoffman had given evidence about the arrest of the alleged murderer. Once again, the mistake they had made was explained: that baffling fragment of skin in Nacka. How on earth had it happened? And the information about investigations in other countries worried him. So much had changed in recent years and the rules of the game were different: everything was traceable. It was almost unsporting, but such was the way of the world now. He understood that, and his adversaries would have to as well. Why should he alone play by the rules? They couldn't cause pain and assume that there was no price to pay.

He closed his eyes. The case was secure above his head. Tomorrow he would be there, ready for the next step.

The gentle rocking of the carriage took him back to their trips to Storblåliden with their father, going fishing on the lake, the wooden cabin where they used to sleep. That was where they had discovered the delights of their abilities, when the fish they had caught were lying in the bottom of the rowing-boat, gasping for oxygen, and they would stick the knife into their stomachs and empty them of life and guts.

The sign on the door was made of brass, all four names engraved in black in the same font:

HALENIUS SISULU
BENGTZON SAMUELSSON

Nina looked at it for a few moments before she rang the bell. There was something solemn about the little metal plaque: it was a declaration as much as a mere description of who lived there. They had decided it was going to work: you and I, my children and yours.

Serena opened the door. Oh dear – weren't the children in bed yet? Nina had delayed the visit as long as she could – she could hardly have turned up any later.

'Hi, Nina,' Serena said, and gave her a radiant smile. 'Have you caught any murderers today?'

She had grown tall, almost up to Nina's shoulder, and was even wearing mascara. Hundreds of tiny plaits cascaded down her back.

'I tried,' Nina said, forcing herself to smile. 'It didn't go very well.'

Serena laughed and skipped along the corridor that led to the bedrooms.

'Hi,' Annika Bengtzon said, coming out into the hall with a tea-towel in her hand. 'Do you want something to eat? There's some chicken stew left.'

'Thanks, I'm fine.'

'Decaf? From the machine?'

'That would be great.'

'Sit yourself down on the sofa. I won't be long. Jimmy's doing the kids tonight.'

Nina kicked her shoes off and put them on the rack, then took her briefcase and went into the living room. She heard a tap running in the kitchen, then the characteristic whirr of one of those coffee-machines that swallowed expensive little metal capsules.

She was always relaxed with Annika, partly because of everything they had been through together, the shared experiences they never spoke about, but also because there was something bruised about Annika that Nina recognized: she shared it.

While she waited she took out the copy of the preliminary investigation into the Josefin Liljeberg case and put it on the coffee-table, a thick folder containing everything from pictures of the crime scene, forensic reports, the medical officer's statement and details of witnesses to interviews with the two men who had been suspected of the crime: the minister for foreign trade at the time, Christer Lundgren, and Josefin's boyfriend, Joachim Segerberg.

Annika brought two mugs in and sank on to the sofa. Her eyes opened wide when she saw the bundle of papers. 'All of it? Really?'

'Q said you could see it,' Nina said. 'It might help the investigation. But source confidentiality applies, so you can't quote from it.'

'Wow!' Annika put the mugs down and grabbed the papers. She flipped through them and stopped at the photographs of the crime scene. They were colour photocopies and the quality wasn't great.

Nina waited for her to speak.

Eventually Annika said, 'I was there. I saw her lying there. But I was outside the railings, of course.'

Nina hadn't thought about that: the police pictures of the crime scene had been taken at a different angle from the media's.

'I went up there yesterday,' Annika went on. 'It's

133

almost a shame that they've cleared away the bushes and sorted out the headstones. Some of the magic of the place has gone.' She closed the folder. 'Thank you so much. I'll read it through carefully, but I won't quote directly.'

They reached for their mugs at the same time.

'I heard the defence lawyer gave you a hard time yesterday,' Annika said.

Nina kept a firm grasp on her mug: her failure in court still stung. If Berglund was released, she would never forgive herself. She blew on the drink. She didn't much like coffee, but it gave her something to do with her hands. 'It wasn't that bad,' she said, and sipped. 'Exchanges in the high-security courtroom are usually like that. They're much harsher in tone than other trials.'

Annika's eyebrows rose, as they did when she didn't understand something.

'It's all to do with the courtroom,' Nina said. 'The parties start off in separate rooms and enter the court through different doors. The prosecutors and defence lawyers never meet outside the courtroom.'

'So they don't bump into each other at the coffee-machine?' Annika said, raising her mug.

'Exactly. They never exchange pleasantries, never talk about the weather. The atmosphere in court can get very fractious.'

'So, what do you think? Will he be convicted?'

Nina warmed the palm of her hand against the bottom of the mug. 'If the DNA evidence is accepted, then he was there. Even if he wasn't the perpetrator, he helped. But the match isn't a hundred per cent, although they very rarely are . . .'

Annika looked down at her lap. 'I need to ask you about something else,' she said. 'Birgitta, my sister, didn't come home from work the day before yesterday. No one knows where she is, and she sent me two text messages asking for help, but I don't know what with. I've spoken to the duty officer at Regional Crime and she's filed a missing-person report, but is there anything else I can do?'

Nina took two large gulps of coffee, and decided she could leave the rest with a clear conscience. 'I presume you've tried calling her?'

Annika nodded.

'Could something have happened to her?'

Annika hesitated. 'Something doesn't make sense,' she said. 'The texts asking for help were sent on the twenty-fifth and thirty-first of May, but she hadn't gone missing then. The second was sent just before half past four on Sunday morning, and she disappeared on Sunday evening.'

'What does her husband say?'

'He's reported her missing as well, with the police in Malmö – that's where they live. He's really worried.'

'Most people who go missing turn up again fairly quickly.'

Annika gave her a fleeting smile. 'I know.'

'Seven thousand people are reported missing each

year,' Nina said, 'and that includes short-term disappearances, teenagers running away from home, asylum-seekers who go off the radar, people snatching their own children . . .'

Annika emptied her mug and put it down. 'What happens with the ones who don't show up?'

'They're officially registered after sixty days,' Nina said. 'That functions as a sort of control, because someone might have forgotten to report a person coming home. And asylum-seekers who've gone missing are also discounted.'

'How many don't show up again?'

'A hundred or so, and they're entered in the central police database of missing people. That's when we make sure we've got a current description, dental records – that's done through the Forensic Dental Unit in Solna.'

Nina had paid it a visit when she was studying, a red-brick building with blue awnings; it was kept in a state of constant readiness because a mass casualty situation could occur at any time. The machinery was able to swing into action at once, identifying the dead and injured.

'And then what?'

'There are usually about thirty left on the register after a year.'

They sat without speaking for a while.

'And how many are there now? In total?'

'In the entire register? Thirteen hundred.' Nina's brother, Filip, was among them.

'All Swedes who've just disappeared?' Annika exclaimed. 'Like they've been swallowed by the earth?'

'Some of the cases are old, dating all the way back to the fifties.'

'When are they declared dead?'

'That's a judicial formality. It used to take a minimum of ten years, but after the tsunami that was reduced by half. So, for instance, if you see someone drown but their body is never found, that person can be declared dead after just a year or so. It's all to do with judicial and economic factors, getting bank accounts closed, claiming on insurance policies . . .'

'What if no one misses them or wants them declared dead?'

'They remain on the register, as non-existent persons . . .'

'Well, she'll probably turn up soon,' Annika said, looking down into her empty mug, as if it might miraculously have refilled itself.

'If she's been reported missing in both Stockholm and Malmö, her disappearance may end up being coordinated by National Crime,' Nina said. 'I can have a word with the duty officer at Regional Crime and see what we can do.'

'That would be great,' Annika said.

Nina stood up. 'I won't disturb you any longer.'

'You could never do that,' Annika said, 'as you know.'

Nina went out into the hall. Jimmy Halenius was

standing there in his socks, looking for something in a jacket pocket. 'Hi, Nina. All right?'

'Fine, thanks. You?'

'The opinion polls could be better, but otherwise everything's great. You haven't got any chewing tobacco, have you?'

She smiled apologetically and bent down for her shoes. Jimmy evidently found what he was looking for because he let out a sigh of relief and went into the kitchen with a small tub of tobacco in his hand.

'What are you doing for Midsummer?' Annika asked from the doorway to the living room.

Nina's answer came automatically. 'Working. How about you?'

'Don't really know. Kalle and Ellen are going to be with Thomas this year, and Jimmy's kids are off to see their mum in South Africa as soon as school breaks up. We were wondering about getting a group of friends together and going off somewhere. Shame you're working.'

Nina tied her shoelaces and stood up, her hair falling over her face. 'I'll be in touch if I hear anything from the duty officer at Regional Crime.'

The door closed behind her and she found herself standing in the stairwell in her silent rubber-soled shoes. Why had she lied about having to work at Midsummer? It might have been fun to go away with a few friends, on the condition that it was just adults. There was nothing wrong with Annika Bengtzon and Jimmy Halenius's children; they were a decent bunch: Ellen a fair-skinned blonde, Serena as dark as her mother, Kalle with Annika's green eyes, and Jacob a swarthier version of his dad. But she had trouble dealing with families: she felt uncomfortable with the whole dynamic.

She ignored the lift, walked down the stairs and out into the street. She stood there for a while. It was still warm, almost muggy. Sometimes she missed her brother and sister so much that it hurt. She had never really lived with them – they had been so much older than her, and only appeared in her life at irregular intervals. Yvonne, with her sun-cream, the one that smelt of coconut, rubbing it into Nina's shoulders, nose and knees: *You mustn't let her burn like that! What sort of mother are you?* Filip, with his books, reading to her in Swedish, Spanish and German: *Es war einmal ein Mädchen, das mit seinem Vater und Stiefmutter lebte . . .*

But Yvonne had been shot and killed by the police in the forest north of Örebro six years ago. Filip, her saviour and big brother, registered missing, would never be coming back. She had shot him on the family's hash farm outside Asilah in northern Morocco. In two weeks' time it would be exactly five years ago.

She held the moist air in her lungs until it hurt.

Then she walked home through the stone-lined streets of the city.

The sound of an American sitcom with a laughter track filtered into the kitchen from the living room. Jimmy was talking on the phone, presumably to the minister – Annika could hear his voice as a wordless melody, rising and falling. The children were asleep – she could almost sense their breathing as a gentle breeze through the rooms.

The preliminary investigation into Josefin's murder lay spread out across the kitchen table in front of her. She had picked out the sections dealing with Joachim's alibi for the night of the murder and had read them twice, all the way through.

She remembered some of it from before.

Joachim claimed he hadn't seen Josefin on the night in question. He hadn't been to Studio Six at all but had been drinking with his friends at the Sture Company nightclub until it closed. Just after five o'clock in the morning, he and six friends had gone in a limousine taxi to a private after-party on Rörstrandsgatan. There, he had fallen asleep on the sofa.

She leafed through the witness statements. His alibi really did look watertight.

All the young men backed up Joachim's story. A waiter at Sture Company confirmed that Joachim had been there. The driver of the limousine taxi stated that he had driven a group of intoxicated young men from Stureplan to Birkastan. Joachim had the receipt. The woman who owned the flat on Rörstrandsgatan said that Joachim had fallen asleep on her sofa.

But Annika knew that Joachim had been at the sex club just before five o'clock that morning. He and Josefin had had a violent row: Josefin's friend had overheard them.

And the waiter hadn't been able to say exactly what time it had been when he saw Joachim that night. It might have been as early as two o'clock. The driver of the limousine could neither confirm nor deny that Joachim had been in the taxi because he couldn't see who was sitting right at the back. Robin Bertelsson had paid for the ride. A number of the friends who had been in the limousine were so drunk that they probably didn't know what was going on during those critical hours.

She could still remember Commissioner Q's conclusions that summer fifteen years ago: the witnesses had been prepared, coached in what they had to say. She had managed to get hold of two. The first had ended the call as soon as she introduced herself, then switched off his phone. The second had denied that he had been involved in the case at all, despite indisputable evidence to the contrary.

The woman who owned the flat had been extremely drunk. She was sure she had seen Joachim asleep on her sofa, but she didn't know what time he'd got there.

Annika pushed aside the preliminary investigation and took out a picture she had managed to get hold of from a contact at the Driver Licensing Agency in Strängnäs. She had spent over an hour trying to find Robin Bertelsson, but this was the only photograph she had been able to track down. He seemed to take the surveillance society very seriously, and had no Facebook account under his own name, nothing on Twitter or Instagram, no blog. He didn't appear anywhere on the internet.

She looked at his symmetrical features, blond hair, sharply cut jaw.

He knew.

Robin Bertelsson had paid for the limousine. And then he had given the receipt to Joachim. If any of them had coached the others and got them to synchronize their stories, it was him. He had been in charge of 'security' at the sex club, and protecting its wretched owner was probably part of his job description.

These days, he was married and living in Denmark. Neither he nor his wife had a listed phone number, no businesses. They had been registered as emigrants by the Swedish Population Register, but trying to find someone's address in Denmark was considerably more difficult than it was in Sweden. Asking the Danish Population Register had been hopeless: they had referred her to the local council, but she was pretty sure that to get hold of someone's address you had to know either their name, previous address and date of birth, or their ID number, past or present. She wasn't entirely sure, though, because she hadn't really been able to understand the woman's Danish. The only information she had managed to uncover was that he worked for Doomsday Denmark, listed as a consultancy firm specializing in 'internet security, analysis and programming'.

Security again.

Annika heard Jimmy laugh in the living room, but

couldn't tell if it was at something the minister had said or the television programme.

Robin Bertelsson had left the club after the murder. Why hadn't he wanted to carry on working there? Did he think Joachim had gone too far? She put her hand on his face. The photograph felt cold beneath her palm.

WEDNESDAY, 3 JUNE

The room looked the same as before, apart from a chrome-plated fan in one corner. It moved slowly back and forth with a gentle hum, and every fifteen seconds the air hit Annika in the face, making her blink.

'You mentioned that you don't have much contact with your sister. Why is that?' The psychologist had switched to her summer uniform, a knee-length denim skirt and white T-shirt. She was looking down at her notepad, which made Annika feel anxious: what had she written in it? Was it like other medical notes? What if the pad got into the wrong hands, if someone else read it?

Annika gulped. The fabric covering the armchair was so scratchy that she rested her forearms on her lap. 'Birgitta and I are totally different.'

'In what way?'

Annika squirmed on the chair, defiance spreading within her. 'Birgitta's got no drive, no ambition. She just wants to be liked. Her goal in life is to sit in the pizzeria in Hälleforsnäs drinking beer with the cool kids from the nineties.'

There, she'd said it, revealing her snobbish, big-city attitude. She readied herself for criticism and derision, but the psychologist wasn't even blinking. Annika felt almost disappointed.

'Does your sister still live in the town where you grew up?'

'Apparently she's moved to Malmö . . .'

Should she mention Birgitta's disappearance? The thought got no further and she said nothing. This wasn't Birgitta's hour. For once, everything wasn't all about her.

'Do you have any contact with anyone else from when you were growing up?'

Annika sat in silence for a moment, mostly to give the impression that she was thinking. 'Not really . . .'

'Your boyfriend, the one who died, what about his family, friends, his parents, perhaps?'

'No!'

The answer was so abrupt that it surprised even her. The psychologist scribbled in her pad.

The darkness was swirling, and a shiver of unease ran down Annika's spine. She saw Sven's parents in her mind's eye, his beautiful mother and well-built father, Maj-Lis and Birger. She hadn't seen them since Sven's death: she hadn't gone to the funeral, and they weren't at the trial. Maj-Lis was dead, she knew that, breast cancer, a few years ago.

'Your father died when you were seventeen. How did that make you feel?'

The fan reached the psychologist, making her short hair quiver and the tissues in the box flutter.

'Terrible,' Annika said.

'How have you dealt with it?'

The air grew heavier.

'I don't think about it.'

'How did it happen?'

'He was drunk, and froze to death in a snowdrift.' By the turning for the beach at Tallsjön, where she always looked the other way when she drove past.

'Were you close to him?'

She had been Daddy's girl, Birgitta Mummy's. 'I guess.'

The psychologist looked at her. 'You felt "terrible" when he died?'

Because he had abandoned her. Because she was left all alone. Because he had done it in such an embarrassing way, like an old alcoholic. People felt sorry for her, not because her dad had died but because he'd been stupid and weak, a disgusting old drunk. To begin with she wished he'd died of cancer or in a car crash. She'd imagined it would have felt different, that she would have experienced a higher class of grief, and people would have felt sorry for her for the right reasons. It didn't matter now, but she could still remember how she had felt.

'I remember that it felt terrible,' she said simply. 'I was very sad, but it passed.'

The psychologist frowned, but dropped the subject. 'You said last time that your mother doesn't like you. Can you expand on that a bit?'

Annika forced herself not to look at the clock on the wall: it would be disrespectful to start checking when she had only just sat down. 'Well, what can I say?' she said, and looked at the clock anyway. 'It's no secret. Mum tells anyone who's prepared to listen.'

It really was incredibly hot in the room. The breeze as the fan swept over her left a stillness behind it that made the air feel thicker.

'What does she say, your mum?'

Annika tried to concentrate. She had to make an effort, or why was she here? And it was only words. If she tried hard enough she could summon a story she had heard about someone else she barely knew. 'That I've ruined her life. She and Dad and Birgitta would have been a happy family if it hadn't been for me.'

The proportions of the room seemed to change: it got narrower but seemed to stretch at the same time. The sound of the fan became more distant.

'Does she ever say what you did?'

Annika's voice echoed oddly inside her head, as if she had discovered herself telling a lie. 'Mum says there was something wrong with me when I was born, that I'm brain-damaged. That I was born . . . bad.' Her cheeks burned. It sounded so silly, as if she were making it up.

'Bad? What does she mean by that?'

Annika shut her eyes, trying to disappear. 'I don't actually know,' she whispered.

The fan hummed. When she opened her eyes again, the psychologist was looking at her intently. This was the sort of thing they liked, she felt sure, mothers who weren't up to scratch.

'You said it isn't a secret that your mother doesn't like you. What does she say to other people?'

Annika looked towards the window. It wouldn't be long before forest fires broke out. If she was still at the paper she'd be sent as close to the flames as possible. 'That I almost killed Birgitta when she was a baby.'

The psychologist adjusted her position, then rubbed her forehead. 'Can you elaborate?'

'Birgitta was in an incubator,' Annika said. 'She was born prematurely, and it was my fault.'

'What did you do?'

'I tripped on the front steps and cut my knee. My mother was so distressed by the accident that she started to get contractions and her waters broke.'

'So your share of the responsibility was . . . what? That you tripped over? When you were two years old?'

Annika nodded. 'Mum didn't want me. She got pregnant and couldn't go to art college.'

The air from the fan hit her again. Her hair flew up in front of her face and she pushed it back.

'Would you like me to turn the fan off?' the psychologist asked.

'No, it's okay.'

151

'How would you describe your feelings towards your mother?'

Annika was breathing through her mouth now, and her eyes were stinging. 'I don't like it when she calls. I avoid her as much as I can.'

The psychologist wrote something down. 'In psychology we generally talk of the "basic emotions",' she said. 'The majority are negative – anger and fear, sorrow and shame, disgust and revulsion – but there are a few positive ones. Usually joy, curiosity and surprise. If you were to use some of those to describe how you feel about your mother, which ones would they be?'

Annika swallowed. 'I don't know.'

'Does it feel uncomfortable to think about it?'

Did it? Was she feeling uncomfortable? What basic emotion was that?

She let the darkness fill her lungs and stomach. What did it consist of? Demands and accusations, reproachful eyes, clumsy fingers dropping things, the shouting: *Go away!* Her eyes filled and she took a deep breath to hold back the tears. 'I'm ashamed,' she said. 'I wasn't good enough, I was always doing things wrong. Mum was angry, and used to get so upset. I wish . . . I wish, well, that I could have been . . . better.'

'No joy?'

Annika checked deep down in the darkness: was there anything light and joyful? Any peals of laughter, a smell of fresh baking? With Grandma, yes, and Dad. *Can you see the magpie? He's got such beautiful feathers, all shiny and blue, like a late summer's night. Anyone who says they don't like magpies has never really looked at them, not properly . . .*

She shook her head. No, no joy, not with Mum. Longing: what sort of basic emotion could that be? Sadness, maybe? Unfairness? Maybe that was part of anger. She didn't know. What a mess . . .

The psychologist wrote something on her pad, then flipped back a page and read in silence for a moment. 'We talked last time about an accident, when your boyfriend died. Can you tell me some more about that?'

The air closed in around her. She didn't want to go there.

'He . . . fell into a blast furnace.'

'A blast furnace?'

The fan roared.

'At the ironworks, back home. It was abandoned by then, shut down, when it happened. They've put a discount outlet there now, in the old factory building.'

'What happened?'

Annika was clinging to the arms of the chair, hard, hard, hard, to stop herself falling. 'He was chasing me with a knife, and he killed my cat. I tried to defend myself, and he fell.'

'Did he often do things like that? Chase you, threaten and hit you?'

You can't leave me like this. What am I going to do without you? Annika, for fuck's sake, I love you!

'He . . . Yes, he used to . . .'

153

'Is it hard to talk about it?'

The darkness closed around her. Her lungs were screaming, her hands burning, and she fell and fell and fell.

Nina steered the hire-car over a long bridge with wide arches. The Lule River shimmered below the concrete, almost a kilometre wide here at its mouth.

The care-home where Ingela Berglund lived was in a part of the city known as Björkskatan, 'birch magpie' (although the name had nothing to do with magpies or any other bird, according to the manager of the care-home: *skatan* was dialect for 'headland'). She had to turn left when she reached the Hertsö roundabout, then follow the signs. Just to be sure, Nina had hired a car with a built-in satnav.

The bridge came to an end and she drove into the city, low brick buildings clad with panelling, gnarled deciduous trees with bright foliage. Off to the right, on the far side of a broad expanse of water, she could see a vast industrial area. She passed a warehouse by the harbour, a few brick buildings, and then she was out of the city centre. The housing became sparser, and the traffic around her melted away.

Sure enough, she reached a large roundabout with two different petrol stations, just as the manager had told her, and bore left towards Skurholmen. A couple of minutes later she reached the turning for Bensbyn and Björkskatan (perhaps Bensbyn was just as misleadingly named, and it wasn't really a village of bones).

She rolled slowly past the houses. This was a side of Sweden she very rarely saw. Simple, well-kept homes, glassed-in balconies, neat lawns, playhouses and ornamental shrubs. This was where people lived with their families, in a country they were proud to call their own.

The satnav was flashing on the dashboard: she had reached her destination. She gazed out through the windscreen at what looked like a suburban shopping centre. There was a health centre clad in orange panels that also housed a chemist and a chiropractor's clinic. She swung round and found an empty space in the car park, checked that her mobile was in her pocket, then switched off the engine and got out, locking the car behind her.

A cold, sharp wind was blowing that she hadn't noticed inside the car. The sky was low and blue. She looked at the time – she was a bit early, but that couldn't be helped.

The care-home was a two-storey, panel-clad building with geraniums in the windows. A sign saying WELCOME in ornate script was screwed to the front door. Nina rang the bell and heard it echo inside the building.

A woman of her own age opened the door. She was wearing jeans and sandals, holding a bunch of keys, and looked anything but welcoming.

'Evelina Granqvist?' Nina asked.

'That's right,' the woman said. She was the manager. For the past four years she had had power of attorney for Ingela Berglund, and was her official trustee.

155

'Nina Hoffman,' Nina said, shaking the woman's hand. 'Sorry I'm a bit early, but there wasn't any traffic.'

'Come in,' Evelina Granqvist said, and walked off towards what looked like a kitchen. Her movements were slightly jerky and abrupt, as though she was already finding the visit uncomfortable. 'You can take your shoes off,' she said, over her shoulder.

She spoke in a pronounced local accent, slow and melodic, a lot like the way Ivar Berglund talked.

Nina stood by the door and made a quick appraisal of the home. There were framed pictures on the walls, probably painted by the residents, and there was a large noticeboard with names, pictures and descriptions of various activities: 'Sandra climbed to the top of Ormberget!' and 'Today Peter did some baking!' Off to the left there was some sort of dayroom – she could hear people talking and laughing on television.

'Do you want coffee?' the manager asked, without looking at Nina. The question was probably so deeply embedded in local tradition that not even an unwelcome visit by a police officer from Stockholm could shake it.

'Thanks. I'd love some,' Nina said, taking her shoes off.

A man with Down's syndrome poked his head out of the dayroom and looked at her.

'Hello,' Nina said. 'My name's Nina, what's yours?'

'Peter doesn't talk,' Evelina said, from the kitchen.

The man withdrew his head and shut the door. The voices from the television faded to a muffled murmur.

The hall floor was covered with pale linoleum. Nina's

stockinged feet slid on the chilly surface. The kitchen looked like an ordinary kitchen in an ordinary house, not like that of an institution. Two mugs of coffee and a plate of cinnamon buns, probably the ones Peter had baked, waited on the table.

Evelina Granqvist closed the door behind her. 'I thought I made myself clear yesterday,' she said. 'I'm opposed to the idea of you questioning Ingela. She can't stand witness in a trial.'

Nina sat down at the table, picked up a bun and took a bite. 'Naturally, you're perfectly entitled to your opinion,' she said.

'I heard that you've requested to see Ingela's medical records as well. What are you hoping to get from this? You can't seriously think that she had anything to do with the things her brother is standing trial for?'

Nina took another bite and studied the woman. Her arms were folded and her legs crossed in an obviously defensive posture. She looked challenged and affronted, possibly also sad and anxious. 'I don't think Ingela is mixed up in Ivar's activities,' Nina said. 'Could I have some milk in my coffee, please?'

Evelina Granqvist's jaw tensed, but she went to the fridge, and took out an open carton of milk.

'Thanks,' Nina said, and poured some into her mug. She took a sip. The coffee was now lukewarm and as grey as dishwater.

'So why are you here?' the manager asked.

Her arms were no longer folded.

157

'Because Ingela matters,' Nina said.

Evelina Granqvist's eyes widened. Nina sat in silence, eating the bun, waiting for her opponent to speak.

'How . . . What do you mean?' the woman eventually asked.

Nina reached for a napkin and wiped sugar from the corners of her mouth. 'The preliminary investigation into the crime that Ivar Berglund is standing trial for has been going on for more than a year. A dozen detectives have been involved, but no one has given any thought to Ingela.'

She stared at the manager, hoping that was true.

'I've said no whenever they've asked to question her,' Evelina Granqvist said stubbornly. 'I've explained to them that it isn't possible.'

'That's what I mean,' Nina said. 'No one made enough effort to talk to Ingela.'

'She doesn't know anything about what her brother has done.'

'Now you're thinking in exactly the same way as those detectives,' Nina said. 'You're speaking for Ingela, as if you knew better than her.'

The manager folded her arms and crossed her legs again. 'It's for Ingela's sake,' she said. 'I don't want her to get upset.'

'Your concern is understandable,' Nina said.

'I've got a good relationship with Ingela. She trusts me. Why should I allow you to see her?'

Nina straightened her back. 'Everyone working on this

158

case has dismissed Ingela Berglund as stupid. I think that shows a lack of respect.'

The manager's face took on an almost defiant look. 'I don't see why it's so important,' she said. 'Nothing that man might have done is reason enough to upset Ingela.'

Nina looked at her intently. 'The trial concerns the murder of a down-and-out in Nacka last year. The perpetrator tortured the victim, pulled his nails out, hung him naked in a tree above an anthill and smeared him with honey. The cause of death was asphyxiation, by a plastic bag. We're going to look beneath every last little stone to find the killer, even if it means upsetting your routines.'

Evelina was staring at her.

'Ivar Berglund is suspected of having committed other crimes,' Nina went on. 'We haven't got enough evidence to charge him with them yet, but we're linking him to the assault of a local politician, Ingemar Lerberg, in Saltsjöbaden last year. I don't know if you read about the case in the papers?'

Evelina blinked several times. Perhaps she was searching her memory.

'The perpetrator spread Ingemar Lerberg's legs apart until the muscles ruptured. His hands were tied behind his back and he was strung up by his wrists, which meant that both his shoulders were dislocated. The soles of his feet were whipped, five of his ribs were broken, his jaw was smashed and one of his eyes was crushed. He's still in a coma, a year later, with severe brain damage.

Unfortunately he's still breathing by himself, so there's no ventilator to switch off.'

The manager's face was completely white. She gulped audibly and lowered her gaze.

'Ingemar's wife is missing, without trace, so it's very likely that Ivar Berglund murdered her as well,' Nina went on. 'His three children are in a foster-home. No one visits him in his care-home. Not that it matters, because he probably doesn't know what's going on around him.'

Evelina Granqvist stood up and went over to the sink, poured herself a glass of water and drank it. Then she sat down again. 'Ingela can't stand witness in a courtroom,' she said quietly. 'That's impossible. She has seizures when she gets stressed.'

'It's very unlikely that she'd ever be called as a witness,' Nina said. 'The trial is almost over. I'd just like to talk to her, ask her about their childhood.'

She found herself thinking about Peter, the young man who had baked the buns. Could Ingela talk?

Evelina Granqvist looked at her, her fingers wandering round her coffee mug. 'What do you want to know?'

'What life was like when Ingela was small, what Ivar was like. I don't know how much she can communicate. Do you think she'd be able to answer a few questions about her childhood?'

The manager reached for a bun. She peeled off the paper and folded it into a tight little ball.

'I'll get hold of her medical records,' Nina said. 'It's

just a matter of time. It's up to you whether you choose to help me or not.'

'Ingela is unusual,' Evelina said. 'Her diagnosis isn't clear, but she has a number of handicaps – ADHD with elements of autism. She may have been deprived of oxygen at birth, but nobody knows. Her IQ is fairly high, almost normal, but she doesn't function very well with other people. She gets on better with animals, but Peter is allergic to them so she can't have a dog here, which is a great shame.' She fell silent.

'Do you want to be there when I talk to her?' Nina asked. 'You've every right to be present, but you don't have to be.'

Evelina Granqvist closed her eyes tight. 'She's in her room,' she said, and got to her feet.

Nina followed the manager out into the hall and up a flight of stairs. Someone had started singing in the dayroom.

Ingela Berglund's room was the last but one in a dark corridor with doors on both sides. Evelina Granqvist knocked. 'Ingela? You've got a visitor. There's a lady here who'd like to talk to you. Can we come in?'

No answer.

She opened the door and a shard of light spread across the corridor. 'Hello, Ingela,' she said, walking into the room.

Nina hesitated in the doorway. The room was bright and nicely furnished in shades of pink and pale blue.

The manager went to a woman sitting at the window.

She put a hand on her shoulder, and leaned forward. 'Ingela, you've got a visitor. There's a lady here from Stockholm. She's come to see you.'

The woman's colouring and build were reminiscent of Ivar Berglund's. She was relatively short and thick-set, light brown hair with traces of grey. She was dressed in a pink tracksuit. She turned her head and glanced shyly at Nina.

'Hello, Ingela,' Nina said. 'My name's Nina. I'd like to talk to you, if that's all right?'

The woman had the same eyes as her brother, but with an entirely different resonance, shiny and shallow. She turned away quickly. 'I don't like strangers,' she said.

She had the same accent as her brother and the manager.

Nina took out her mobile and began to record the conversation. 'Interview with Ingela Berglund,' she said, 'in the Flower Garden care-home in Luleå, Wednesday, the third of June, at ten fifteen a.m. Also present is Evelina Granqvist, manager of the home.'

Evelina Granqvist flushed, but she didn't protest.

Nina tucked her phone into her jacket pocket. The microphone was powerful and worked fine through the fabric. She fetched a rib-backed chair from the other end of the room and sat down next to her witness so that they could look out of the window together. The car park spread out below them. Nina could see her hire-car behind a gnarled birch tree. Ingela Berglund ignored her.

'When I was little I had a dog called Zorro,' Nina said, looking at her car. 'Zorro means "fox" in Spanish. I was living in Spain at the time, and I thought my dog looked like a fox. He was red.'

She sat quietly, looking at her car. The room smelt stuffy and enclosed. After a while she felt Ingela Berglund look at her. 'I used to play with Zorro every day,' Nina said. 'He was my best friend. He learned how to swim and fetch balls from the sea. Zorro liked all sorts of balls, but his favourite was a red one, maybe because it was the same colour as him.'

Now Ingela Berglund was staring at her, wide-eyed. Nina turned her head slightly and met the woman's gaze. She looked away at once. 'Do you like dogs?' Nina asked.

Ingela Berglund nodded.

'The witness is nodding,' Nina said. 'Have you got a dog at the moment?'

Ingela Berglund snorted. 'Peter,' she said. 'Dogs make him ill, stupid bloody Peter.'

Evelina opened her mouth, presumably to correct the woman's choice of words. Nina quickly raised a hand to stop her. 'What was your dog called when you were little?' she asked.

'Buster,' Ingela Berglund replied straight away.

'Was he just yours, or Ivar's as well?'

She snorted again. 'Ivarandarne's dog died.'

She pronounced her brothers' names as a single word.

'Ivar and Arne,' Nina repeated. 'It's sad that their dog died.'

Ingela Berglund was staring out of the window.

'Was it mostly Ivar's dog, or Arne's?' Nina asked.

'Ivarandarne,' Ingela Berglund said. 'Ivarandarne. They're the same.'

The radiator was on in spite of the time of year, radiating warm dust towards Nina's face. 'Ivar and Arne,' she said. 'Your brothers. They shared the dog between them?'

Ingela Berglund got up clumsily from her chair, then walked with short steps to her bed and lay down with her back to the room. Nina watched her, that thick-set body, the brown-grey hair. *They're the same?*

Evelina Granqvist hurried over to the woman and put a hand on her arm. 'Ingela, are you okay?'

Nina stood up, walked to the bed and sat down. 'What happened to Ivar and Arne's dog?' she asked.

'He . . .' The woman curled up. Her arms and legs began to shake. 'The tools,' she whispered. 'Father's tools, the saw . . .'

Nina held out her mobile. 'What did Ivar and Arne do with the saw?'

Ingela was staring blankly at the ceiling. 'Paws,' she said. 'He tried to walk without paws . . .'

Nina leaned over her.

'The bomb,' Ingela gasped. 'They detonated the bomb. Over Nausta.'

'What did you say? Naus—?'

The manager stepped in and pushed Nina away. 'Ingela,' she said loudly and clearly. 'I'm here. I'm here,

164

Ingela.' She sat down beside her and put her arms round the woman's shoulders. 'There's nothing to worry about, nothing to worry about . . .'

The woman's arms and legs were cramping badly now, and a gurgling sound was coming from her throat. She coughed and spluttered a few times, then began to scream.

She screamed and screamed and screamed as Nina walked slowly down the stairs to the ground floor, while the staff rushed in the opposite direction.

Thomas's feet hit the tarmac at a steady speed of approximately seven minutes per kilometre. That wasn't fast enough for him to be wheezing, like a truck along the quayside, but quick enough for his top to get sweaty and stick to his chest, and for his hair to hang down in front of his eyes in moist clumps.

He was getting sweaty because he was running in a long-sleeved top, with the hook in a relaxed posture, its fingers gently curled, just like his right hand. His legs were muscular and tanned – there was a solarium just a couple of doors away from his horrible flat, and he had got into the habit of using it a few times each week. The tan lent his appearance a pleasantly sporting touch.

He could feel people's eyes on him, men's and women's. It was surprising how many people still remembered him, even though it was eighteen months since it had happened. Thousands of stories had passed through the television news and newspaper headlines since then, but his was one that had stuck in people's heads, the civil servant who was kidnapped and mutilated but managed to escape, a truly heroic story.

The American woman speaking from the app on his mobile informed him that he had run 2.1 kilometres in fifteen minutes; he was maintaining exactly the right tempo.

He lengthened his stride and picked up the pace slightly.

He wasn't going to work today.

Just thinking about work sent an angry shudder through him.

Tomorrow he was supposed to have presented his report at the cabinet meeting. He would have sat at one end of the table with all the ministers, opposite the prime minister, explaining how important and well-considered his legislative proposal was. The government would have praised his work, and his report would have been sent out to fifty or so individuals and institutions who would have thought about his proposals and made suggestions and comments. He had been prepared for brickbats and plaudits, as well as constructive criticism, but Halenius had sabotaged his work.

There was a bitter taste in his mouth. His feet pounded the ground. The water of Riddarfjärden sparkled to his left as he ran past a woman with a pushchair.

He was to have held a big press conference in the main government offices, he and the minister who had officially led the inquiry, but as Thomas had done all the work, he would have answered any questions. He would have appeared in all the television news bulletins, on the radio and in the morning papers too (but not the *Evening Post*: Annika's gossipy little rag only covered murders and scandals, not serious stories about important changes to the law).

Now the press conference had been postponed.

He had been due to write a major article for *Dagens Nyheter* as well. In fact the text was almost finished: he had written a draft that Facelift had polished up very nicely – she was good at expressing herself. (Okay, so he hadn't exactly been given the green light by *DN*, they wanted to read the text first, but he was convinced that the editor would have taken it.)

If it hadn't been for his boss, Jimmy Halenius, the man who had taken his family away from him while he had been kidnapped by terrorists in Somalia, who had made sure he wouldn't be able to watch his children grow up . . .

The woman in the app spoke again: he had run 2.6 kilometres in twenty minutes. He had slowed down. He speeded up: he had to stay in shape; he was no victim.

He wouldn't go to Sophia's party: he had no desire to socialize with her stiff, standard-issue financial-industry acquaintances. Sophia might be attractive and wealthy, but there was something bland about her. He needed a woman with firm opinions. Someone like Annika, but with a bit of class and style.

His mobile started to vibrate in the back pocket of his

shorts. Runkeeper wasn't the only reason he took his phone with him: it was important for his work that he could always be reached. Talk of the devil, he thought, as he looked at the screen.

'Hello, Annika,' he said, slowing to a walk.

'Hello,' his ex-wife said. 'Am I interrupting anything?'

'I can give you a minute,' he said curtly.

'Great,' she said. 'I was hoping to ask you about something.'

He swung the hook idly as he walked. 'Sure.'

'You've remembered the kids are coming to yours tonight?'

Shit. He'd forgotten. 'I'm glad you've called,' he said. 'I was going to talk to you about that.'

'Don't tell me you'd forgotten about them again!'

'I don't know if Jimmy's spoken to you about my inquiry, but a couple of things have cropped up and I—'

'Thomas, if you don't want to look after the kids, it would be much better if you just came out with it. Kalle is always so disappointed when you back out at the last minute.'

He gulped. 'Oh, no,' he said. 'It's fine. The kids are more than welcome.'

'Are you going to Sophia's party?'

He stopped at a jetty. Two schoolgirls looked at him and giggled. He turned away, screening the hook with his body. 'Are you?' he asked.

'I said I would, but I'm not sure I'm going to have time, and that's what I'm really calling about. I'm at

Kastrup. I need to be in Denmark today, and Jimmy's had to go to Brussels. There's something I need a bit of help with . . .'

Oh, so it was okay to come crawling to him when she needed help? A shiver of anticipation ran through him. 'What is it?'

'Jacob and Serena can cook and feed themselves, it's not that, but they've spent quite a bit of time at Sophia's, and would like to see her on her birthday.'

He looked out across Lake Mälaren. He wouldn't have wished his former lover a happy birthday if it hadn't been for that email.

'Okay, so how . . .?'

'I know this is really last-minute and a bit of a nuisance, but if you could maybe take them with you to Sophia's when you pick up Ellen and Kalle. What do you think?'

She was unbelievable! He was supposed to babysit Jimmy Halenius's kids? Clearly it wasn't enough that he and Annika had taken Thomas's family away from him. And she was calling from an airport in another country. Talk about taking him for granted! Seriously, how bloody presumptuous could she be?

'Sure,' he said abruptly. 'I suppose so. Seeing as I'll be there anyway.'

'God, that's brilliant, thank you so much. You really have saved the day. See you tonight, then?'

They hung up, and the American woman told him he had run 2.7 kilometres in twenty-five minutes.

*

169

He walked between the furrows with a rolling gait, swaying rhythmically, the way Signar Allas had taught them when they followed the reindeer to their winter pasture. The soil wasn't stony moraine, like it was at home, but stiffer, like clay, maybe even glacial. His body felt heavy but stable; he was sure of his feet and clear in his thoughts. The treetops above his head were singing, a lonely song that made him feel melancholic. He let his eyes roam up the trunks to the sky. They were all straight as flagpoles, evidence of very well-managed forest, scrupulously thinned out. They were between sixty and seventy years old, ready for cutting in another decade or so.

He took a deep breath, letting the smell of pine needles fill his lungs.

It was almost a shame that the forest needed to be cut down. If it was left to its own devices it would stand for several hundred years, as long again as dried pine, getting whiter and more brittle, until it collapsed and was swallowed into the earth, which would take another century.

A midge buzzed in his ear, and he slapped his head, leaving a bloodstain a centimetre across on his thumb. Who had the midge bitten? Not him, anyway. An animal? It must have been an animal: there wasn't another human being within a three-kilometre radius, he was sure – he'd crossed the terrain several times in the past twenty-four hours. The forest tracks were closed to road traffic, and no one had cycled or walked there recently, perhaps since the last mushroom and berry season.

The suitcase swung heavily from his left hand.

He thought about Signar Allas, the old man from Udtja Sámi village, who had taught them about the forest. He and his brother had liked Signar a lot. But Father had disliked the Sámi and their culture – *Bastard Lapps*, he used to call them. *Only fit for Lapps and sea-birds* meant something was very bad, and he would swear about the Sámi as he sat on the sofa drinking his schnapps.

Father had been a poor example of *Homo sapiens*, angry and bent-backed. Mother's body was weak and she was a little soft in the head. He had thought about them a lot lately, now that he was on his own, but in truth he barely remembered them. Their faces had been erased over the years, dissolved, their voices faint and distant, but he remembered their frequencies, the vibrations of their souls. He remembered how they sounded inside him.

The landscape opened up around him. The water of the lake shimmered. Between the trees, he could make out the house. The land around it hadn't been looked after with the same care as the forest, and had been allowed to fall into disuse, which was a shame, from a cultural point of view.

He was almost there now, in so many ways.

It would be nice to have everything finished.

*

Annika looked up at the building, Købmagergade 62. A publishing company was based on the top floor, an advertising agency at ground level, and the IT business where Robin Bertelsson worked was in the middle.

The entry-phone had three buttons. She pressed the one marked DOOMSDAY.

A woman answered, and Annika took a deep breath. 'I'm looking for Robin Bertelsson,' she said.

The woman's reply was so fast and incomprehensible that she was baffled. Did Annika have an . . . something? She wondered what the last word might be in Swedish. It had to have been 'appointment', surely. 'Er, no, I don't have an appointment . . .'

'You're welcome to make a booking via our website.'

The telephone clicked. She took a step back.

Two young women came out of the door. She moved a few steps back and studied the window of a branch of H&M. There was probably no point in trying the entry-phone again: that would only make the people in the security firm suspicious.

She looked around. Copenhagen felt completely unlike Stockholm. The buildings were lower, more uniform, old and attractive. The cityscape felt genuine, somehow, although she couldn't put her finger on why that was. Maybe it was just the absence of multi-storey car parks and ugly new buildings.

The young women went off in the other direction, laughing and chatting, Annika didn't understand a word they were saying. She felt stupid: she had lived her whole life under the delusion that Danish and Swedish were practically the same language. She had spent hardly any time in Denmark. Kalle had wanted to go to Legoland for years, but Thomas had thought he was setting his ambitions way too low. If you were going to go to an amusement park, it ought to be Disneyland Paris, in his opinion, but just as Annika was about to book the trip he'd decided it was too expensive, and they'd ended up staying with her parents-in-law out in the archipelago. Again.

She walked a short distance until she reached a large square, then turned and walked back. The heat had made the tarmac soft under her shoes, but she still felt frozen. Her throat was sore and her hands were shaking. Her panic attack in the psychologist's armchair was lingering, like a damp fog.

Her bag weighed heavily on her shoulder and she dropped it on to the pavement. If Robin Bertelsson was at work today, he would have to come out of the building sooner or later. Her plane back to Stockholm didn't leave until 18.05, so she had time to wait.

She brushed the hair from her face and concentrated on number 62.

A group of four middle-aged men, dressed in almost identical jackets, emerged from the door and headed towards her, giving her a chance to study them carefully. None of them was him. One gave her an encouraging wink. She turned away.

A man and a woman passed her, stopped at the

entrance to number 62 and tapped in the entry-code. He looked just about rumpled enough for her to guess that he worked in the advertising agency.

She looked around. There was a café on the other side of the street. Maybe she should get a cappuccino, but then she'd need a pee and might miss Robin Bertelsson.

She got her mobile out, no messages.

The door of number 62 opened and Annika held her mobile in front of her as she watched the doorway from the corner of her eye. A blond man in his mid-thirties, in a long-sleeved T-shirt and camouflage trousers, rushed out and half ran across the pavement. Was he Bertelsson?

The man turned towards the square, checked quickly for traffic, then crossed the street. Annika's mouth opened. It was him – it must be. She took a few steps after the man, saw him go into the café, say something to the barista, and they both laughed. The Danes, the happiest people in the world, and among the highest consumers of antidepressants.

She turned her back on the café and stared into the window of H&M. In the reflection, she saw the man who had to be Robin Bertelsson step out on to the pavement with a large paper cup in his hand. He waited until a taxi had passed, then set off back towards number 62.

Annika raised her mobile and filmed him as he ran across the street, then walked quickly towards the doorway.

The man was about to tap in the door-code when

Annika caught up with him. 'Robin?' she asked, making her voice sound surprised and happy.

He looked at her in surprise.

Yes, it was him. No question. She gave him a broad smile. 'God, Robin, it is you!' She threw herself forward and wrapped her arms round his neck, pressing her body against his. The man took half a pace back, clearly horrified, and held out his arm to protect his coffee.

'Wow!' Annika said. 'What are you doing here?'

A mass of thoughts were flying round in the man's eyes, and he tried to smile, but without quite succeeding.

'Don't you recognize me?' Annika asked, surprised but not upset.

She held her arms out. 'I'm Annika! From the club! On Hantverkargatan! God, it's so long ago – it must be fifteen years! I was on the roulette table, used to wear a sequined bikini . . .' She thrust out her breasts and pretended to look seductive.

A tentative light flickered in the man's eyes. 'Bloody hell,' he said. 'I was getting worried.'

Annika laughed loudly. Robin Bertelsson still had no idea who she was. 'Oh, sorry,' she said. 'I didn't mean to scare the life out of you. How are you?'

He gave her a crooked smile and shrugged uncomfortably. 'I live here now,' he said. 'You know, wife and kids . . .'

A clear message: don't expect anything.

'It's great to see you again!' Annika said. 'Are you still in touch with any of the others?'

He took a step back. 'Others?'

'From the club. By the way, did you hear about Ludde?' She pulled a sad face and he looked confused.

'About . . . what?'

'Did you go to the funeral?'

He brushed his hair back. 'Oh, no,' he said. 'No, I didn't. I . . .'

'So tragic,' Annika said, with a sniff. 'Bastard cancer.'

He nodded hesitantly. Three women were heading towards the door, and Robin Bertelsson grasped the handle as if he were about to go inside, but Annika stepped in the way. 'Have you heard anything from Joachim lately?' she asked.

Robin Bertelsson looked at her warily. 'No, it's been a while.'

Annika sighed. 'The last I heard, he was in Croatia,' she said, 'working as an estate agent. Can you imagine? It was just after that young girl withdrew her complaint.'

'Well, I'd better be—' Robin Bertelsson said.

'I think about it sometimes,' Annika said quietly, moving a step closer to him. 'The way everyone lied to protect him from the police.'

Robin Bertelsson stiffened.

Annika smiled and shrugged. 'That was a bit of a problem, back at the start, of course,' she said. 'Protecting a criminal, that's the name of the offence, but it passed the statute of limitations a long time ago. Today everyone's free to say what really happened that night. There's no risk any more.' She moved even closer to him.

'Haven't you ever thought about the fact that Josefin never got any justice, that Joachim got away with murder, and that it's the fault of the witnesses, your fault, for giving him an alibi?'

The man's face drained of colour. He was clutching the cup hard. 'Who are you?' he asked. 'What are you doing here?'

She waved vaguely towards the entry-phone, where the logo of the publishing company shone out from a brass sign. 'I'm going to write about it,' she said. 'About Josefin and everything that happened that night.'

Robin Bertelsson backed away from her. 'You can't drag me into this.'

'You must have thought about it,' Annika said. 'You could give her justice. If you contact the police in Stockholm, or the prosecutor, Sanna Andersson, and tell them what really happened . . .'

Robin Bertelsson turned on his heel and stalked off along the pavement.

Annika hoisted her bag on to her shoulder and ran after him. 'Robin,' she said loudly. 'Think about it. You can—' She collided with a large woman who swore at her angrily, but she hurried on and grabbed hold of his sleeve. 'Robin, wait!'

He stopped abruptly, spun round, his lips pressed together in a thin line. He tore the lid off the cup of coffee and threw the contents at her. She took a step back but wasn't quick enough, and the coffee hit her chest and left arm. She lost her breath – it was still very hot. She opened her mouth to scream, but no sound came out, as she felt the coffee run down her fingers and drip on to the pavement.

Robin Bertelsson headed off into the crowd. For a while she saw his head bobbing between other people's, but then he was gone.

Nina stepped out on to the red-painted landing. The lift doors closed behind her with a sigh. Her workplace had its own unique sounds and smells; the sealed building murmured and echoed. Above her was Kronoberg Prison, in all its impenetrable inhumanity; buried in the ground below were the culverts and the large high-security court-room, used when the smaller one up near the roof wasn't big enough; between the two sat all the police officers and detectives. Together they formed an integrated whole, an organism that ground criminal acts of violence down to a manageable structure of process and formality, all of it archived in ring-binders.

She held her pass card up to the magnetic reader and tapped in the code. The lock clicked and the glass doors of the National Crime Unit slid open. On her way to her office she fished her mobile out of her jacket pocket and dialled the duty officer at Regional Crime, but got no answer. She held her breath as she peered into her office, then noted with immense relief that Jesper Wou still hadn't returned from his trip abroad. She breathed out, took off her jacket and hung it on the back of her chair. Her T-shirt was wet with sweat across the back.

She sat down at her desk, drank some mineral water, and thought.

She began by conducting a basic search on her computer, and logged into the national identity and address database. She searched for anyone with the surname Berglund who was born on 28 May fifty-five years ago.

One result: Ivar Oskar Berglund, born in the Älvsbyn council district, currently registered as living in Täby.

No Arne.

She clenched her jaw, then filled her lungs with air.

It had to be true. She just needed to find a different way to check. An historical search, same criteria . . .

The circle on the screen turned. *No result*.

She logged out of the database, and let her fingers rest on the keyboard as she thought some more.

Her unit had access to a large number of different databases, both Swedish and international (all of them not necessarily legal), but she shouldn't need any of the confidential ones here. Instead she jotted Arne Berglund's details on a sheet of paper, then took it, with a printout of Ivar Berglund's record and her pass card, and headed out into the corridor. She went down one floor to the blue landing and the communications centre on the seventh floor. The room was gloomy, lit only by the flicker of computer screens and the indirect daylight from the next room. A number of officers, some in plain clothes, two in uniform, were concentrating hard at their terminals.

'Hello, Nina. Do you need help with something?'

asked a man in plain clothes with a moustache. She couldn't remember his name.

She smiled and handed over the sheet of paper with Arne Berglund's name and place of birth. 'Is there a way of finding this individual in the registers?' she asked. 'He's fallen out of the main population database. He emigrated in the late eighties or early nineties, and died about twenty years ago.'

Moustache Man took the sheet of paper and sat down at a terminal. Nina scanned the room in the hope of finding something with the guy's name on it, but there was nothing. She held her breath as he logged in and conducted the search, as his computer whirred and flashed.

'Are you sure about the date of birth?' he asked.

'No,' she said.

'But he's dead, you say? You know that for certain?'

'He died in a traffic accident in Alpujarras twenty years ago.'

'Alpu-what?'

'The mountains south of Granada, in Andalucía, the southernmost part of Spain.'

She waited quietly while he logged out of one system and into another. The page loaded.

'No,' he said. 'There's no Arne Berglund with those details here.'

'Can you try Ivar Berglund, same birth details, and see if he has any family listed?'

The computer whirred.

'Yes, here we go. Parents Lars Tore Berglund and Lilly Amy Berglund, died 1975, province twenty-five, council district sixty, parish two.'

The province of Norrbotten, and the council district and parish of Älvsbyn.

'Is there anything about siblings?'

Moustache Man shook his head. 'No,' he said. 'You'd have to check the National Archive.'

Church records, in other words.

Moustache Man handed the details back to her. As she took them, he didn't let go of them straight away. 'Anything else I can do for you?'

The corners of her mouth tensed. 'Thanks very much,' she said, snatched the sheets of paper and went back the way she had come.

The province of Norrbotten was covered by the National Archive office in Härnösand. She looked up the number on the internet, called, asked to be put through to their research office, and found herself in a queue. It didn't take long to get through: people had better things to do on a hot day in June than genealogical research. She introduced herself with her name and title, and explained that she was after the birth details of an Arne Berglund, deceased. They would be in either the register of births and christenings or the book of deaths and funerals covering province 25, council district 60, parish 02.

The woman at the other end paused before replying, 'You can't come and look for yourself?'

181

'I'm at the National Crime Unit in Stockholm,' Nina said. 'I'd really appreciate it if you could help me with this.'

'I'd be happy to. If you fill in the form on our website, we're usually able to respond to requests for information in about two weeks.'

'This concerns a murder investigation,' Nina said. 'The person I need information on is suspected of committing a murder in Nacka last year.'

'Didn't you say he was deceased?'

Nina took a deep, silent breath. 'I'm happy to wait on the line.'

It took ten minutes. Then the woman returned. 'I found the register of christenings,' she said. 'Arne Johan Berglund was born on the twenty-eighth of May. He'd have been fifty-five years old now. He died on the sixth of February at the age of thirty-five.'

Nina scribbled the information on the sheet of paper with Ivar's birth details. 'Thanks for your help,' she said, and hung up.

She went straight to see Johansson and knocked on his door. 'Have you got a minute?'

The secretary was hunched over his keyboard and looked up at her mournfully. She walked across to his desk, and concentrated hard on not seeming stressed and pushy. 'I think I've got the answer to that DNA sample from Orminge,' she said. 'Ivar Berglund and his brother Arne were identical twins.'

Johansson looked up. She passed him the birth

details – Ivar Oskar Berglund, born 28 May, Arne Johan Berglund, born 28 May, same location and year.

Johansson studied the information.

'Arne emigrated to Spain just before the Tax Office took over the population register in July 1991,' she went on, trying to stick to the facts. 'He was no longer in the main database, and it hasn't occurred to anyone to check him out specifically.'

'I don't quite understand,' Johansson said, handing back the printout.

Nina sat down on the chair opposite him. 'That would explain the DNA result from Orminge. The profile is almost identical, but not quite, because our DNA is affected by environmental influences all the way through our lives, by illnesses, diet and substance abuse.'

'Nina,' Johansson said, 'it doesn't explain anything. The man's been dead for twenty years.'

Nina tried to relax her shoulders. 'I know he died in a car crash, but we ought to look into that accident. Which police force conducted the investigation?'

Johansson sighed. 'What makes you think they were monozygotic?'

'Mono . . .?'

'Identical.'

He picked up the printout again, then looked quizzically at Nina. No, it wasn't clear from the details on the database that they had been identical twins.

'Their sister, Ingela Berglund,' Nina said. '*They're the same.* That's what she said.'

183

Johansson looked at her thoughtfully over his glasses. 'They're the same?'

'Ingela has problems with social interaction,' Nina said. 'Questioning her wasn't all that straightforward.'

Johansson opened Ivar Berglund's file. 'I think you're complicating this business of the DNA match,' he said. 'It's as close at it can be, ninety-nine per cent.'

'Could we check the circumstances surrounding that car crash in Spain?' Nina asked. 'Just to find out what really happened?'

The secretary sighed. 'I'll look into it, but don't hold your breath. We should probably be happy if we get a reply before the year is out.'

Nina stood up and tried to smile.

'A duty officer from Regional Crime tried to get hold of you earlier,' Johansson said, pressing some chewing tobacco into a little clump. 'Something to do with the search for a mobile phone?'

'Thanks,' Nina said, feeling as if she had just been reprimanded. She could be on the wrong track entirely, she was aware of that.

Maybe she was chasing ghosts.

The train had passed Ørestad and was approaching Tårnby. Annika glanced at her watch. Her flight back to Stockholm left at 18.05. She had four and a half hours. She looked down at her top. The coffee had almost dried, making the fabric hard and stiff. She would have to buy a new T-shirt.

The conductor was moving slowly through the carriage. Annika strained her ears to listen, and yes, thank God, he was speaking Swedish.

'This train goes all the way to Malmö, doesn't it?' she asked, as he checked her ticket.

'It goes all the way to Gothenburg, love,' he replied.

Tårnby was a modern station of stone and grey concrete, ice-cold, clean Scandinavian design. She'd never been to Malmö. The paper had its own newsroom there, so violent crimes, riots and fights between football supporters were covered by local reporters. She knew little about the city, and what she did know was restricted to fragments of old headlines and stories that probably weren't true: Sweden's Most Dangerous City, the ghetto of Rosengård, the football team that had qualified for the Champions' League, hostility to immigrants, shutdown shipyards – and, of course, Zlatan Ibrahimović.

Why had Birgitta moved there? No one in their family had any connection to Malmö. Perhaps Steven had friends or contacts there. She could understand them trying to move to Norway – loads of Swedes did that to earn a bit of money – but Malmö?

She had lived with the vague but straightforward conviction that she knew her sister: she knew when Birgitta had had her first period, what food she hated, how she hummed to herself when she was painting, and what she sounded like when she cried in her sleep.

Why had she chosen Malmö? What was she doing there? Who had she become?

185

The train set off with a jolt.

Annika got out her mobile, no messages, then discovered that there was Wi-Fi on the train. She opened Birgitta's Facebook page, which was dominated by photographs of its owner, selfies and pictures in mirrors, Birgitta's beautiful face and glossy blonde hair; she was almost always smiling, always nicely dressed. Annika lingered over a summer photograph taken on a restaurant terrace, the wind tugging at Birgitta's long hair. Her eyes were sparkling and she was laughing. Annika scrolled down, and found a number of childhood pictures, including one with herself in it, from the beach at Tallsjön. She and Birgitta were sitting side by side on a blue rug, wrapped in towels, each eating an ice-cream. Birgitta was smiling coquettishly at the camera, Annika was looking away, her face in profile. Dad had taken it.

Annika clicked to the personal information section. Birgitta hadn't mentioned that she'd moved to Malmö.

The sign at the end of the carriage lit up: next station Kastrup.

People around her gathered their belongings, closed cases, checked their passports and tickets. The train slowed and stopped. The man beside her groaned and got to his feet.

She stayed where she was.

The carriage was quiet once most of the passengers had got off, and the train stood at the platform for another minute or so, as a breeze that smelt of warm rubber swept through the open doors. The floor of the carriage rumbled and vibrated.

The doors closed.

She knew nothing about Birgitta and Steven's relationship, not even how they had met. She had already moved away, leaving Hälleforsnäs behind her, and Sven was dead. She had met Steven just once, on that night when he and Birgitta had missed the last train after a Rammstein concert. They had both been seriously drunk, and Steven had dozed off on Annika's sofa. Birgitta had pleaded with her to leave him alone, or he'd get angry. Halenius had got them out of the flat by saying he was a police officer, which had had a sobering effect on Steven. The situation had told Annika that her sister was frightened and her brother-in-law some sort of criminal, but that was hardly an objective interpretation.

Was she confusing herself with Birgitta? Did she see an abuser in every man who couldn't hold his drink?

The sky broadened and the waters of Öresund surrounded her, sky and sea a vast expanse of blue, with just a narrow strip of mainland on the horizon. She could make out blocks of flats, roads and a power station, presumably Barsebäck – but that had closed down, hadn't it?

The boundary between Denmark and Sweden was around here – maybe she was crossing it at that very moment. She looked out over the water and let her thoughts run free.

Birgitta had visited her flat on Södermalm twice, when

she'd dropped off and picked up Destiny, her daughter, at either end of her trip to Oslo to look for work. She had seemed tired, and there was an edginess that Annika recognized from herself but had never seen in her sister before. Birgitta, who had always loved nice things, had looked at the crystal chandelier, the paintings and the hand-woven rug on the living-room floor and said, 'Clever Annika and her lovely job. Now she's got the perfect home too.'

The only thing she knew about Steven was that he had never had a proper job and was on sickness benefit, but did undeclared building work, which wasn't unusual in dying industrial communities.

Her eyes fell on a sloppily folded newspaper on the seat opposite, a copy of the early edition of the *Evening Post*. She reached for it and turned to pages six and seven. The spread was dominated by her interview with Kjell Lindström. They had chosen to focus on his comment that Gustaf Holmerud's convictions were a miscarriage of justice. The police thought they knew who had killed Josefin but the night editors had played that down: it was in the article, but not the headline. From a news perspective, she could hardly object – a fresh mass murderer was more interesting than a girl who had been dead for fifteen years – but it still rankled.

A wrecked boat appeared in the water just to the right of the bridge. Annika gasped and dropped the paper. It was a fishing-boat, which had run aground and toppled over. She sat up higher to get a better view. The hull, navy blue and white, had split open, and the mast was gone. She glanced around, but the remaining passengers were staring down at their phones or blankly at the sky. That boat must have been there for a long time, she thought. A familiar tragedy aroused neither alarm nor fear.

Embarrassed, she picked up her phone again and went back to Facebook. Birgitta Bengtzon hadn't posted any updates all year. When she lived in Hälleforsnäs she had been fairly active on Facebook. Why had she stopped?

The train halted at the first station on the Swedish side – or the last, depending on where you were going.

Her mobile buzzed: Kalle, wondering if he really had to go to Dad's that evening. Guilt flared inside her, sharp and irrational: no matter what she did, someone was always disappointed. As the train pulled away she sent a reply to Kalle, explaining that these were his dad's days, that was what had been arranged. 'But I'll see you at Sophia's later,' she wrote, adding a cheerful smiley at the end.

She sat back and let herself be jolted along as the train entered a tunnel.

It stopped at Triangeln Station, blasted into a huge cavern in the rock, all stone and concrete, a world of varying shades of grey.

A mother with a little girl got on and settled down next to Annika, the woman glancing at Annika's coffee-stained top. The child was blonde and blue-eyed, and looked a bit like Destiny.

189

'Hello,' the little girl said. 'What's your name?'

'Annika. What's yours?'

The little girl hid her face against her mother's arm, as the woman tapped at her mobile.

Destiny must have grown a lot by now. She was about the same age as this child, almost three. The last time Annika had seen Birgitta, her sister had implied that there was something wrong with her daughter, that she was a slow developer. That ought to have become more apparent now, if it was true.

Four hours and fifteen minutes until her plane took off.

The train rolled into Malmö Central Station. She stood up, clambered past the mother and daughter, and the little girl waved as she got off. The mother didn't look up from her phone.

She went up a long escalator to the station building. In contrast to the granite and concrete stations, it was old and warm, light and beautiful, red bricks and painted ceiling. Shops and cafés lined the passageway that led to the various platforms, warm air pouring out of the open doors. She stopped in the middle of the gangway and people streamed past her, everyone on their way somewhere. She felt suddenly dizzy so she went into a café, ordered coffee, then sat down at a table and took out her phone. She pulled up a map of Malmö and looked for Branteviksgatan 5, and a branch of MatExtra supermarket in a place called Värnhem, Birgitta's home and work.

She found them straight away. Branteviksgatan was in Östra Sorgenfri, which sounded familiar. Wasn't that

190

where Zlatan Ibrahimović was from? The 'hooligan from Sorgenfri': wasn't that what he was called as a child? Värnhem was a square that seemed to be a hub for local traffic, and MatExtra was located in a shopping centre alongside. It looked as if it was within walking distance, almost directly south-east from the station.

She drank her coffee.

It wasn't against the law to leave home. Adults were allowed to come and go as they pleased. Maybe Birgitta *did* want to be left alone for a while.

She sent a message to Nina Hoffman, to see if she'd heard anything about the tracing of Birgitta's phone.

But there was another reason too, one that lurked in the back of every editor's mind: the person who appeared in the local press calling for information about someone who was missing was usually the one who had killed them.

Life was so fragile that killing someone was simple. Suddenly she could feel the iron pipe in her hand, cold and rough, the flakes of rust.

She rubbed the palm of her hand on her jeans and finished her coffee.

The wind outside the station was hard and hot. She crossed a canal and entered part of the city that felt medieval, low buildings with heavy façades, windows that seemed to bow in the sun. She passed squares lined with half-timbered buildings, and came to a row of clothes shops. She went into H&M, bought a new T-shirt and threw the old one away.

She crossed another canal and found herself in Rörsjöstaden, with taller, more ornate buildings, and boulevards lined with chestnut trees.

Birgitta's childhood dreams had been very grand: she was going to be a princess, a prima ballerina, Madonna. She liked lace and tulle and pretty colours, was frightened of the dark, rats and spiders, so perhaps this place suited her. She used to paint watercolour landscapes that Mum loved, and portraits of Annika and their mother and grandmother that were stuck to the fridge door with magnets. Annika remembered the conflicted feeling of pride and envy that the pictures aroused, her astonishment that Birgitta could create something so beautiful and real.

Her sister would have enjoyed painting this avenue – it was certainly clichéd and grand enough. The sun filtered through heavy treetops, forming flickering patterns on the path beneath her feet. At the far end there was an ornate church with showy turrets and pinnacles, as ostentatious as a castle in a fairy tale.

Annika quickened her pace, feeling a little giddy from the heat.

At Värnhemstorget, the character of the city changed: it was now concrete slabs, rumbling buses and diesel fumes. A group of down-and-outs were having an argument about a bottle of schnapps, and Annika looked the other way as she passed them.

'APOLOGIES FOR THE MESS: WE'RE REBUILD-ING', said a sign on the revolving door. Annika was funnelled through with four women in full-length *niqab*s.

The shopping centre was the cheaper sort, a long passageway of plaster walls and low ceilings, brown paper stuck to the inside of shop-windows. The MatExtra supermarket lay some way into the complex, with a lottery booth and letterbox by its entrance. The row of checkouts led directly onto the passageway. Only half of them were open, but the queues were short. This was where Birgitta worked.

Annika stopped in the passageway and studied the cashiers. Four were young women, two middle-aged. They were wearing matching red blouses with the store's logo on the back, scanning items with expressionless faces, handing back change and tapping instructions for debit cards.

The cashier closest to Annika switched off her conveyor-belt, then got up from her chair and hooked a chain across the gap between her and the next checkout. Annika went up to her. 'Hello,' she said, 'my name's Annika Bengtzon. My sister works here, Birgitta.'

The woman had her arms full of moneybags. She was young, twenty-five at the most, with glossy dark hair and heavily made-up eyes.

'I need to get hold of her,' Annika said. 'It's important.'

'I have to put the money away,' the young woman said.

Annika saw the tiredness in her eyes, the heaviness in her arms after a long shift, and suddenly it was her mother standing there, her arms laden with food she had brought home from the shop. *Just peel the potatoes, Annika, don't be so bloody lazy.*

'Do you know if Birgitta's working today?'

'Birgitta's left,' the woman said, taking a step back.

'When?'

The cashier's eyes glinted. 'You're not a bit alike.'

A flash of irritation. *Of course we are. It's just that Birgitta is fair and I'm dark.* 'Do you know where I can get hold of her?' Annika asked. She forced herself to smile.

The young woman looked at her watch. 'Come with me to the office,' she said. She turned on her heel and walked off towards the greengrocery, and Annika hurried after her. The young woman stopped beside an unmarked door fitted with a coded lock. 'Wait here,' she said.

Annika was left standing outside next to a wooden crate full of new potatoes from Holland. A minute or so later the cashier returned. The air smelt of soil. 'Why do you want to get hold of Birgitta?' she asked, her eyes sparkling with curiosity. 'Has something happened?'

Her accent was more Västergötland than Skåne.

Annika took a deep breath and forced herself to stand still. 'I didn't know she'd stopped working here. When did she leave?'

'Two weeks ago. It came out of the blue – she just texted Linda. I didn't even know she'd applied for a new job. She hadn't mentioned it. Pretty shitty, if you ask

194

me, you can tell her that from me. She could have called in to say goodbye and all that.'

Annika was rooted to the spot. 'A new job? Do you know where?'

'Another supermarket, Hemköp at Triangeln. She could have let us know she'd got a permanent job. People usually get cake for everyone when they leave . . .'

So Birgitta had got a permanent job. Not even their mother knew that. If Barbro had known, she would have phoned Annika at once and crowed about how well Birgitta was doing, how clever and appreciated she was. Or would she? After all, she'd never mentioned that Birgitta and Steven had moved to Malmö. Why had she kept quiet about that?

'And Linda is?'

'Our boss. Okay, so Birgitta was only a temp, but you should still hand your notice in properly, I reckon.'

'Is your boss here?'

The young woman shook her head. 'She's opening up tomorrow. So what's happened?'

'How long had Birgitta been working here?' Annika asked.

The young woman tilted her head. 'She started last autumn, doing odd shifts. Then at the end she was filling in for Fatima, who's on maternity leave. Are you really her sister?'

Annika shuffled her feet, feeling stifled by the smell of potatoes. 'Elder sister,' she said. 'It's been a while since we were in touch.'

'Birgitta never mentioned that she had a sister.'

'Do you know her well?'

The young woman shrugged. 'Birgitta was Linda's favourite. She told her she'd get the next permanent job, even though there were others who'd been here longer.' The cashier pulled a face that said she was one of them.

'Elin, come in and close the door. The alarm's gone off!' someone called, from the inner reaches of the store.

The young woman glanced over her shoulder.

'If Birgitta gets in touch,' Annika said, 'can you ask her to call me?'

'What do you want me to say? What is it that's so important?'

'Just tell her I got her messages,' Annika said.

The cashier gave a disappointed shrug and disappeared. The door closed with an electronic click.

Annika remained where she was, relieved. Birgitta was changing her life. She was no longer relying on the favours of workmates but teaming up with her boss and aiming for permanent employment. Leaving her loser of a husband and creating a new life full of responsibility and success. Maybe she was looking for somewhere new to live as well, and as soon as she'd found a decent flat she'd fetch Destiny. She just wanted to get everything sorted out before getting in touch.

Annika left the supermarket and hurried along a grimy passageway as she called Directory Enquiries and asked to be put through to the Triangeln branch of Hemköp in

Malmö. The call was answered by a receptionist with a thick Skåne accent.

'I'm trying to get hold of one of your employees,' Annika said. 'Her name is Birgitta Bengtzon. Is she working today?'

'Who?'

'Birgitta Bengtzon, she—'

There was a loud noise in the background.

'I can't put you through to any of the cashiers.'

A tiny glimpse of progress.

'So she is working today?'

'I don't know. Has she got a mobile?'

'Yes, but—'

'If it's urgent, you'd better call her on that.'

The call was disconnected. She looked round, trying to get her bearings. She found Triangeln Hemköp on the map on her mobile. It was next to the railway station so she could look in on her way back to Kastrup.

A bus on its way to Bunkeflostrand pulled up with a belch of fumes at the stop in front of her. Two of Malmö's more unfortunate citizens had fallen asleep on a bench, a scruffy German shepherd sitting next to one, panting. An empty schnapps bottle lay on the ground. The bus set off with a bestial roar.

She dropped her phone into her bag and started walking towards Birgitta's home in Östra Sorgenfri, trying to make sense of the sequence of events. According to Steven, Birgitta had gone off to work as usual on Sunday, but hadn't come home. According to her workmate, she had left her job two weeks ago. She had asked Annika for help first thing on Sunday morning when, according to Steven, she had been at home, and would soon have been setting off to work.

One thing was clear: Steven was lying.

There was a large cemetery ahead of her, neatly maintained graves stretching as far as she could see, granite stones, raked gravel paths.

Just to be on the safe side she tried calling Nina Hoffman, but there was no answer. She sent a quick text: *Hi, I'm on my way to see Steven and wondered if you've heard anything I can pass on to him. I'll call later. Annika.*

Now Nina knew where she was.

She walked along beside the cemetery fence and looked across the gravestones. Such a short time we are alive, and such a long time dead.

Birgitta could have gone missing two weeks ago, but for some reason Steven had kept quiet about it until this Monday. He could have sent that text from Birgitta's mobile, or forced her to send it,

Maybe she hadn't left home at all. Maybe Steven was holding her captive in the flat. Perhaps she wanted a divorce or to move home to Hälleforsnäs. *The critical moment is when the woman says she's leaving.*

Behind a wooden fence she could hear laughter and children playing. The sun was blazing as she crossed a main road and found herself among three-storey yellowbrick buildings. She could smell freshly cut grass, and

198

some boys were playing football. She walked quickly along a footpath. Two girls with lollipops in their mouths cycled past her. She ought to be there by now, and she stopped outside a library to check the map. To her surprise, she found that she had wandered into Rosengård, Sweden's most notorious ghetto, the housing estate that the Danes used to scare their kids.

She'd walked past where Birgitta lived, on the other side of the main road.

Branteviksgatan 5 was a block of flats with several different doorways. She walked round the whole building before she found the right one. The door had a coded lock and she waited several minutes until an elderly man came out and she was able to slip in.

Her sister and brother-in-law lived on the eighth floor. The lift rattled up through the core of the building. The landing contained four doors, and smelt of cleaning fluid. There was a hand-painted wooden sign on theirs, with flowers and butterflies and their surnames.

She stopped outside it and listened for sounds from inside the flat, but could hear nothing except the air-conditioning in the stairwell. She held her breath and rang the bell. Footsteps approached, a key rattled.

Steven opened the door. He loomed in front of her, like Hercules, tall and broad-shouldered. He had cut his hair. 'Annika,' he said, clearly surprised, taking a step back. 'What are you doing here?' He sounded bemused, but not hostile.

'I was in Copenhagen on a job and had a few hours spare,' she said, stepping into the hall and dropping her bag on the floor. Now he'd have to throw her out if he wanted to get rid of her.

'Diny, look who it is! Auntie Annika!'

The little girl popped her head out of a room immediately to the left of the door, in a pink dress and pink hairclips. Annika knelt down, feeling Steven's eyes on the back of her neck. 'Hello, Destiny, remember me? You came to visit me once. I've got two girls, Ellen and Serena.'

The girl ran to Steven and hid behind his legs. Annika stood up.

'I wasn't expecting this,' he said. 'What do you want?'

She met his gaze. He was big and heavy, his eyes red-rimmed. What did Birgitta see in him? 'Have you heard anything?' she asked.

He turned away. 'Diny,' he said, 'would you like to get some biscuits out for Auntie Annika?'

The child ran down the short corridor and disappeared to the left.

'Something must have happened to her,' Steven said, in a low voice, not loud enough to reach the kitchen. 'Something awful.' His hands were shaking.

'We don't know that,' she said, thinking about the new job at Hemköp. She had decided not to mention it, because if Steven didn't know, it was probably because Birgitta wanted to keep it a secret.

He stood where he was, swaying, leaning forward.

'Would you like anything?' he asked, after a few moments. 'Coffee?'

'Coffee would be good,' she said.

He all but shuffled towards the kitchen.

Annika took her shoes off and put them on the pine rack. The building was very quiet – she couldn't hear a sound from the neighbours. The little girl was talking in the kitchen, but she couldn't make out what she was saying. Destiny's room was in front of her, small and sparsely furnished, a bed and a desk. A doll's house. Toys on a Billy bookcase. Annika took a few silent steps to a door that stood ajar, and pushed it open. A bedroom. The bed was made, with a bedspread from Ikea. Scatter cushions. A couple of wardrobes along one wall, ordinary size, no locks on the doors.

She stood for a few seconds in the hall, trying to get her heart to slow down. Then she walked into the living room. A few canvases were lined up against one wall, butterflies and flowers, the same style as the sign on the door. She went over to them and tipped a couple forward to see what was behind them. Destiny looked back at her, strikingly realistic, but with bright red lips and long eyelashes. Annika lingered over the portrait, which was lovely but disquieting, a glamour picture of a three-year-old.

'She's good, isn't she?' Steven said from behind her, the pride in his voice unmistakable.

Annika let go of the painting. 'Birgitta's started painting again?'

'She's been doing an evening course, even though she sometimes works late and can't always get there.'

Steven went to the window at the far end of the living room. Outside there was a glassed-in balcony. Annika joined him; she reached his shoulder.

The view was remarkable. Red rooftops spread out as far as she could see, foliage, towers and housing blocks in the distance.

'What a lovely flat,' she said.

'It's my cousin's,' Steven said. 'He's moved to Kiruna, got a job in the mine. We're subletting.' He was still gazing at the view. 'It feels like you can see the whole world.'

'Why did you move here?' Annika asked.

A coffee-machine gurgled. Steven turned and disappeared towards the kitchen. Annika followed him slowly. The floor was cold in spite of the warm weather.

A packet of Ballerina biscuits, with a chocolate filling, lay on the table. Destiny had climbed up into a child's chair and was munching one. Steven put a glass of milk in front of his daughter, then took out cups for himself and Annika, saucers, spoons, sugar lumps and milk. He sat down heavily. Annika bit into a biscuit.

Steven poured the coffee. 'Birgitta's got problems,' he said. 'I . . . We had to do something about it.'

'What do you mean?'

He cast a quick glance at her, then turned to his daughter. 'Diny, do you want to watch television? *Pingu*?'

She nodded. He lifted her down from her chair and

they went into the living room together. Annika heard the theme tune of the children's programme.

He came back into the kitchen and slumped on to his chair. 'Birgitta drinks,' he said. 'So do I, sometimes, but I'm not an addict.'

Annika looked hard at him, scepticism stinging her throat. 'How do you mean, "drinks"?'

'She was out of control. It just couldn't go on like that. There were so many excuses, so many reasons to have a drink. It's Friday, it's Saturday, it's been a bad day at work and you need cheering up, it's been a good day and you want to celebrate.'

'So you've got a problem as well. You do admit that?'

'Who the fuck hasn't got problems?' he said. 'Haven't you?'

Annika took another bite of the biscuit and the crumbs swelled in her mouth.

Steven covered his eyes with his hand. 'I'd been at a building site in Fjällskäfte. The roof was being relaid. When I got home, Birgitta was lying on the sofa. She'd been drinking wine and a whole bottle of Absolut. I couldn't wake her up. Diny was in the bathroom, she'd done a poo and had managed to pull her pants off . . .'

Annika washed the biscuit down with coffee.

Steven fixed his eyes on the wall above her head. 'Birgitta spent a week in the Kullbergska. She almost didn't make it.'

It was the hospital in Katrineholm.

Annika stared distrustfully at him. 'Does Barbro know about this?' she asked.

Steven drank some coffee. 'No. She'd have had a fit. I told her we were on holiday in Finland.' He finished the rest, grimaced and put the cup down on the saucer. 'Birgitta had to get away from her friends and her mum. Away from all those people who drink to stop life seeming so shit.'

'They just discharged her after she'd spent a week in the Kullbergska? Didn't she get any aftercare, any rehab?'

'She kept going as an outpatient until we moved.'

'And Birgitta wanted to move to Malmö?' Annika asked.

'She was really sick of your mother.'

Annika's eyes narrowed: *isolate, control, manipulate.*

'So what happened? Did she stop drinking when you got here?'

'We both did. For me it wasn't a problem, but Birgitta felt awful to start with.'

She looked at his cheeks: he'd shaved. His clothes, jeans and T-shirt, were clean and ironed. Did that mean anything? If so, what?

'I was thinking about Birgitta's appearance,' Annika said. 'What was she wearing when she went missing?'

Steven looked down at the table. Annika thought the colour of his face darkened slightly.

'Her normal clothes. She gets changed at work.'

'Mummy,' Destiny said from the door. 'Mummy's at work.'

She spoke with a Skåne accent. Great. That meant she went to nursery.

'That's right.' His voice wobbled. 'Mummy's at work. She'll be home soon.'

'Do you remember which clothes?'

He stood up and got more coffee. May had been unusually cold throughout the country, with night frosts even in the far south. If Birgitta had disappeared two weeks ago, she ought to have been wearing a jacket, trousers, proper shoes, maybe even a scarf. By Sunday the heatwave had already reached Skåne, so if she'd disappeared then she would have been wearing summer clothes.

'I don't remember, off the top of my head,' he said.

'Try to think.'

He swallowed. 'I think she was in shorts and a T-shirt. Sandals. Hair in a ponytail.'

His hand was shaking more now.

'Anything else you remember? A bag of any sort?'

'The one she always uses, that pale one, leather.'

Annika didn't know it.

He put his hands on top of each other and the shaking diminished. 'What am I going to do if she doesn't come back?' he said.

Annika didn't know what to say. 'Has she been the same as usual over the past few weeks?' she asked instead.

'Daddy, *Pingu*'s finished,' Destiny called.

He went out into the hall. When he came back he sat down again.

'Have you got a job?' Annika asked.

He shook his head. 'I might be able to get invalidity benefit,' he said.

'What's wrong with you?' she asked. She had spoken more sharply than she had intended.

'Parkinson's,' he said. 'It's got a bit better since they put me on Madopar.'

'Have you had it long?'

'Ages,' he said. 'But I was only diagnosed last autumn. I should have got checked out earlier, I'd been feeling shit for so long, but you always think it'll pass, don't you?'

Annika blushed. She had always dismissed him as a useless layabout. Had Birgitta had enough of her sick husband and decided to make a new life for herself? 'I've got a friend at National Crime,' she said. 'She's putting a bit of pressure on them to trace Birgitta's mobile.'

Steven hid his face in his hands. 'Where do you think she could be? You grew up with her. Where could she have gone?'

Annika felt inadequate. She ought to know. 'I'll be in touch as soon as I hear anything,' she said.

Destiny was sitting in her room, wearing an enormous pair of headphones and staring at a little iPad as Annika put her shoes on. She decided against disturbing the child. She closed the front door quietly behind her, and took the stairs down.

The air smelt intoxicatingly fresh when she stepped out of the door. She walked quickly without looking back until she was out of sight of Steven's balcony. Then she stopped and leaned against a wall. She needed a toilet. She rested her head against the bricks, took some deep breaths, then called Nina Hoffman. No answer. She tried calling the Hemköp supermarket at Triangeln again, but found herself talking to the same receptionist. 'I'd like to talk to someone in charge,' she said.

'What's it concerning?'

'I've found a piece of glass in a jar of baby food.'

The receptionist disappeared, and the line crackled. Then a different woman came on the line.

'Good afternoon, my name's Annika Bengtzon, I'm trying to reach my sister, Birgitta Bengtzon. I wondered if she was working today.'

'Who?'

'Birgitta Bengtzon, from Hälleforsnäs. She's only just got the job. Maybe she hasn't started work yet.'

'Where did you say she works?'

'On the checkouts.'

'No, that can't be right.'

Annika swallowed. 'Could I talk to the store manager?' she asked.

'That's me,' the woman said. 'You said you'd found a piece of glass in a jar of baby food?'

'Oh, no, not at all,' Annika said. 'There must have been some sort of misunderstanding. Sorry for disturbing you.'

She disconnected the call.

Everyone was lying.

GREGORIUS
(posted 3 June, 16.53)
To me, equality means fucking a sexist feminist
whore in the vagina with a large knife. The best thing
you can do for equality in Sweden is go out with a
baseball bat and beat a sexist feminist bitch to death.

The rockface felt warm and rough beneath Anders Schyman's hands. If he closed his eyes he could almost have been on his island in the archipelago: the smells and sounds were similar, the movement of the water and the tang of seaweed. The background noise was different, though, people and traffic.

He didn't know where he was. But that didn't bother him: he had satnav in the car.

He squinted at the surface of the water. The reflections dazzled him in a way he loved – he was overwhelmed with light.

He had taken off his shirt and put it beside him on the rocks. His pale body had turned pink in the sun, and his shoulders stung. He was somewhere out on Värmdö, he knew that much, on a rockface where the road ended and the sea began. He could see islands.

He had been stuck in traffic on his way to the newspaper, just like every other morning, when something inside him had snapped. He had put the car into gear and driven along the hard shoulder, overtaking the entire queue on the inside, jolting along the verge at times, but what else was his SUV for?

He had driven without any clear destination, and with even less hesitation. For the first time ever he called his secretary and said he wouldn't be at work today. She had sounded curious, but didn't ask why.

A boat engine started up some distance away, then spluttered and died.

He ran his hand over the rock, gathering grit and pine needles between his fingers. The sea was his solace, his desire and eternity. When he imagined Paradise, it looked like the Rödlöga archipelago, all grey skerries and hissing sea. Unfortunately his wife's idea of Paradise was rather different. She liked the theatre and neatly trimmed lawns. As long as they lived together he wouldn't be able to disappear to his island.

He wasn't expecting any reward in the afterlife but his wife was a believer, a characteristic he secretly envied. They had discussed religion at the start of their relationship, but the subject had been dead and buried for decades. For him faith, no matter what the religion, was incomprehensible. How was it possible for educated, intelligent adults to believe in fairy tales? In all seriousness?

He could understand the cultural, traditional, ethical and moral aspects, that you could be raised as a Catholic or a Jew or a Muslim, in the same way that you were Swedish, a Social Democrat, or a Djurgården fan from birth, but truly *believing*? Living under the delusion that we had been created by a higher power who, for no discernible reason, also happened to wish us well?

To him it seemed blindingly obvious that the exact opposite was true.

When human beings became aware of their own existence, they also realized they would die. And they couldn't handle that awareness, so they constructed a higher purpose for their pointless life on Earth.

Man had created God in his own image, someone who protected and looked after him: an all-encompassing power for us to lean on, pray to and rely on.

To start with, God had been a woman, the good mother who gave life and food. As humans abandoned their lives as hunter-gatherers and settled in fixed abodes, conflict had broken out, the patriarchy had taken control and God had become a man.

He sighed, sifting the pine needles between his fingers. The boat engine started up again, and this time the sound continued. It merged with that of his mobile phone, and he looked around the rock in some confusion. It had been silent all day. He had told his secretary he wouldn't be taking any calls, but it was definitely ringing now. His wife, perhaps?

He fumbled for his shirt. His phone was in the breast pocket. No, not his wife. It was the paper. He sighed and took the call.

'I've got that serial killer on the line,' his secretary said. 'Gustaf Holmerud. He's very persistent and insists on talking to you.'

These days, religion was rather overlooked. Schyman had read somewhere (probably in his own newspaper) that more Swedes believed in ghosts than in God. That probably wasn't true, but the fact remained that Sweden was probably the most secular country on the planet. That didn't mean they were more rational or heedless of guidance than earlier generations, just that they relied on other things instead.

'What does he want?' Anders Schyman asked.

God had been the guiding principle: his will had shaped people's daily lives, established society's norms and moral boundaries. His word could be read in the Bible; that was the Truth. He had given humanity his stories. People begged him for mercy, confessed to him, and prayed for the forgiveness of their sins. God judged and condemned, crushed and forgave. But not any more.

'He sounds very angry,' his secretary said.

The newspapers and television were where people confessed now: celebrities who had been caught speeding, sports stars who had taken performance-enhancing drugs, politicians who had drunk too much, murderers who claimed they were innocent.

'Okay, put him through,' Schyman said.

'Hello?' a voice said.

Yes, hello, this is God.

'This is Anders Schyman,' he said. 'What can I do for you?'

Gustaf Holmerud took a whistling breath. 'This is harassment!' he said, sounding strained. 'Bullying!'

Schyman moved the phone to his other ear. 'You sound upset.'

'The tabloids are tormenting me!' Gustaf Holmerud said, his voice trembling. 'You just lie and make things up.'

Then came what sounded like a sniff.

Schyman wasn't clear what was going on. 'You're welcome to give your own version of any stories we print,' he replied amiably.

'You said in your paper that I'm a miscarriage of justice! That I didn't commit the crimes I was found guilty of! How can you print something like that without talking to me first?'

Ah, so that was it, the old prosecutor speaking his mind.

Anders Schyman stood up. He had got rather sweaty in the sun and the wind was soothing. 'What would you like us to do to put things right?' he asked.

'I'm the only person who can say that I'm not guilty. I have to retract my confessions or there can't be a retrial in the Supreme Court.'

Anders Schyman felt the hair on the back of his neck stand up. This was unquestionably one of Fate's little ironies.

The notion of a mysterious serial killer in the suburbs of Stockholm had arisen during a particularly dull editorial meeting at his own paper. If he wasn't mistaken, Patrik Nilsson had come up with the idea, and they had pushed the issue in their prime news pages, persisting with it to the point that the police were eventually obliged to consider it, if only for the sake of appearances. Naturally, the whole thing would have run into the sand if the unfortunate Gustaf Holmerud hadn't suddenly decided to confess to the murders, then manage to be convicted of all five. He was probably guilty of one, a chiropractor called Lena with whom he had had a relationship. Schyman had spoken to her mother at some point.

'It must have been extremely hard for you,' he said, 'being convicted of all those murders when you were innocent.'

Gustaf Holmerud was definitely sniffing now. 'They tricked me,' he said. 'The police lured me into confessing and the doctors drugged me with powerful medication. They were interested and kind as long as I kept saying what they wanted me to say. I wanted to feel important. I wanted to be helpful . . .'

Anders Schyman's stomach was churning. 'So you're entirely innocent?' he said, forcing himself to sound trustworthy and neutral.

'Completely,' Gustaf Holmerud said. 'I'm going to be demanding serious compensation from the Swedish state for snatching all these years of my life from me.'

Well, it wasn't that many, Schyman thought.

'You're very welcome to speak out in the paper,' he said. 'I can send a reporter to Kumla first thing tomorrow, if you like.'

'I want you to write it.'

Of course.

'My reporters write what I tell them to. They do as I say.'

There was silence on the line. The water lapped against the rocks, and the boat engine was coming back. 'Hello?' Schyman said.

'Okay,' Gustaf Holmerud replied. 'But I need to approve every single word.'

'Naturally you'll be able to check any quotations attributed to you. You'll need to arrange the visit with the authorities at your facility. Let us know when that's done and we'll come and see you.'

Silence again.

'You're all liars, really,' Gustaf Holmerud said, and hung up.

Anders Schyman stood where he was, gazing out to sea. It had been an immense responsibility, but it would soon be over. Whether or not they closed the *Evening Post*, it was in its death throes. The notion that journalism was omnipotent was obsolete. With the internet and social media, power and responsibility had been placed in the hands of each individual. Everyone was their own Creator, and the only place that was likely to lead was straight to Hell.

But if he could end his days as a journalist with an appeal in the Supreme Court, then, in spite of everything, it wouldn't all have been in vain.

He put his shirt on.

Now that he came to think about it, he was extremely hungry.

*

Thomas used to love mingling. Before the hook, he could glide through a room with a glass of red in one hand, the other nonchalantly in his trouser pocket, his jacket and shirt slightly open, his hair tousled and his eyes full of laughter. He could talk and flirt in a state of constant movement, sailing across the floor, talking to anyone and everyone, striking a chord with both sexes. The men wanted to *be* him; the women wanted to be *with* him. Now he didn't even know how to handle his glass. If he held it in his right hand he couldn't shake anyone's hand. Okay, he could tuck it into the hook, but that would look mad.

He took a sip, then put his glass on the dresser in the hall. The flat was full of people, kitchen, living room and dining room: Sophia's unbearable financial-services friends, stockbrokers and analysts, business lawyers and risk capitalists, and the occasional failure who did something arty. They thought they were so special, that they'd succeeded in life, but none of them had anything to say, no influence. None had any real power.

He moved towards the kitchen, unimpeded. The hook was in his trouser pocket, and he hoped he wouldn't meet anyone he knew. The kids, thank God, had installed themselves in the small bedroom, the one that had been Kalle and Ellen's room when he'd lived there with Sophia. Apparently an old PlayStation was still gathering dust in there.

'Are you having a good time?' Sophia had slid up alongside him, her hand reaching under his left arm and giving it a familiar squeeze.

He stiffened. What if she felt the hook? He smiled and pulled away. 'One thing's for sure,' he said. 'You're very good at organizing parties!'

She laughed. 'Don't you want anything to drink?'

He tilted his head and pretended to think. 'A whisky, maybe?'

He could down it in one and, God knows, he'd need the alcohol if he was going to stick this out until Annika showed up.

Sophia smiled her most beautiful smile. 'Coming right up. Don't go anywhere!'

He went over to the wine-rack and inspected the bottles. Incredibly, she still hadn't got round to buying a wine fridge. He recognized a few bottles from when he had lived there – probably undrinkable by now.

'I know what you're thinking,' she said, handing him a glass containing two fingers of deep golden liquid.

He raised an eyebrow and took a sip of the whisky, which tasted like diesel.

'I'm going to buy a wine fridge,' she said, 'but I might keep it at Säter. I'm thinking about moving up there.'

He forced himself to swallow his mouthful, then put the glass on the counter rather too hard. Säter was the Grenborg family's estate in northern Uppland. 'Are you abandoning the city? What are you going to do out there in the sticks?'

She gave a melancholy smile. 'Dad can't look after the estate by himself now, and I've probably been treading water as a bureaucrat for long enough.'

A woman with very obvious breast implants pushed between them and showered Sophia with flowers, hugs and alcohol-addled birthday wishes, then turned to Thomas with clear interest in her over-made-up eyes. 'And who have we got here, then?' she said, running her tongue over her lips.

From the corner of his eye Thomas saw Sophia's face cloud, and he held his hand out to the woman as he moved closer to Sophia, so close that their bodies touched. 'Thomas Samuelsson,' he said, with a smile. 'An old friend of Sophia's.' He said this in an insinuating way, and with warmth. The woman picked up the hint and drifted off.

Sophia stayed where she was, her bottom pressed against his thigh. 'Okay,' she said quietly. 'What was all that about?'

He ran his hand through her hair, and at that moment he saw Annika step through the front door. She looked tired and sweaty, and her hair tumbled in front of her face as she bent down to take off her shoes (who took their shoes off at a cocktail party?). She was holding a plastic bag from the duty-free shop at Kastrup airport.

'Happy birthday!' she said, giving Sophia a hug, and ignoring him.

'Oh!' Sophia said, as she pulled a bottle of champagne out of the bag. 'Thanks very much. That's so kind.'

'Hi, Thomas,' Annika said, glancing at him quickly. 'Did it go okay with the kids?'

Sophia put the bottle on the table with the other gifts.

'Fine,' he said, downing the whisky. He had ordered a taxi to pick them up, all four children, and had paid for it when they turned up at Sophia's.

'Thanks very much,' she said. 'I really appreciate it.'

He leaned over her. 'I know these are supposed to be my days to have the kids, but I've got such a lot on at work . . .'

For a moment he thought she was going to topple over.

'I'm going to Kumla first thing tomorrow morning,' she said.

'I understand,' he said, 'but—'

'Don't worry,' she said. 'I can take them home with me. It's no sacrifice.'

'Great,' he said. 'You know I'm always happy to help, but . . .'

She gave him a thin smile. 'Thomas, I said it was okay. Okay?' She turned and went off to the room where the children were.

The warmth of the whisky spread through his stomach. There were plenty of people who *did* appreciate him. Maybe he should have another whisky.

Nina padded quietly down the dimly lit corridor. Most of the signs on the doors had fallen off, and she counted them in silence as she went. She stopped at the ninth door on the left and listened as she reached for the handle. Quick steps echoed behind a plasterboard wall, and a fluorescent light crackled and hissed. The ventilation system sounded like a never-ending inhalation, and the regular bleeping of a security camera reached her from some distance away.

She didn't bother to knock.

The room lay in semi-darkness. The night-time lighting was on, a few yellow lamps over in the far corner casting long shadows over the ward. Eight beds, positioned close together in a very small space, but there was no point in complaining. The patients would never make a fuss: none of them was aware of their situation.

She went over to her usual place, pulled up the chair and saw that the book was still on the bedside table where she had left it. Then she looked at the man in the bed. He had been shaved and seemed well cared for. She didn't recognize the pyjamas. His remaining eye was peering, half closed, at the ceiling.

'Hello, Ingemar,' Nina said, stroking his cheek. 'It's me, Nina. I see you've had a shower.'

He didn't react. She took his hand and warmed his cold fingers. 'The trial continued today,' she said quietly. 'Everything seems to be progressing as it should. We'll just have to see if it's enough.'

Ingemar Lerberg was no longer in any pain. The torn muscles in his groin had been repaired, his broken ribs had healed, and his shoulders were back in their sockets. The vitreous fluid in his shattered eye could never be replaced, but it wasn't causing pain.

'I'm worried about the DNA results,' she went on. 'Johansson says it's fine, that it's fairly common not to get more than a ninety-nine per cent match, but the

219

defence lawyer's playing that card so hard that it's troubling me.'

Right from the start she used to come to the care-home in case he had woken up. Ingemar Lerberg was a key witness in the case against Ivar Berglund: if he could identify the man who had assaulted him, several crimes could be cleared up at once. She sat by his side, evening after evening, listening to his heartbeat, watching him breathe. He was the epitome of absolute loneliness, shut inside his own catastrophe. No one knew if he had any idea of what was going on around him. Probably not, but as time passed she found a peculiar consolation in the total freedom of being able to talk without it making any difference at all.

She reached for the coconut hand-cream she had bought at the airport in Amsterdam last winter when she was on her way back from a Europol conference in The Hague. She squeezed some out and started to massage Ingemar Lerberg's stiff right hand.

'I met Ivar Berglund's younger sister today,' she said. 'She must have had a tough time growing up. I wonder what they did to her for her to end up the way she is.'

She put the man's right hand down gently, then reached over and picked up the left; a bit more cream, soft, gentle movements.

The door glided open and a nurse came in. 'Hello, Nina,' she said.

'Hello, Petra,' Nina said. 'These are nice pyjamas. Are they new?'

Staff Nurse Petra went over to Larsson, one of the

patients on the other side of the room, pulled the covers back and set about changing his colostomy bag. 'Yes, they're lovely, aren't they? We had a new batch yesterday. Have you got coffee?'

'I'm fine, thanks,' Nina said.

Petra smiled and tucked Larsson in again. 'Just say if there's anything you need,' she said, and walked out.

The door closed.

Nina stood up and massaged Lerberg's feet. The scars from where he had been beaten shone in the yellow light, and she traced them with her finger, hard and smooth. Then she sat down with the book in her lap. '*En esto, descubrieron treinta o cuarenta molinos de viento que hay en aquel campo, y así como don Quijote los vio, dijo a su escudero . . .*'

This was her favourite part of Cervantes' classic novel, the eighth chapter, about how the impoverished but pure-hearted nobleman went into battle against the evils of the world, and attacked thirty windmills. She knew that Ingemar Lerberg had once studied Spanish, but this text from the 1600s probably went way over his head, even if he was aware of her reading it. She had decided that it didn't matter: she was reading for her own sake, for the chance to speak her mother tongue aloud, to hear her own voice as it sounded in her head, and perhaps also to remember Filip when he'd read to her, and his soft whisper afterwards, when she was already drifting off to sleep: *Maybe they really* were *giants, Nina, disguised as windmills. Always try to see the truth!*

She had reached Don Quixote's battle-cry, '*Non fuy-ades, cobardes y viles criaturas, que un solo caballero es el que os acomete,*' when her mobile rang. It sounded like a fire alarm and she hurried to answer.

'Where are you?' Johansson asked.

'Reading,' Nina replied.

'We've had a reply from our Spanish colleagues,' Johansson said.

'That was quick,' Nina said. 'Who investigated the crash?'

'The crash?'

'In the Alpujarras mountains.'

'The local police in Albuñol, but that's not why I'm calling. We've got a match for Berglund, one of the old cases. No doubt this time. The result is beyond question.'

Her pulse and breathing picked up. Nina looked at Ingemar Lerberg's half-closed eye. 'Where?'

'A murder in San Sebastián, eighteen years ago.'

She stood up, then sat down again. 'The Basque country?'

'They assumed ETA was behind it, which is why it's taken so long.'

She breathed out through her open mouth. 'And it's definite this time? The DNA match is a hundred per cent?'

'Even better than that,' Johansson said. 'We've got a fingerprint as well.'

She clenched her right fist in triumph. Fingerprints were unique, even in identical twins. 'Thanks for calling,' she said, and Johansson hung up.

She waited until she had calmed down. Then she put away the book, checked that the lid of the hand-cream was on properly, and stroked Ingemar Lerberg's arm.

THURSDAY, 4 JUNE

The walls began at the end of the smart residential area. They stretched off towards infinity, as life sentences must do for the inmates inside. Layer upon layer of concrete and electric fencing, boredom and frustration, barbed wire and steel gates: Viagatan 4 in Kumla, commonly known as the Bunker.

Annika turned into the visitors' car park and found a space, put the handbrake on and switched off the engine. The car radio fell silent, cutting off Adam Alsing midsentence. The heat was making the engine click.

She was a bit late. Ellen had a sore throat and she'd had to wait to see if the paracetamol helped before sending her daughter to school. Not that a few minutes made much difference: Gustaf Holmerud wasn't likely to be going anywhere. Schyman had warned her that Holmerud would probably be difficult, and arriving a quarter of an hour late was hardly going to change that.

She got out of the car and the wind tugged at her hair. The weather was hot and muggy, carrying with it the threat of thunder and lightning. She had been to Kumla before, and knew she couldn't take anything inside with her. All she had was a notepad that fitted her back pocket.

She announced her arrival via the entry-phone, and was welcomed by a female guard. The gate gave an electronic click and she entered the long passageway through no man's land, a gravel path a hundred metres long, lined with steel fencing, that led to the visitors' entrance. Her feet scraped the gravel. Another entry-phone. The same guard. This door was extremely heavy, she remembered that, and wondered why. Was there some sort of hidden symbolism at work? She used both hands to open it, which felt oddly reassuring.

The waiting room was empty. A few keys were missing from the white lockers lining the walls so she wasn't the only visitor that Thursday morning. A third entry-phone, still the same voice.

She waited, not bothering to draw the curtains from the window: she knew what was behind them. White bars and a gravel courtyard. The noticeboard next to the entry-phone contained information about visiting times and how to book the overnight flat.

She brushed her hair from her forehead, struck by life's absurdities. The fact that she was there just then was partly her own fault, and possibly deservedly so, depending on how you chose to look at it. Last autumn, just after she had returned to the newsroom after her stint as the paper's correspondent in Washington, she had compiled a list of all the murders of women that had been committed in Stockholm and its suburbs during the previous six months. There were five, all carried out close to the victims' homes or workplaces, all with different types of knife. In every case it was the women's current or previous partners who were suspected of killing them, which meant that the media silence surrounding the deaths was practically impenetrable. (There seemed to be an understanding within the media that murdered wives weren't real murders, just sordid domestic tragedies, in the same deep-frozen category of news as alcohol-fuelled murders in drug-dens and genocides in Africa.) Naturally, Patrik had dismissed the list as devoid of interest, until Annika uttered the random words that she had regretted so many times since: 'What if there's a serial killer on the loose whom everyone has missed?'

And now she was standing there, five convictions for murder later, wondering who she was about to see: a wretched girlfriend-beater, a ruthless serial killer, or the innocent victim of a miscarriage of justice?

'Please, come through,' a voice said, from the loudspeaker up by the ceiling.

Annika raised her hand towards the security camera in the corner and walked into the secure airlock. Two guards, a man and a woman, watched her through reinforced glass. She put her notepad on a little plastic tray and it was passed through the scanner. Then she walked through the metal detector into the secure zone. She showed her ID and was allowed to borrow a pen, a yellow Bic. She wrote her name, and the name of the person she was visiting, signed to state that she understood the conditions of the visit (that she agreed to be searched by two female guards, if necessary, or by a sniffer-dog, and that she consented to being locked into a confined space with the inmate).

'You'll be in room number seven,' the male guard said, as he hung her driver's licence on a noticeboard behind the desk. 'Would you like coffee?'

She thanked him, but declined.

They walked down a corridor lined with numbered doors.

'You'll have to clean the room afterwards,' the guard said.

As though she were there to have sex.

She stepped inside it.

'You can call the security guards using the intercom, and this is the emergency alarm.'

Annika nodded and thanked him again.

The door closed behind her. She stood in the middle of the floor and looked at the foam-rubber mattress on the bed, the chest of drawers containing sheets and blankets, the toilet and shower, the single chair. The only decoration on the walls was a framed poster for an exhibition at Moderna Museet, in Stockholm, by an artist called Johan Wahlström, naïve faces in blue, red and silver. The picture was called *The Waiting Room*, which seemed appropriate.

She sank onto the chair. They were bringing Gustaf

Holmerud from his part of the prison along some underground tunnel. He would have to go through the same security routine as her, plus a bit extra: he'd have to change his shoes (in the past inmates had hollowed out the heels of their trainers and filled them with heroin). When the visit was over and he went back to his cell, he would have to go through the metal detector naked. The security equipment was checked daily, and the routines worked. There were hardly any drugs in the Kumla Bunker, no escapes and very few murders.

She looked at the bars on the window.

People who never saw the horizon ended up with distorted perspective. She'd read that somewhere. Always finding walls in the way, never being able to let your eyes roam free, your perception of distance shrank. It was unnatural: humans had developed on the savannah where the skies were endless.

The door opened and Annika stood up instinctively. Her palms began to sweat.

Gustaf Holmerud was much bigger than she had expected. She had always imagined him as a short man, hunched and evasive, but the few pictures that existed of him outside the courtroom hadn't done him justice. He practically filled the doorway, tall and thick-set, with long arms and short legs. His hair was wet: he had showered before meeting her.

They shook hands and introduced themselves. His hand was cooler than hers, and the set of his mouth indicated nervous frustration.

231

'So Anders Schyman has sent one of his minions,' he said. 'Oh, well, such is life.'

The door closed behind them. The lock rattled. Annika hurried to sit on the only chair again, unwilling to sit beside him on the bed.

'Thanks for letting me interview you,' she said, resting the Bic pen and her notepad on her lap.

Gustaf Holmerud remained standing. From a statistical point of view, he fulfilled all the criteria for a woman-killer: a native Swede, physically healthy and with no previous convictions, like the majority of ordinary Swedish men. But the majority of the male population didn't kill their women with kitchen knives because they couldn't control them.

'I think you've misunderstood your role,' Gustaf Holmerud said, sitting on the edge of the bed. 'You're not here to conduct an interview, you're here to make sure I get out.'

He moved closer to her, so close that their legs almost touched, and leaned his elbows on his knees. His breath struck her in the face. It smelt of coffee.

Annika sat on the chair without moving. She wasn't going to let herself be intimidated. She looked hard into his eyes, which were watery and red. Perhaps he was on some sort of sedative. 'No,' she said. 'You're the one who misunderstands the situation. I'm not your defence lawyer. I'm a journalist, and I'm going to write an article for the *Evening Post*.'

He stared at her with his mouth half open, then moved back and made himself more comfortable on the mattress. 'It must be very exciting for you to be here with me,' he said. 'This is a real coup for you. You think you're going to win the national prize for journalism now, don't you?' He laughed, a dry little chuckle.

'You told Anders Schyman that you're innocent of the crimes you were found guilty of,' Annika said. 'You said you wanted to give your side of the story. I'm ready to listen to what you've got to say.'

'Oh, sweetie,' he said. 'I make the decisions about who I talk to, and it has to be a proper editor.'

A middle-aged white man, maybe. Someone who's been on television, preferably one with an aristocratic surname? She held his gaze. 'You were imagining someone with a bit of authority and experience? Someone who looks like the person you wish you were?'

He looked at her with vacant eyes. 'Annika Bengtzon,' he said. 'Why are you out there, and I'm stuck in here?'

A chill ran through her. 'How do you mean?'

'You really did kill someone. I didn't. You can put that in your paper.'

She felt her throat tighten.

'*He claims that my screams are pleasure rather than pain*. That was very pleasant reading.'

He'd read her diary, which had formed part of the preliminary investigation. How had he got hold of it? But, of course, it wasn't hard: anyone could request a copy from a district court: once the verdict had been pronounced, it was in the public domain. She made an effort not to gasp for air, but her body felt heavy and powerless.

233

He smiled. 'There are several of you from the papers who ought to be in here. Your colleague Patrik Nilsson was convicted of imitating a public official, did you know that? He dressed up as a police officer and took witness statements from a crime scene. And Bosse, from the other paper, he's got problems with the Enforcement Service. His attempts at trading in shares didn't turn out very well. And Berit Hamrin, the old Communist, she'd be counted as a terrorist, these days.' He clasped his hands over his stomach, evidently enjoying the situation.

Annika made some notes. 'It's clever of you to have done your research,' she said. 'That's how you managed to get convicted of those crimes. You learned what to say when questioned, and how to react when you were taken to the crime scenes.'

He stopped smiling, and pursed his lips. 'I want some influence over the person I talk to,' he said.

'I'm sorry,' she said, 'but today you're going to have to make do with me. How come you've changed your mind? Why have you retracted your confessions?'

He shoved himself even further back on the bed so that his back was pressed to the wall. His legs stuck straight out and he was wearing a pair of Prison Service plastic sandals.

'You think you can trick me into talking,' he said. 'I want this to be big, not some single shitty little article in one paper. A book, a television programme, and lots of articles for days on end.'

She took a silent breath, then picked up her pen and

notepad. 'Let's see if I've understood you correctly,' she said. 'You want a synchronized media launch on every possible platform. Television, newspapers, social media, radio, too, maybe, and a book. Is that correct?'

He hesitated for a few seconds, then nodded. 'Yes, that's it,' he said.

She looked at him, his bulging stomach, his slowly drying hair. 'Why did you do it?' she asked.

His smile faded. 'Do what?'

'Confess to all those murders.'

He pursed his lips and folded his arms.

'You told Anders Schyman that the police had lured you into confessing,' Annika said. 'That the police and doctors made you feel important, and as long as you kept confessing you were given drugs and plenty of attention.'

'Anders Schyman promised that I could check every word.'

'He said you could check quotes attributed to you,' Annika said.

Gustaf Holmerud sat in silence, staring at Johan Wahlström's picture.

Annika stood up. 'I'll convey your demands to my editors,' she said. 'Seeing as you don't want to talk to me, I'll have to draw my own conclusions about our conversation. Do you want to know what I'm going to say?'

He lit up.

'That you confessed to a series of crimes you didn't commit to get attention and stand in the spotlight, but

235

that now the lamps have gone out, it isn't so much fun, so you want to get back into the spotlight, this time by claiming to be innocent.'

She tucked her notepad into her back pocket and pressed the intercom.

'Annika Bengtzon in room seven,' she told the control room. 'I'm ready now.'

Gustaf Holmerud shuffled to the edge of the bed and got to his feet, his eyes rather anxious. 'Are you leaving?'

'There's not going to be an interview,' she said. 'I've got better things to be getting on with.'

'When will I hear from you again? What's the next step?'

She heard footsteps in the corridor. 'You're not as good at research as you think you are,' she said. 'Or else you're lying. Patrik Nilsson may have been found guilty of wearing a police uniform, but he never took witness statements from a crime scene. The uniform was part of a prank for a men's magazine when he was a freelancer. He was fined ten days' wages, which doesn't really warrant being locked away in the Kumla Bunker.'

The lock rattled and the door swung open.

She shook his hand. 'I'll see to it that someone informs you of whatever we decide. Thanks for seeing me.'

She went out of the door, passed through the security zone and waiting room, and returned to her car without a backward glance.

*

Her failure chafed like a stone in her shoe. She had sent a short text message to Schyman: *No interview today, Holmerud obstructive. Still possible, details this afternoon.* He hadn't replied. Adam Alsing had finished for the day, so she switched the radio off.

What could she have done differently? Not much, probably. Gustaf Holmerud wasn't stupid, even if he was half mad. He had managed to get himself convicted of four crimes he hadn't committed, which demanded considerable perceptiveness and application. He was probably guilty of the fifth: the murder of his former girlfriend.

She was fifteen minutes into her drive back to Stockholm when her mobile rang, a number she didn't recognize.

'Good morning,' a mournful male voice said. 'My name is Johansson, I'm calling from the National Crime Unit.'

Unconsciously she sat up straighter in the driver's seat. Was she allowed to talk on the phone while she drove? She felt suddenly uncertain.

'Am I talking to Annika Bengtzon?'

Yes, he was. She slowed down.

'My colleague Nina Hoffman has asked me to let you know the results of a trace on a mobile phone.'

'Yes,' Annika said. 'My sister's phone, she's gone missing.'

'Of course, yes, I can see the report here. Two reports, in fact, one in Stockholm and the other in Malmö.'

'Sorry,' Annika said, 'but why isn't Nina calling?'

'She's away on official business. It's a little unortho-dox, giving the results in this way, but if I've understood correctly, you and Nina have an ongoing collaboration.'

Well, Annika wasn't sure she'd put it quite like that, but never mind.

'We've looked back over the whole of the past month, from the first of May onwards, it says here. Should I tell you the results now, or would you like me to—'

'Now is fine,' Annika said.

'Until two weeks ago the pattern was the same. The operator picked up signals from masts mainly located in central Malmö, between Rosengård and Värnhemstorget.'

She heard the rustle of paper.

'Then, on Sunday, the seventeenth of May, there's a gap in the signal. The phone is switched off, and the next time it gets switched on is Tuesday, the nineteenth of May – two days later, in other words. On that day two text messages are sent, one to a woman called Linda Torstensson, and one to a Steven Andersson. Was this something you already knew?'

Annika knew that Birgitta had written to Linda: she had lied about getting a permanent job in another super-market. Why? She had been her boss's favourite, so why burn her bridges?

Because she'd wanted Linda to be upset. She didn't want Linda to contact her. She wanted to be left alone. As for what Birgitta had written to Steven, only he knew that.

'I can see here that those two texts were sent via a mast in Södermanland, in a place called Hälleforsnäs.'

Annika braked, and the car behind blew its horn angrily. Tuesday, two weeks ago, Birgitta was in Hälleforsnäs? 'Is it possible to see where the phones that received the text messages were?' Annika asked.

Johansson coughed. 'They were both in Malmö when the messages were received.'

For some reason that news calmed her. The technology was cold and definite. Steven had been in Malmö when Birgitta had vanished. At least he wasn't lying about that.

'The mobile was switched on two more times during the following week, on the twenty-second and the twenty-fifth of May. Three messages were sent, two to Steven Andersson, and one to Annika Bengtzon, to you, all via the same mast.'

Annika, please get in touch, you've got to help me! Birgitta

'One final text was sent to your mobile on Sunday, at four twenty-two a.m., from Luleå.'

Annika's brain froze. *Annika, help me!* 'Luleå?'

Annika could see the city in her mind's eye, snowdrifts against panelled buildings, the heavy pulse of the steelworks, shiny railway tracks on a winter's night. She had been there several times in connection with Benny Andersson's murder and the hunt for Red Wolf – dear God, the children had been so young. It had been during those trips to Luleå that Thomas embarked on his affair with Sophia Grenborg.

239

'Is this any help to you? Does your sister have any connection to these places?'

'We come from Hälleforsnäs,' Annika said.

The man let out a sigh. 'She must have gone for a visit.'

Annika thanked him for the information and ended the call. She came off at the next junction, turned round and drove back a couple of kilometres. Then she took the road that led to Hälleforsnäs.

The Dirección General de la Policía in San Sebastián lay on Calle de José María Salaberria, a narrow alley with roadworks on one side and scaffolding on the other. Nina looked up at the brick building, which reminded her of a block of flats in a Stockholm suburb.

She stepped into the police station, a little unsteady on her feet through lack of sleep. Her Ryanair flight to Biarritz in France had taken off from Skavsta airport at the crack of dawn and she'd tried to get some sleep on board but the seat wouldn't recline more than a millimetre, and her knees were aching just half an hour into the flight from being pressed up against the seat in front. She had given up and focused instead on how best to present the Ivar Berglund case to her Spanish colleagues.

The taxi from the airport had taken just under an hour. On the way they had crossed the border between France and Spain, but she hadn't even noticed.

She asked for Police Commissioner Axier Elorza in Reception, and showed her driving licence, as a civilian. Her status as a police officer was as yet unsanctioned.

240

Europol would be granting authorization later that day, and she didn't want to pre-empt the decision. She would be permitted to act as an observer rather than an active representative of authority, but that would be enough.

The receptionist told her to take a seat and wait.

She sat on a hard wooden bench and looked out of the window. The trial in the high-security court was due to finish tomorrow. There was a risk that Ivar Berglund would be released immediately after the main hearing, but that was unlikely. She had to gain access to the whole of the Spanish investigation into the old case in which the DNA evidence had been secured today, ideally that morning, in order for official procedures to be set in motion and to make sure that Berglund remained in custody.

'Third floor,' the receptionist said, pointing to a lift.

Nina got to her feet and made her way up through the building.

She found the chief of police in a cramped room with a view of the building site on the other side of the street. Axier Elorza was a small, skinny man in plain clothes, with a drooping moustache. He could easily have been one of the old men who fed the pigeons in the square in Alisios where she had grown up. But Nina knew that appearances were deceptive: Commissioner Elorza had tracked down, arrested and eliminated more ETA terrorists than any other Spanish policeman alive today.

'Señorita Hoffman,' the old man said, his eyes twinkling. 'It's an honour.'

'The honour is entirely mine,' Nina told him. 'Thank you for seeing me at such short notice.' She was a head taller than him.

'Please, let's set aside formalities. Do come in!' He gestured her into his little office, evidently keen to keep her visit as informal as possible, at least at this stage. No conference room, no large delegation to share information. She sat on a chair on the other side of his desk, which was empty, apart from two bottles of carbonated water and two small glasses.

'So, Señorita, tell me why our DNA result from an eighteen-year-old murder is of such interest to the Swedish police,' he said, twisting the cork stopper off one of the bottles of water with his fist.

Nina sat still, her back straight. His way of stressing her title fulfilled two functions. First, he was making it very clear that she was there as a private person: it had been sensible of her to present herself to the receptionist in that capacity. Second, he was stressing her gender: female police officers were still unusual in Spain's macho culture. His way of dealing with the water-bottle was a less than subtle way of showing his strength. She was actually rather thirsty, but couldn't see a bottle-opener. She'd never be able to get the cap off with her bare hands but had no intention of asking for his help.

'A murder trial is currently under way in Stockholm District Court,' she said, even though she assumed that Commissioner Elorza already knew a fair amount about why she was there. 'A man named Ivar Berglund has been charged with the crime. He's a Swedish citizen, single, a businessman with a forestry company, no previous criminal record. The evidence consists of a DNA match found under the victim's fingernail, a match that isn't a hundred per cent but which would probably be enough in a normal case. The problem is the nature of the crime and the defendant's irreproachable background. The murder was unusually calculated, and there's nothing to suggest that the defendant has a criminal nature.'

Commissioner Elorza took a sip of water, and Nina moistened her lips.

'We're also satisfied from an investigative perspective that the same culprit is guilty of an extremely brutal assault on a Swedish politician, a crime that was committed just a couple of days before, in the same part of Stockholm.'

'But he hasn't been charged with the assault?'

'No,' Nina said.

The old man sucked his teeth, demonstrating obvious disapproval. 'How come?'

'There was insufficient forensic evidence.'

'So what leads you to the conclusion that you're dealing with the same perpetrator?'

Nina chose her words carefully. 'A number of reasons. The murdered man was legally responsible for a Spanish company that was owned by the assaulted politician's wife. A child's drawing was found at the scene of the murder that could well have been drawn by the politician's children.'

243

The commissioner screwed up his eyes. 'But that isn't the whole truth,' he said. 'You're absolutely certain. Why?'

She held her hands still in her lap. 'Both victims were subjected to established torture methods.'

The policeman leaned forward in his chair. She had his interest now.

'Which ones?' he asked.

She straightened her shoulders, and used Spanish terminology in so far as there was any. '*Fakala*,' she said, 'the soles of his feet were beaten. *La Bañera*, suffocation with a plastic bag. Spread-eagle, in which the victim's hands were tied behind his back and he was then strung up by his wrists. *Cheera* – the victim's legs were pulled apart until the muscles tore. The second victim was subjected to *La Barra*: his wrists were tied round his knees, then he was hung from a tree by his knees.'

The commissioner looked almost amused. 'Tell me, Señorita, why have they sent you to give me this information?'

She met his gaze. 'Because these are my conclusions,' she said. And because I speak Spanish and we're in a hell of a hurry.

'You visited the scenes of these crimes?'

'Of course.'

'Didn't you find it unpleasant?'

She looked at him in surprise. 'Naturally. They were terrible crimes.' How could she explain the shadows inside her, the ones that meant she could see in the dark? That she wasn't afraid of a lack of light because she had

244

been born into it? 'Criminals are predictable,' she said. 'They work in the same way as everyone else. They have the same motivations and ambitions. One common denominator is that they regard themselves as powerless, and are prepared to do anything to change that. What we call evil is really only a consequence of their choice of tool, because they use violence to gain power. We have to look beyond that, and not allow their methods to stop us seeing what's really important.'

A fleeting smile passed across the old policeman's face. He leaned forward and twisted the cap off the other bottle, then poured the bubbling water into her glass. 'What do you know about ETA?' he asked.

She took a small sip. 'Not much. A separatist group whose aim was to create an independent Basque state.'

'*Euskadi ta Askatasuna*,' the commissioner said. 'Basque for "The Basque country and freedom". Between 1968 and 2003, eight hundred and nineteen people were killed in various acts of terrorism that we believe were caused by ETA. Ernesto Jaka – have you ever heard of him?'

She assumed the question was rhetorical and said she hadn't.

'No,' the commissioner said. 'Why should you have? Ernesto Jaka was a Basque businessman, from Bilbao. Not too small, but not too big either. He dealt in raw materials, mostly oil. He was found tortured to death in a garbage container at a building site controlled by ETA. It was thought he had neglected to pay his revolutionary tax, another way of describing ETA's protection racket.'

Nina clasped her hands. 'I thought ETA mostly stuck to bombings,' she said.

The commissioner nodded. 'But sometimes they had a go at something different. In this particular case they had used the tools that were available on the building site, saws and hammers and drills. Well, you can imagine the injuries the victim suffered.'

Nina could, all too well. 'Where did you find the DNA?'

'On one of the tools, a saw blade, if I'm not mistaken. Obviously, most of what we found on the tools was the victim's blood, but there were also traces of different DNA, and a fingerprint that we never managed to identify.'

'The perpetrator cut his hand or finger when he was using the saw,' Nina said.

The commissioner nodded enthusiastically. 'That was what we concluded as well. We compared it to all known members of ETA but without any result, and that's where we were for eighteen years, until yesterday.'

Nina thought. 'Ernesto Jaka traded in oil,' she said. 'Russian?'

'Mostly, but also Nigerian,' the commissioner confirmed.

Nina relaxed her hands.

When the Soviet Union had collapsed, vast quantities of state assets were privatized, among them forestry and oil. During the 1990s a small number of oligarchs became some of the richest men in the world: the Yukos Oil Company and its owner, Mikhail Khodorkovsky, were perhaps the most famous examples, but there were others, not as large, not as particular, and the infighting between them was appalling. Ivar Berglund's company had traded in a lot of Russian timber: he had the contacts, he had the opportunity.

Commissioner Elorza sighed happily. 'Imagine,' he said. 'It isn't every day we manage to reduce the number of ETA's victims, but we can do that today. From eight hundred and nineteen to eight hundred and eighteen.' He stood up. 'We've prepared all our documentation about the case,' he said. 'If you'd like to follow me, I'll—'

'There was one more thing,' Nina said, getting slowly to her feet. 'I was wondering if you could help me with another matter.'

Elorza stopped in the doorway, surprised.

'It concerns our suspected perpetrator or, rather, his brother,' Nina said. 'The perpetrator's twin brother died in a car crash in Alpujarras twenty years ago. I'd like to know more about what happened.'

There was a glimmer of interest in the old man's eyes. He took a step back into the room and closed the door again. 'That could be difficult,' he said. 'An ordinary accident gets buried deep in the archives, if the file still exists.'

'Yes, it would be difficult, and I have no mandate to request it,' Nina said. 'But it's extremely important that I get to see any records.'

'And what can I do about that?'

' "Commissioner Axier Elorza" is a very well-known

name throughout the whole of Spain,' Nina said. 'The sort of name that can open doors.'

The old man smiled.

Thomas woke up with a pneumatic drill pounding inside his skull. He tried to open his eyes and was met by shiny, polished knives. Dear God, what the hell had happened?

He lay perfectly still in the merciful darkness behind his eyelids and became aware that he was breathing, so at least he wasn't dead. Somewhere in the distance he could hear traffic. His mouth tasted like a sewer.

Where was he?

He groaned, and made a fresh attempt to look around.

A white room, stuffy, light falling in through a sky-light above his head. Oh, no! Sophia's bedroom, which had once been his too.

He twisted his head to see if anyone else was in the bed, and there she was, her tangled blonde hair on the white pillow. How had he ended up here? What exactly had happened last night? He moved his left arm and was struck by a terrible realization. What had he done with the hook?

Leaning on his elbow, he heaved himself off the mattress. The drill began to thud twice as fast and he groaned again.

Sophia lifted her head and blinked sleepily at him. 'Good morning,' she said groggily, smiling.

He thought he was going to be sick. 'Good morning.'

The words cut through his brain like a laser scalpel.

Sophia reached out a hand and stroked his chest. 'Oh, it's so lovely having you here,' she said.

He held the stump outside the bed so she wouldn't see it and tried to smile at her. It hurt his facial muscles. How the hell was he going to get out of this? Creeping away without her noticing was out of the question now. Where was the hook? And how was he going to put it on, and his clothes, without her seeing?

'That was quite some party,' he said tentatively.

She laughed quietly. 'Yes, you were certainly in party mode. I don't think I've ever seen you on such a roll.'

On a roll? He'd been *on a roll*?

She leaned over him and he pressed the stump towards the floor, pursing his lips to avoid breathing sewage at her, but she kissed him anyway. She tasted of toothpaste. She must have snuck out to brush her teeth, then crept back into bed and pretended to be asleep: what a phoney. Her eyes were very close to his, so close that he couldn't see them clearly. He tried to avoid breathing in her minty breath.

'If you only knew how much I've been longing for this,' she said. 'I'm so very fond of you.'

He swallowed. 'And I'm very fond of you,' he said.

It was almost true, he felt, as he said it, at least in part. He didn't have anything against her. Sophia was a bit silly and nondescript, but she was loyal and simple-minded.

She ran her hand down his left arm towards the stump. He felt panic growing in his stomach.

249

'I think I need to go to the loo,' he said, and pushed himself up with his right hand. A firework went off inside his head and he groaned again but swung his legs over the side of the bed. His right foot landed on something rubbery. Nausea welled inside him but he forced himself to look down at the floor. He had trodden on the hook, but what the hell had he done with his clothes?

'Would you like breakfast?' Sophia asked.

'In a bit,' he said, bending down to pick up the prosthesis.

'It's so lovely that you wanted to stay,' Sophia said, behind his back. 'And I really appreciate the fact that you trust me, that you let me get close to you. I know how hard it's been for you since the accident.'

Accident?

He had been mutilated by Somali terrorists when he was on official business for the Swedish government. That wasn't an accident, a random occurrence. Accidents were old people slipping on ice and breaking their hips, like his mum had done last winter, or people getting whiplash in their cars. What had happened to him was an act of terrorism with international consequences!

'I know you find it difficult, but your hand really does look completely natural,' she said. 'No one who didn't know what you went through would realize that it . . .'

Grabbing the hook with his right hand, he hid the stump in front of his body and stood up. His legs were a bit shaky but he stayed upright. Where was his shirt? He looked round desperately, his mouth dry. There, on the floor by the door. And his underpants – oh, thank God, they were next to his shirt.

He fled into the bathroom, dropped his clothes on the slate floor, put the hook in the washbasin and locked the door behind him. Exhausted, he slumped on to the toilet, the seat ice-cold against his naked buttocks. His heartbeat was thudding in his head in time with the drill. He found himself staring at his cock. Did they have sex last night? He had no memory of it, but one of his talents was the ability always to get it up. It was almost always an advantage, but there were exceptions. Last night was one of them. He leaned over and sniffed. They'd had sex. Bloody hell.

He sighed. Out in the hall he could hear Sophia humming, the way she did when she was in a really good mood. She was on her way to the kitchen to make breakfast. The very idea made him feel ill. He swallowed hard and closed his eyes.

Oh, well, he had the hook and his clothes with him, so if he could just put them on he'd probably be able to get out of there. He stood up and turned on the cold tap, filled her pink tooth-mug and drank. (When he'd lived there he'd had a pale blue one.) He met his own gaze in the mirror, red-rimmed and hollow-eyed. He looked down at the hook.

A cosmetic hand, it was called. It was supposed to look as much like a natural hand as possible, but the problem was that you could barely move it. You could use it as a brace, or hang things from it. Its outer layer

251

consisted of a PVC glove that could be replaced, and had been chosen to match his natural skin tone. He hated it, but not as much as he hated the other hand, the one he called the Terminator. That was at home, buried at the bottom of a drawer. The Terminator consisted of metal fingers attached to straps round his back and shoulders, and it was considerably more manoeuvrable. He was supposed to use it when he was 'pottering about at home' (as the doctor had put it).

Back at the start he had tested a myoelectric prosthesis as well, an advanced contraption that could be controlled by electrical impulses from the stump. It ran on batteries that needed charging, it was heavy, and whirred when he moved the fingers. There wasn't space for it in the drawer so he had handed it back.

The thought of the whirring hand made his stomach churn, and he fumbled with the toilet seat, only just managing to lift it at the last minute before the evidence of last night's drinking came back up.

Afterwards his whole body felt sweaty. He flushed but stayed on all fours, panting.

'Are you okay?' Sophia asked, from outside the door.

Christ, he couldn't even throw up in peace. 'Fine,' he said, amazed at how normal he sounded. 'I'll be out soon.'

'Would you like scrambled egg?'

He stood up cautiously. 'Just some coffee,' he said. 'I've got to get to work.'

She didn't answer. He could feel her silent disappointment through the bathroom door.

'Okay,' she said eventually, and went back to the kitchen. No humming this time.

He rinsed his mouth: he wouldn't be able to escape a farewell kiss. He pulled his underpants over his sticky cock and picked up the hook. It wasn't hard to attach: he could strap it straight on to his arm. The silicon on the inside smelt bad – it got very sweaty when the weather was as hot as it had been. The hook scratched and slipped.

He looked at his reflection. A man in early middle age in his shirt and underpants and hook, cloudy eyes, messy hair and uncertain future prospects. He felt like bursting into tears.

He cleared his throat, unlocked the bathroom door, went back into the bedroom and found the rest of his clothes scattered across the floor. With fumbling fingers he managed to put on his chinos, socks, shoes and jacket. He stuffed his tie into his pocket. Then he went down the hall and into the kitchen.

Sophia was wearing underpants and a T-shirt, and suddenly looked naked in comparison to his formal dress. It made her a bit shy. 'Coffee's ready.'

He gazed at the dull wooden top of the island unit, the old-fashioned cupboard doors. 'How tatty it all looks,' he said.

Her smile grew unsteady as she handed him a mug of coffee, standing close to him. 'Are you sure you won't stay a little longer?' she whispered against his neck.

He took a dutiful sip of the coffee, then kissed her

gently on the lips. 'All the plans we made for renovations. You never got any further with them?'

She took a step back from him and lowered her gaze. 'It didn't seem as much fun when I was on my own,' she said.

He made an effort to conceal his derision when he looked at her: how small and pathetic she was. 'I suppose I could stay a bit longer,' he said.

The clouds were gathering over the ironworks. The wind tugged and tore at the tops of the birches, making them rustle like rain. Half a dozen cars were parked outside the discount outlet: cut-price clothes weren't in demand that Thursday morning.

Annika drove up past Tattarbacken and forked right towards the Konsum supermarket. She was careful to avoid looking towards the turning to the beach at Tallsjön. She saw some girls sitting at the bus-stop swinging their feet, each of them eating an ice-cream. She had sat there just like that, with ice-cream and the same swing in her legs, but there and then was an utterly different place from here and now, thirty years later. Both she and the little industrial town had changed, but the main difference was in her perspective. Back then the works had been the world, a self-evident and integrated whole. Everything had fitted together and she was part of it. Today she saw the town as separate splinters, individual entities that just happened to have ended up in the same place, buildings and people alike, coming together for a few brief moments.

Where should she start looking?

She stopped outside the supermarket. Her mother didn't work much, these days. Other people could stand in behind the till whenever someone was ill. Despite all the years she had spent as a temp, Barbro had never had a permanent job in the shop. For some reason that made Annika feel ashamed.

If Birgitta had come here in secret, without telling her mother or her husband, where would she go? What would she have done here? Why was it such a secret?

She drove back towards the works, again avoiding looking at the turning to Tallsjön, and let the car roll past the grey factory buildings towards the discount store. Her family had toiled there for generations, possibly since the works were established in the 1600s. When her father had started there were more than a thousand employees, and when he had died, they were down to a hundred or so. The number had kept shrinking until it sank below ten, and now the ironworks had been shut down for years. Other enterprises had moved into the premises, the Kolhus Theatre and a museum, various artists' groups, and now the discount store. The manor house, all one thousand square metres of it, had been sold a few years ago for the same price as a three-room flat on Södermalm. She could just see the crenellated façade beyond the theatre.

She parked the car behind an old Volvo, took her bag and went inside the building. The store was called Warehouse 157. It was poorly lit, but the ceilings were high and the cement floor had been polished. Displays of cut-price clothing stretched as far as she could see.

She took out her mobile and pulled up the photograph of Birgitta sitting on the terrace, her hair fluttering in the wind as she smiled at the camera, and headed towards the checkouts. Only one of the six tills was open. A woman of Annika's age, her hair in a ponytail, was sitting there reading a magazine.

'Hello,' Annika said. 'Sorry to bother you, but can I ask you something?'

The woman looked up. There was something vaguely familiar about her. Did they know each other? Annika stopped, uncertain.

'Annika Bengtzon!'

Annika took a deep breath and forced herself to smile. So who was the woman? 'Hello,' she said feebly.

'Are you back?' the woman asked.

Who was she? No one from her class, maybe the year above, or below. 'Only for the day,' Annika said. 'I need to ask you something.'

'Hey,' the woman said, 'I heard about your husband. God, that was rough.'

The penny dropped. Helene Bjurstrand. That was her name. From the parallel class.

'I mean, kidnapped by terrorists,' Helene Bjurstrand said. 'Awful.'

'Yes, it was,' Annika said.

'You don't think something like that could happen to anyone you know,' the woman said.

Oh, so she knew Thomas, did she?

'Do you remember my sister, Birgitta?' Annika asked.

She held out her mobile with the Facebook picture, but Helene Bjurstrand didn't look at it. 'Of course I do. She moved to Malmö last autumn.'

'That's right,' Annika said. 'You haven't seen her recently? In the last week or so?'

The woman took the phone and looked at the picture. 'No,' she said. 'No, I haven't seen Birgitta since she moved. How are they getting on down there?'

'Oh, they're fine,' Annika said. 'Do you know if anyone else has seen her lately?'

'If anyone has, it would be Sara. Sara Pettersson.'

'Does she still live on Tallvägen?'

Helene Bjurstrand sighed. 'The fight over that will's going to outlive us all. But how are you? I've moved back, as you can see. Lived in Huddinge for ten years, but after the divorce I thought I might as well come home. Are you still living in Stockholm or . . .?'

Annika smiled and put her phone in her pocket. 'It was lovely to see you again,' she said, and headed towards the café.

The two baristas behind the counter probably hadn't been born when she'd left Hälleforsnäs, so there was no danger of them recognizing her. Neither of them had seen Birgitta in the past couple of weeks, they said, but they didn't look at the photograph particularly closely.

Annika bought a cappuccino and a ciabatta roll, then took her tray out on to the terrace. At once she knew where she was. This was where the photograph of Birgitta had been taken, the picture she had just shown the baristas. She sat down at a table in the corner, possibly the same one from which Birgitta had been laughing at the camera. The sky had grown even darker and the wind was stronger, stirring up the muggy air. There was a sulphurous smell. She took a bite of the roll.

'Is this seat free?'

She looked up. She'd recognize that face in her sleep: Roland Larsson, an old classmate of hers. Jimmy's cousin.

'Of course,' she said. 'Sit down. Good to see you.'

The first time she had had dinner alone with Jimmy, years ago now, they had talked about Roland. *We used to lie in the hayloft at Grandma's on summer evenings, down in Vingåker,* Jimmy had said, *and Roland would spend hours talking about you. He had an old photograph he'd cut out of the paper, of you and a few other people, but he'd folded it so only you showed. He kept it in his wallet . . .*

Roland Larsson sat down, scraping the chair. His stomach had expanded considerably. She pulled her tray back to make room for him on the other side of the table.

'What brings you to these parts?' he asked.

'I was on a job not far away and thought I'd stop off here,' Annika said. 'I don't suppose you've seen Birgitta recently?'

Roland took a large bite of the carrot cake in front of him, then began to talk with his mouth full. 'How's

258

Jimmy doing? Haven't heard from him in ages. Is he still slaving away for the government?'

'Yes, I suppose he is.'

He drank some coffee. 'You should all come and visit this summer! I know Sylvia would really like that.'

Sylvia Hagtorn was a former classmate and an old enemy: she had hated Annika from their very first day at school.

Roland adjusted his tie. 'We're expecting number two in September,' he confided.

'That's great!' Annika said. 'Congratulations.'

Roland Larsson laughed. 'Things are really happening here. I'm going to be chair of the local council, if things go the way we hope in the election, and it looks like they will.'

'Yes, the Social Democrats are bound to hold on to Flen,' Annika said.

'We're doing a good job,' he said. 'People can see that. We care about each other out here.' He popped a piece of carrot cake into his mouth, and some icing got caught on his moustache. 'Take the ironworks, for example. Ten years ago it looked like Poland in the fifties. Now, with the discount outlet, the museum, the lattes, it's great.'

Annika couldn't disagree with that.

'Sylvia runs Mellösa Pod-Radio, and *Hälleforsnäs Allehanda* is switching from monthly to weekly publication. There's plenty of news for them to cover. We've had a wave of break-ins in the summer cottages in the forests round here over the last few weeks. We're talking about recruiting a freelance editor to take care of things, if you're interested?'

Annika coughed.

'Just think of the quality of life we've got out here,' Roland said. 'Everyone knows everyone else so no one falls through the net. Everyone can afford to live in a decent home, there's all the nature, and we're only an hour from Stockholm if we want to go to the opera or theatre.'

'You haven't seen Birgitta recently, have you?' she asked again.

Roland looked at her cheerfully. 'I have, actually,' he said. 'I saw her outside Konsum in Malmköping, but I didn't talk to her.'

Annika sat up straight. 'You did? Can you remember when? What was she doing?'

Roland ate some more carrot cake and reflected. 'It must have been last Friday, because Sylvia and I were going to a party that night and I stopped to buy a bottle of red to take along. Not that Sylvia can drink at the moment but . . .'

'Why didn't you talk to her?'

Roland looked rather taken aback. 'She was sitting in a car,' he said. 'I was going to go over and knock on the window, but she was asleep so I didn't bother.'

'What time of day was it?'

'Afternoon, about five, half five, maybe. Why? Has something happened?'

'Oh, no,' Annika said quickly. 'I was just wondering. What sort of car was she in?'

Roland was looking worried, and Annika tried to smile reassuringly.

'Goodness, what sort of car? A Ford, maybe? Or a Nissan? I'm not much good at cars.'

Birgitta had been in Hälleforsnäs. Roland would never have got that wrong. After all, he'd been on the point of knocking on the window when he had seen that she was fast asleep.

'Tell her to stop by in Mellösa next time she's here. I know Sylvia would love to see her.'

Yeah, right.

'So you're still living with Jimmy? On Södermalm?'

She nodded and took a bite of her ciabatta roll.

Roland Larsson pushed his empty plate away and wiped his moustache with a napkin. 'I sometimes wonder what life would have been like if I'd gone away,' he said. 'If I'd concentrated on my career, maybe got a job with the government. Who knows? Maybe I'd have been living on Södermalm.' He winked pointedly at Annika.

Annika stuffed the rest of the bread into her mouth and drank the last of her coffee. 'It was really great to see you,' she said, getting to her feet.

'Are you going?'

She smiled and took the car keys out of her pocket. 'Got to get back to work,' she said. 'Take care.'

'Say hi to Jimmy,' he called after her. 'And try to get out here again this summer. We've got our own place by the lake.'

'Sure,' Annika said. 'I'll tell him!'

She could feel his eyes on the back of her neck as she walked away.

Sara Pettersson's home was a single-storey villa with a basement and a small garden, which was mostly scruffy lawn, on a side-street off Flensvägen. She rented it from Olle Sjögren's estate: his family couldn't agree if the house should be sold in its present state, or renovated first. Any eventual profit from the sale would go to pay legal fees but for the moment Sara went on living there.

Annika parked the car on the street and walked up to the porch. There was no doorbell, so she knocked, then tried the handle. It was unlocked, and she pushed it open. 'Hello?' she called.

A dog barked.

'Don't let him out!' a woman shouted from inside the house.

Annika quickly closed the door, and the dog went on barking like mad inside.

'Charlie, go and lie down!'

The dog whimpered, then fell silent. The door opened.

Sara Pettersson had put on weight. Her hair was long, streaked various shades of red and mauve. She was holding the dog's collar, and the look on her face was one of unfeigned astonishment. 'Annika? Bloody hell, is it really you? What are you doing here?'

Annika didn't move from the porch. 'Am I disturbing you?'

Sara pulled out her mobile and glanced at the screen.

'I've got a client at one o'clock. Come in, come in ...'
She dragged the dog into the kitchen. It was a mongrel,
German shepherd mixed with Labrador, perhaps. Its
tongue lolled from its mouth as it struggled to get free.
Annika stopped in the kitchen doorway and looked at
the well-preserved 1970s décor: brown cupboard doors
and orange tiles. On the kitchen table there were lots of
small bottles of nail varnish, arranged in rows, colourful
pots of files and cotton buds, strips of foil and a pile of
white hand-towels. There was a strong smell of acetone.

'It's probably best if you introduce yourself to him,'
Sara said. 'Otherwise he'll never give up.'

Annika held out her hand to the dog, which leaped up
at her.

'Charlie!' Sara Pettersson herded the dog into the next
room and slammed the door. It started to howl in protest. 'Well, it's certainly been a while,' she said, turning
to Annika. 'How can I help you, then? Do you want your
nails done?'

Annika and Sara had known each other for thirty
years, ever since Sara had moved to Tattarbacken with
her mother just before she started school. She and Birgitta had been best friends ever since, in the same class all
the way through school. Annika was never allowed to
join in when they played together, not that she wanted to.
They played at being hairdressers, models, make-up artists, and Annika had preferred football, snowball fights
and cross-country skiing. Sara was now thirty-seven, the
same age as Birgitta, but she looked older.

'Are you running your own salon?' Annika asked, nodding towards the paraphernalia on the table.

'Diamond Nails,' Sara said, walking over to the fridge. She took out a can of Diet Coke and held it towards Annika, eyebrows raised.

'No, thanks,' Annika said.

'Lacline, *hard as diamond*, you burn the polish on with UV light. It works really well, lasts for weeks. Do you want to try?'

'Not really,' Annika said. 'I actually came to ask if you'd seen Birgitta recently.'

'I got everything online. The internet's brilliant, don't you think? It doesn't matter where in the world you are, you have the same access to things as everyone else.' Sara poured the fizzy drink into a glass, took a large swig, then went over to Annika and took her hand. 'Ouch,' she said. 'When did you last have a manicure?'

Ellen had painted Annika's nails last winter, but that probably didn't count. 'It's been a while,' she said.

'You've got good foundations, just like Birgitta,' Sara said, patting her fingertips and pointing to one of the rib-backed chairs. 'Would you like anything else, coffee, some wine, maybe?'

There was a box of South African merlot on the worktop.

'Thanks, I'm fine.'

'What colour would you like?'

Annika sat down on the wooden chair and looked at

the rows of little bottles, utterly bewildered. 'Has it been long since you last heard from Birgitta?'

'Your mum asked me the same thing the other day. What's going on?'

'Did you know she was up here last week?' Annika asked.

Sara Pettersson's eyes widened. 'No way,' she said. 'She'd have come to see me. Do you want me to do your nails, or . . .?'

Annika tried to relax. 'Sure.'

'I'll see if I can make them look a bit more modern,' Sara said, taking hold of Annika's left hand and rubbing her cuticles with yellow cream. 'What makes you think she was here?'

'Roland Larsson saw her outside Konsum in Malm-köping last Friday.'

Sara's lips tightened at the mention of Roland Larsson's name. They had been seeing each other before he'd moved in with Sylvia Hagtorn in Mellösa. Sara worked on Annika's nails with fast, firm movements. The sticky yellow cream was now smeared on the cuticles of both hands. She picked up a file and began to shape the nails into elegant curves. 'I haven't seen Birgitta since they moved, although we Skype sometimes. I know she was back at Christmas, but we didn't meet up then. I was away seeing Mum and her partner in Bälgviken. Can you relax your arm? Thanks.'

Annika hadn't realized how tense she was, and let

Sara pull her hand towards her. She was poking at the cuticles with a chrome-coloured implement, and it hurt a bit. 'The last time you Skyped, did she say anything particular?'

Sara glanced up, then carried on working. She soaked a ball of cotton-wool with something that smelt like surgical spirit, then energetically rubbed off the cream she had just smeared on. The dog began howling on the other side of the door again.

'Shut up, Charlie!' Sara yelled.

The dog fell silent.

'We talked about the summer. She said she'd come and see me during her holiday, but she didn't want to stay with your mum, and staying here wouldn't work, not with Steven and the kid, so we talked about places she could rent. She was going to get in touch with Margareta Svanlund, because she's got that little cottage in her back garden.'

Annika was watching Sara's face. She didn't seem to be very fond of Birgitta's family. 'Do you know why Birgitta and Steven moved to Malmö?' she asked.

Sara's movements as she applied the undercoat of polish became slightly jerkier. 'Don't you know?'

'We haven't really had that much contact,' Annika said.

'You didn't even come to the wedding.'

Ah, there it was again.

Her sister had got married on 20 January, the same day that the newly elected American president had assumed office, which also happened to be Annika's first big reporting job as US correspondent. It would have been professional suicide to fly back to Sweden for a wedding, but she still wished she'd done it. Staying in the USA was clearly a failure to prioritize properly. She had apologized, but it hadn't helped.

'Stick your hand in,' Sara said.

Annika looked at the box Sara pushed in front of her, rather taken aback: it looked like a small oven made of plastic. Dubiously she pushed her hand through the opening of the box. Sara pressed a red button on top and it filled with neon-blue ultraviolet light.

'I know Steven thought Birgitta was drinking too much,' Annika said.

Sara snorted and painted undercoat on the nails of the other hand. 'Sweden's so puritanical,' she said. 'Look at Spain. They drink wine with their lunch every day and they live just as long as we do. We ought to have a more relaxed attitude to alcohol, if you ask me.'

Maybe Sara didn't know about Birgitta's stay in hospital with alcohol poisoning.

The light in the box went out and the world was left rather greyer. Charlie was whimpering feebly on the other side of the door.

'Change hands,' Sara said, then pressed the red button again.

While the undercoat was burned on to Annika's right hand, Sara, with a great deal of concentration, set about painting Annika's nails different colours. Her thumb ended up blue, her index finger orange, the rest of her hand all the colours of the rainbow.

'Do you know if Steven's ever been violent?' Annika asked.

'Only the once.'

Annika's head spun. The lamp went out.

'What happened?' she asked.

'They'd been out to a party and had an argument on the way home. He hit Birgitta in the mouth, split her lip. Okay, I'm just going to put a top layer on, then you're done.'

Annika switched hands again. 'What happened? Did Birgitta report him to the police?'

'No, she talked to Camilla, the social worker. Steven was given an ultimatum – either he went on one of those aggression-therapy courses or Camilla would talk to the police. He was in therapy for six months. What do you think? Don't they look lovely?'

Annika spread her fingers out and admired Sara's work. The polish had gone over the edges in a few places, but otherwise it was very professional. 'Really great,' she said.

'The move to Malmö was Steven's idea. I think it's a bit pathetic to give in to whatever a man wants – I wouldn't do that. But apparently it was more important for Birgitta to play at being a nuclear family than to live the life she wanted.'

'Maybe she needed to get away from Hälleforsnäs,' Annika said, unable to stop staring at her fingernails.

Sara snorted. 'This might not be the most exciting place in the world, but it's good enough for me, and it's good enough for Birgitta. That'll be five hundred kronor.'

Annika almost gasped. Sara noticed her reaction. 'It's much cheaper than it is at Stureplan,' she said reproachfully, 'and I pay my taxes and national insurance. You can have a receipt if you like.'

A knock on the door made Sara leap up. Charlie began barking again in the other room. 'It's my one o'clock,' she said apologetically, and disappeared into the hall.

Annika put a five-hundred-krona note next to the wine box on the counter, said hello to the next customer, thanked Sara for her time, and left.

Margareta Svanlund, Birgitta's art teacher, lived on Karlavägen, one of the small streets behind the supermarket. The buildings were older there. Annika's mother didn't think they were anything special: she preferred modern houses, preferably made of white bricks.

Annika rolled along the cracked tarmac, looking at the villas. This part of town could easily pass as Bromma or Mälarhöjden in Stockholm, but houses here cost a tenth of those in the suburbs of the capital. There, house prices were based on status and dreams, and no one dreamed of moving here.

Annika parked in Margareta Svanlund's drive, and saw movement behind the curtain. The little house dated back to the 1920s. It was pale yellow with a hipped roof, white shutters on the windows and a smaller cottage by the edge of the forest in brown and green. The paint was peeling. The flowerbeds were empty or covered with bark chippings – nothing had been planted this year.

She got out of the car and locked it. The art teacher had been Birgitta's form mistress at secondary school, and when their father had died she had acted as Birgitta's support person. Barbro used to drink wine occasionally before then, but after she was widowed she'd started to drink seriously. She'd even spent a while in hospital – how had Annika almost forgotten that? Had she been in a psychiatric unit or rehab? Annika didn't know. She had moved in with Sven for a month or two, and Birgitta had stayed with Margareta. She'd had her own little room in the attic, with a crocheted bedspread and sloping ceiling.

'Well I never!' the woman said, as she opened the door. 'What a surprise!'

Annika shook her hand. Margareta's grip was firm and warm. She had grown old, her hair white and her back bowed, but her eyes were the same: sharp and bright blue.

'I'm sorry to turn up unannounced. Am I disturbing you?'

'Not at all. I don't do much, these days. Come in and sit down and I'll get you a cup of coffee. I've just made some.'

Annika noticed that Margareta couldn't walk very well. She was dragging her left leg, and supporting herself on the wall with her right hand as she shuffled into the kitchen.

'What's happened?' Annika said. 'You seem to be having a bit of trouble walking.'

'Stroke,' Margareta said. 'Like your grandmother, only I survived mine. Sit yourself down.' She gestured towards the kitchen table.

Everyone here knew all about everyone else: Annika finding her grandmother on the floor of her house at Lyckebo after her stroke would have done the rounds, if not as much as her killing Sven had.

Annika pulled out the old-fashioned chair and sat down. The room looked as she remembered, only smaller. She rested her hands on the table, which was shiny and worn with use. She noticed things she either hadn't seen or hadn't appreciated as a child: the kitchen had been carefully restored using traditional techniques and materials – wooden panelling, lime-wash, the pine floor like velvet after decades of scrubbing with lye soap.

'It really is lovely to see you,' Margareta said. 'Now, tell me all about what you're doing, these days. Are you still working at the newspaper?' She put two mugs on the table. Annika recognized them: they were from Höganäs – Berit had some the same.

'For the time being,' Annika said.

Margareta poured the coffee. 'Milk or sugar?'

'Black, thanks,' Annika said.

Margareta sat down heavily. 'And you're living with Jimmy Halenius?'

'His children, too, as well as mine,' she said. 'I've really come to ask if you've heard from Birgitta recently.'

'You're the second person to ask. Your mother phoned the other day, wondering the same thing. Why do you both want to know?'

'I heard that you'd talked about her maybe renting your little cottage for the summer. Is that right?'

'The water pipe to the cottage froze last winter and I haven't got round to getting it repaired – they'd have to dig up half the lawn – so I said she was welcome to stay there if she wanted, but that there was no water. She said she'd think about it.'

'Was that long ago?'

'The beginning of May, so about a month ago.'

'She didn't call in last week, by any chance? Or the week before that?'

'I was staying with my sister in Örebro last week, so I don't know.' Her eyes narrowed. 'Why don't you just tell me what's happened?'

Annika shifted on her chair. 'No one seems to know where Birgitta is. Steven says she went off to work as usual on Sunday morning and didn't come home that evening, but he's lying. Birgitta hasn't been to work for two weeks. I know she was here in Hälleforsnäs last week, and she's resigned from her job and lied to her boss. Have you got any idea where she might be?'

Margareta got up and fetched a plate of almond biscuits. Annika took one and bit into it.

'What makes you think Birgitta's been here?' the old teacher asked.

'Roland Larsson saw her in Malmköping last Friday,

and her mobile phone has been traced here the previous week.'

'So she's officially missing, then?'

Annika nodded.

'Well, let's not jump to conclusions,' Margareta said. 'When I spoke to her she said she was going to come up and look for somewhere to stay this summer. Maybe she doesn't think my little cottage would work – it would be hard to live there without running water if you have a small child.'

'Did she say when she might come?'

Margareta shook her head. 'We talked about other cottages that might be available. She asked about Lyckebo, your grandmother's old place. She said she was going to call Harpsund and ask if it was available to rent. Do you know if it's still empty?'

A jolt of anger and jealousy ran through Annika: Lyckebo was nothing to do with Birgitta. She didn't even like it there. Lyckebo was *hers*. 'I think so,' she said quietly.

'Steven and Birgitta rented Old Gustav's place a few summers ago, of course, but that's been sold now. A young family from Stockholm.'

Annika drank some coffee. No one else was allowed to rent Lyckebo. 'How did she sound, the last time you spoke to her?' she asked.

'Happy,' Margareta said. 'Said she'd started painting again. It sounded like the move to Malmö had done her good.' A black cat strolled in from the hall and jumped on to her lap. She stroked it absently and it started to purr loudly. 'Birgitta could have been a good artist. Her feeling for colour and form was exceptional. I remember her as having great technical ability, in both oil and watercolour . . .' She tailed off and gazed out across the kitchen.

'But?' Annika said.

Margareta changed position and the cat jumped down. It disappeared again. 'Birgitta only ever chose things that were easy and beautiful. She always shied away from anything dark and difficult. She had a lot of talent, but to develop she would have had to get to grips with things she found difficult, and she didn't want that. Birgitta was content, and that's not a good quality to have if you want to move on.'

'Do we have to want to move on?' Annika asked.

Margareta smiled. 'Oh, yes,' she said. 'I think so. If you've been given a talent, you ought to try to do something with it. We have a responsibility towards the gifts we're given, even intellectual ones.'

Annika glanced at her watch. She should be going.

Margareta pushed her mug and half-eaten biscuit away. She got to her feet with an effort, waving away Annika's offer of help. 'I'll see you out,' she said.

In the hall, as she was putting her sandals back on, Annika glanced into Margareta's living room. The mirrored door was ajar, and light was flowing in through the curtainless windows. The floor was covered with corrugated paper, and she caught a glimpse of an easel and a half-finished painting. Stacks of paintings were propped against the walls.

'Since the stroke I haven't been able to crochet,' Margareta said. 'You need two hands for crafts, but I can hold a brush.'

'Can I see?' Annika asked.

Margareta gave a slightly apologetic shrug.

The room smelt pleasantly of oil and turpentine. Annika looked in amazement at the paintings. She was no connoisseur of art, but these were spectacular modernist portraits in strong colours. She stopped in front of an abstract portrait of a bald man in bright pastels, his penetrating eyes sharply critical. He looked out at her from the canvas with arrogant derision.

'That's Georg Baselitz,' Margareta said. 'A German artist. He said women can't paint. He uses a lot of pastels himself, which is why I chose to show him like that.'

'It's wonderful,' Annika said. 'Is it for sale?'

Margareta laughed. 'I don't sell my pictures. I'm not an artist.'

'No, seriously,' Annika said. 'An artist, who says women can't paint, painted like this by a woman? I'd like to buy it.'

The old teacher shook her head. 'If you like it you can have it.'

Annika shuffled her feet. 'That's not what I meant.'

Margareta smiled. 'I know. That's why you can have it, if you want it.'

Together they wrapped the picture in corrugated paper, then Annika carried the parcel out to the car and laid it on the back seat.

Margareta waved as she drove off.

Had Birgitta really tried to rent Lyckebo?

Dark clouds were chasing across the sky. She steered away from the town, past the turning to the beach at Tallsjön, towards Granhed.

Neither her mother nor Birgitta had been especially fond of Grandma's place. Mum thought the walk through the forest to reach it was too long, and complained about the midges that hatched in the marsh where the stream ran out into the lake.

Had Birgitta gone ahead and called Harpsund?

The fork that led to the cottage appeared on her left, so she slowed down and turned on to the patch of grass in front of the barrier.

She wouldn't have to sign a contract if she simply made an enquiry. It cost nothing to ask. If Birgitta could do it, so could she.

She pulled on the handbrake and switched off the engine. Leaving her bag on the back seat, she put her mobile into her pocket, locked the car and headed off quickly through the forest. She could still see her footprints from earlier in the week on the grass. The pines sighed; the air felt electric.

It couldn't be that expensive to rent somewhere with no access by road, no electricity or running water. Maybe she could set up her own business and work as a freelance, writing for consumer magazines and updating websites, then deduct the rental costs as office expenses.

She reached the old meadow and the abandoned cottage. The black sky made the house look even smaller. She walked up to the kitchen window and peered in. It looked so naked, lonely and abandoned. If she ever had the chance to rent it, she'd buy a cloth for the table, a rag-rug to cover the hatch to the cellar, and a picture of angels watching over children on the edge of a cliff.

She leaned against the wall and fished out her mobile. She gazed at the grey water of Hosjön as her call to Directory Enquiries was connected. She asked to be put through to Harpsund.

'Good afternoon, my name is Annika Bengtzon,' she said, sounding over-polite and almost obsequious. 'I was wondering if it might be possible to rent one of your cottages?'

'One moment, please,' the woman at the other end said. 'You'll need to talk to Per.'

Annika introduced herself again and explained that she was interested in renting one of the estate's cottages. Her grandmother had lived there for many years – she had actually been the housekeeper at Harpsund: perhaps he remembered her. No?

'Lyckebo?' Per said. 'It's listed as available to rent on our website. I had an enquiry about it just a few weeks ago.'

'From Birgitta Bengtzon, by any chance? She's my sister.'

'Yes, that was her. She thought it was a bit too expensive. We're only renting it on a yearly basis.'

So Birgitta had tried. 'How much is it?' She held her breath as Per leafed through some papers.

'The cottage has a kitchen on the ground floor and one room upstairs,' he said, sounding as if he was reading aloud. 'There is also a guestroom with an open fire, an outhouse and woodshed, and an outside toilet. The cottage has no electricity or running water, but there is a well on the site. The contract is on an annual basis, and runs from the first of April to the thirty-first of March. The quarterly rent is 3,850 kronor.'

Almost thirteen hundred kronor per month. Could she afford that?

'Would you like to take a look at it?' Per asked.

'Thanks,' Annika said, 'but I know it very well. I grew up there.'

'Perhaps you could share the cost with your sister,' Per said. 'Then you'd both be able to enjoy it. It's a wonderful location.'

'I'll think about it,' Annika said. In her new life as a freelance, would it be hard to justify the expense to an accountant? Explain why she had to rent a cottage beside a lake in Södermanland to carry out her work? If the worst came to the worst, she could always take the job at the *Hälleforsnäs Allehanda*.

She walked back and sat down on the porch step. Had Birgitta been here last week? Had she looked through the kitchen window and missed the tablecloth, the rag-rug and the angel on the wall?

Why had Steven lied about when she'd disappeared?

She raised her phone again.

Steven answered straight away. 'Have you heard anything?' he asked.

'Yes and no,' Annika replied, and looked towards the old barn. 'The police have traced Birgitta's mobile. She wasn't in Malmö last week, she was in Hälleforsnäs. Did you know that?'

He was silent, so silent that she thought they had been cut off. 'Steven?' she said.

'What was she doing in Hälleforsnäs? Is she there now?'

'Steven,' she said, 'can't you tell me what really happened when Birgitta disappeared?'

He coughed. She could hear the theme tune of a children's programme in the background.

'Have you seen her?' he asked.

'No,' Annika said. 'I'm in Hälleforsnäs now, and I've looked, but I don't know where to try next. You have to tell me what really happened or I can't help.'

She could hear his breathing, and waited in silence for him to answer.

'She had a relapse,' Steven said. 'Nearly three weeks ago, at the weekend.'

Annika looked up at the sky. The clouds were swirling, turning the surface of Hosjön steely grey.

'She went to a bar after work,' Steven said. 'When she came home we had a terrible row. I was terrified she was going to lose it again. She shouted that I was controlling and spying on her.'

'This was the Saturday night?'

'She got in touch on Tuesday, said she felt ashamed. She asked me several times to forgive her and said she wanted to be left in peace.'

Annika was forcing herself not to get angry. 'You've spoken to her?'

'Diny, can you turn it down a bit? I'm on the phone . . . What did you say?'

'You spoke to her?'

The music got quieter.

'No, she sent a text.'

That matched the tracking result.

'Why did you wait two weeks before sounding the alarm?'

He gulped audibly. 'She asked me not to say anything. Said she wanted to think, and that she needed to get hold of you.'

'Me? What did she need me for?'

'I don't know.'

'Daddy,' Annika heard the child say at the other end of the line, '*Pingu*'s finished.'

'Can you hold on a moment?' Steven said.

'Sure.'

There was a thud in her ear as he put the phone down to help his daughter with the television. Did she watch the same programme all day long?

'The description you gave me,' Annika said, when he returned, 'of the clothes she was wearing. It was all wrong, wasn't it?'

He coughed again. 'She went to the bar straight from the shop. She was wearing her work shirt and her brown jacket.'

Annika thought for a moment. 'Have you spoken to her at all?'

'I've tried calling, but she said I needed to give her some breathing space.'

'She replied by text? Breathing space?'

'Daddy!'

'Just wait a moment, Diny. I'll be there soon.'

A gust of wind tugged at Annika's hair. 'What made you sound the alarm on Monday?'

'The art society,' he said. 'Birgitta's been painting all spring so she could take part in an exhibition. Two men from the society came round on Sunday to look at her pictures.'

'What did they say?'

'It was probably lucky she wasn't home, really. They talked a load of crap, said the pictures were too superficial, that they lacked depth, they didn't want them in their exhibition. Birgitta's been talking about it for ages, that they were going to come and look at her stuff. She wouldn't have missed that. Something's seriously wrong.'

'Have you called her work?'

'They say they can't put calls through to the tills.'

'So you haven't been down there?'

The little girl said something in the background and Steven put the phone down again.

'Do you know what she was doing in Hälleforsnäs?' he asked, when he came back.

'She was asleep in a car, a Ford or a Nissan, something anonymous, outside the Konsum supermarket in Malm-köping last Friday.'

'Asleep?'

'She must have been there with someone. Do you have any idea who?'

He said nothing. The silence echoed. She sat there, gazing at the lake and listening to the trees.

Eventually he sighed. 'I'm coming up,' he said. 'I'll rent a car straight away.'

'She's probably not here any longer,' Annika said. 'Her last text was sent from Luleå.'

'Luleå?' The surprise in his voice was unmistakable. 'What's up there?'

'I don't know,' Annika said.

'I'll come anyway,' Steven said.

'That might be as well,' Annika said. 'It doesn't sound like she's in Malmö, anyway.' She took a deep breath. 'There was one other thing. I know you hit Birgitta. Why did you lie about that?'

A few seconds' silence.

'Let's talk about that when I get there.' He hung up.

Annika put the phone back into her pocket.

If you fell asleep in someone's car, you had to feel comfortable with them. Who had she driven off with?

She looked towards the lake. The birches rustled; the ripples sparkled with shards of silver. She took out her

282

mobile again, opened the web browser and found the website of an online business directory. She typed in *matextra malmö*. She found the details of the company's board and MD, Anders Svensson. Then she called Directory Enquiries and asked to be put through to MatExtra in Malmö.

A receptionist answered.

'I'd like to speak to Linda, the store manager.'

She was on the line almost immediately.

'My name is Annika Bengtzon, and I'm the sister of Birgitta, who used to work for you,' Annika said.

'I see,' Linda said warily.

'I've been wondering what happened on Saturday, the sixteenth of May.'

'I don't understand what—'

'Something happened,' Annika said. 'Birgitta was very upset about something, and I'm wondering what it was.'

Silence.

'Either you tell me what it was,' Annika said, 'or I go straight to Anders Svensson and tell him what a useless manager you are.'

The woman gasped. 'What are you talking about? Who did you say you were?'

'Birgitta's elder sister. I want to know what happened. If you tell me, you'll never hear from me again.'

There was the sound of a door closing.

'Well,' Linda said, 'it was nothing much. I just told Birgitta that she couldn't have the permanent job we'd talked about. Other people had been here longer than her, and I had to think about the morale of the other staff.'

'So you withdrew the promise of a permanent job?'

'I wouldn't call it a promise. We'd certainly talked about it but—'

'Thank you,' Annika said, and hung up.

Elin, or one of the other cashiers, had complained to the boss, and Linda had backed down. Birgitta had evidently taken it badly and, instead of going home, had gone to a bar and started drinking.

But why was she staying away? And why had she lied about getting another job?

Annika's hair blew across her face, and she brushed it aside with her newly polished nails. She found herself looking at the front door of the cottage and her mind stood still. There was a pale patch of wood beside the lock. The strip at the side was slightly crooked.

Someone had broken in. The marks were barely visible, but they were there.

Roland had said there had been a wave of break-ins into summer cottages recently.

She took hold of the handle and the door opened, the hinges squeaking. Her heart was pounding. She took a step into the hall. 'Birgitta?' she said.

The place smelt mouldy and stale. The floor was covered with a thin layer of dust that swirled up when Annika moved.

No one had been inside: their footprints would have shown in the dust.

The door slammed and Annika screamed. The wind whistled through the gaps in the wood. She threw herself at the door, which opened instantly, and stumbled outside. It was just as empty and deserted as before. The wind had blown it shut.

She stood there until her heart had slowed down.

Then she closed the door properly.

For the time being she still had a job to go to and work to do. Back to Gustaf Holmerud. She set off towards the car.

He heard the woman long before he saw her.

She moved through the forest like a threshing machine, crushing twigs under her feet, pulling at branches, the fabric of her coarse trousers pushing through the vegetation. She was walking fast, approaching at speed. She was heading in his direction.

Quickly and silently he made his way across the abandoned meadow towards the edge of the forest. He straightened the grass behind him with a small branch. He never left a trail.

He waited behind a pine until he saw her emerge into the clearing and stop.

It was her. He recognized her at once.

She was panting slightly, and stopped to catch her breath as she looked at the house. Perhaps she was in the habit of coming here. That would make things easier.

He studied her movements as she walked up to the cottage and looked in through the kitchen window. She was wiry, a bit skinny – she could probably move quickly.

She stood at the window a little too long and, for a moment, he worried that she had seen something odd. Perhaps her mind was on other things because suddenly she pulled a phone from her trouser pocket and made a call. She leaned against the wall and looked out across the lake as she talked. He couldn't hear what she said, but that didn't matter.

Then she ended the call, went to the steps and sat down, fiddled with her phone, and talked again, read something, talked.

Then something happened. He looked more closely through the branches.

She had noticed that the door had been forced.

Well, perhaps that didn't matter either. He watched with interest as she inspected the lock, then took hold of the handle. She stepped into the hall and said something, he couldn't hear what. She might have been calling for someone, *Is anyone here?* or *Hello?* Fortunately he wasn't as hard of hearing as his brother. His mirror image had been a little too fond of percussive weapons at the start, before they had realized how impractical it was to drag guns around when you could take a toolbox instead. But his hearing had suffered lasting damage. He never complained, accepted the situation and lived with the injury.

He knew his brother was doing his mental exercises in prison. He himself had tried to devote himself to them more actively over the past year, had tried to feel that it bound them together, but hadn't succeeded.

It had been a terrible year, an *annus horribilis*, as the British queen had once put it. He had lived his shadow life more or less as usual, the way they had when they were both in Sweden and one of them was in the villa in Täby, or when they were both in Spain and one was in the terraced house – the other would rent a flat in a shabbier neighbourhood, under an assumed name, and live as the Shadow, the featureless man who didn't exist. He was still able to live quite openly: even though his brother's picture had been in the press countless times, no one reacted when they saw him. It was easiest to get lost in a crowd; they had always lived by that motto. A woman had lain dead in a flat in the stairwell next to his for three years and no one had missed her. No one would miss him.

A gust of wind blew through the forest, and he watched it slam the cottage's door. The woman screamed and rushed out into the meadow. He had been right: she was quick. She looked at the door, and for a moment she turned in his direction, but didn't see him, he was sure. She stood like that for a minute or so, then turned back, closed the door and set off towards the path through the forest.

He waited without moving for seven minutes, the length of time he estimated that it would take her to reach Highway 686, then thought he heard a car start.

He waited another half-hour before emerging from his hiding place and getting on with his business.

*

The arrest warrant from the Spanish Prosecution Authority was presented to Stockholm District Court late in the afternoon. It requested Ivar Berglund's extradition to Spain, on suspicion of the murder of businessman Ernesto Jaka in San Sebastián eighteen years ago.

Nina was sitting on the terrace of a café by La Concha beach when the news reached her. It appeared on her phone in the form of a text message from Johansson, just minutes after the petition was handed in. She read the short message twice, then put away her phone. She looked out at the Bay of Biscay. If he wasn't convicted in Sweden, he would be extradited to Spain and found guilty there. The Spaniards weren't in the habit of letting their murderers out in a hurry. The minimum sentence was twenty years, and the maximum double that.

She beckoned over *el caballero* and asked for the bill, paid and began to walk back towards the police station.

San Sebastián, Donostia in Basque, was a disappointment. Not because there was anything wrong with the city, either the architecture or the setting – on the contrary, the beautiful city centre curled along the famous beaches of the bay – but it wasn't *Spain*. Not her country, her streets, not her language. The Basque being spoken around her bore no resemblance to *Castellano*. The architecture could be French, or Swiss, with its heavy ornamentation and grey stone façades radiating affluence and solidity. There was no trace of the Moorish inheritance that dominated the landscapes of her

288

childhood, with their sun-drenched white stucco buildings and terraced olive plantations.

She returned to the police station as a Swedish police observer: Europol had verified her status during the afternoon.

Commissioner Elorza was waiting for her in his little room. 'I heard that our request for the extradition of Señor Berglund has been registered with the Swedish authorities,' he said. 'That was quick. You have a very efficient administration.'

'Sweden has many good points,' Nina said, settling on her chair. 'Productive bureaucracy is one of them, as is a humanitarian view of criminals.'

'And the bad points?'

Nina reflected for a moment. 'The tyranny of welfare,' she said. 'The constant need for more without having to do more to get it. Small-minded whining about any change or development, and a deep-seated conviction that we're the best in the world at absolutely everything.'

The commissioner laughed. 'I've had a long conversation with Javier Lopez, my colleague in Albuñol,' he said.

Nina waited for him to go on.

'It's funny the way some events stay with you,' the commissioner said. 'Lopez still remembers the accident when a Swedish man got himself killed nearly twenty years ago. It happened during his first year in the force, so that may go some way to explaining it.'

Nina's hands were clenched in her lap, anticipation growing in her stomach.

'Lopez pulled out the old file, just to make sure, and it confirmed what he remembered.'

Commissioner Elorza ran his fingers over his notes. 'It was a Wednesday night at the start of February and it had been raining earlier in the evening. That makes the roads up in the mountains slippery, and with bad tyres it's easy to find yourself aquaplaning. The car containing Señor Berglund drove straight into a ravine above Albondón. It caught fire on impact and was burned beyond recognition.'

Nina tried to imagine the scene in her mind's eye. 'Beyond recognition? In spite of the rain and the wet ground?'

'That's how it was described to me.'

'So how did they know it was Arne Berglund's car? And that he was driving it?'

'The number plate was still readable. The car, a Volvo 164, was registered in Arne Berglund's name. An overnight bag was thrown out of the car when it crashed, and contained Arne Berglund's wallet. The body that was found strapped in the driver's seat was a man of Berglund's size and age. A watch and a necklace that were burned on to the corpse were identified as belonging to Arne Berglund.'

'By whom?'

Commissioner Elorza looked down at his notes. 'The victim's brother, Ivar Berglund.'

Nina clenched her fists tighter.

'Arne Berglund was registered as a resident of Marbella,'

the commissioner continued. 'He owned a small house there and ran a business trading in timber.'

'What happened to the house and the business?' Nina asked.

Axier Elorza looked at her with a twinkle in his eyes. 'I had a feeling you might ask that. They were both bequeathed to his brother, who went on running the business from Sweden, albeit on a smaller scale. The house still belongs to the brother.'

Adrenalin was coursing through her. 'It may not have been the brother who identified the dead body,' Nina said. 'What if he did it himself? He identified himself. He didn't die in that accident. Someone else did. I don't know how they did it, but it wasn't Arne Berglund who was burned beyond recognition in that car crash.'

'That will be hard to prove. The body was cremated.'

Nina had to force herself to remain seated. 'It's not the dead body we should be focusing on,' she said, 'but the living man.'

'You seem very sure about this.'

She straightened in her chair. 'I'm not certain, but it's a possibility that ought to be investigated. The men are identical twins. They could have carried on living two lives, in Sweden and in Spain, under the pretence that they were the same person. As long as they were never seen together, they were safe.'

Commissioner Elorza nodded thoughtfully, with a degree of amusement. 'Today one brother is in custody in Sweden, charged with murder. Which of them is it? And where might the other be?'

'I don't know which of the brothers is which,' she said. 'For the time being it doesn't really matter, because if I'm right, they're both guilty. The one who's free must have been lying very low for more than a year, so they must have access to homes or refuges that we don't know about.'

'Here, or in Sweden, or somewhere else on the planet?'

Nina took a deep breath. 'One last question,' she said. 'You didn't happen to get the address of the house in Marbella?'

Commissioner Elorza smiled.

Disappointment burned in Anders Schyman. He had intimated to the chairman that something big was in the works, that he could see an appeal to the Supreme Court. But Bengtzon's terse text message after her meeting in the Bunker – *No interview today, Holmerud obstructive. Still possible, details this afternoon* – had led him to draw the wrong conclusion. He had believed that the interview would take place the following day, that something had to be negotiated higher up the food chain. He certainly hadn't been expecting this.

Albert Wennergren put the printout of Bengtzon's notes on the desk. 'Well, well,' he said sardonically.

Schyman chose to ignore the sarcasm. 'You sound surprised.'

The chairman of the board smiled. 'Positively surprised,' he said. 'First you got him convicted as a serial killer, and now you're going to get him released. That's what I call proactive journalism.'

Schyman looked at his boss, with his supercilious attitude, his designer sweater and hand-stitched leather shoes. Proactive journalism had paid for it all. 'We need to check the terrain carefully, see what interest there is in the rest of the media,' he said. 'We have to build alliances and synchronize publication. It could get a bit complicated.'

Wennergren nodded thoughtfully. 'I wonder how long the others are going to struggle on with their print editions,' he said. 'We live in interesting times.'

Anders Schyman had nothing to add on that point, so he kept his mouth shut. Wennergren picked up the printout again. 'I'd like to talk to the reporter, find out what Holmerud said. Word for word.'

Schyman looked out at the newsroom. Annika Bengtzon was packing away her laptop. A brightly coloured picture of an old man was propped against the wall near to her desk, and he wondered what it was doing there. 'You'll have to hurry,' he said. 'She's getting ready to go home.'

Wennergren got to his feet, opened the glass door and headed out into the newsroom. He said something to Annika, who looked up in surprise, then they headed for Schyman's glass box.

'He said exactly what I wrote in my notes,' the reporter said, as she walked into the room and Wennergren closed the door. 'He's bored with being locked up and wants to get out. Men who kill women don't have an easy time of it in prison, so maybe his friends are being nasty to him at mealtimes.'

'This is interesting,' Wennergren said, waving the printout. 'I'm on the board of the family's television channel and publishing company. I could stir up my contacts and we could make common cause with this, the same reporter presenting a series of articles, a television documentary and a book-length study. There's a lot of profit to be made from that sort of blanket coverage.'

'What a great idea,' Annika Bengtzon said. 'But why restrict our synchronization to Gustaf Holmerud? If we collaborate closely enough, we'd need only a single journalist in the whole of Sweden.'

Schyman's heart sank, but Wennergren laughed.

'Sit down,' the chairman said, dragging another chair over to the desk.

Bengtzon did so. She looked hollow-eyed and tired, on the brink of exhaustion. Her fingernails sparkled in a range of neon colours – they looked very odd, Schyman thought. 'How are you doing?' he asked.

'Not great,' she said. 'My sister's disappeared.'

He raised his eyebrows. 'Anything for us?' he asked.

'Hopefully not,' she said, and looked down at her nails.

'What sort of impression did you get of Gustaf Holmerud?' Wennergren asked, evidently untroubled by missing sisters.

'He's resourceful and manipulative,' Annika said. 'He

294

appears to have gathered information on the reporters who've written about him – he mentioned personal details about me, Berit, Patrik and Bosse from the other evening paper. And I don't think he's innocent of all the crimes. I've done some research into the first murder he was suspected of committing, and I think he's guilty of that one.'

'So you don't think we should do this?' Schyman asked.

She bit her lip. 'I think we should, actually. For one important reason – to get justice for the murdered women. Four murderers are at liberty as a result of Holmerud taking their crimes on himself. That's why I don't think we should dismiss him out of hand, and certainly not as things stand.'

'But you don't want to do it?' Schyman asked.

'He's not going to accept me. He wants someone prestigious, someone with more authority.'

Wennergren nodded. 'Naturally he wants this gambit to make an impression. He wants someone who's going to be seen and heard in the public debate.'

'But you know all about the case now,' Schyman said to Annika. 'Couldn't you start by pulling together all the research on the subject, conducting background interviews, figuring out how this synchronization might work?'

'So that someone else can scoop up the National Award for Journalism?' She put her hands on the arms of her chair and pushed herself up. 'If you'll excuse me,' she said, 'I've got things to do.'

'What's that picture you've got over there?' Schyman said, nodding towards her desk.

'He's a German artist, who claims that women can't paint.' She walked out, closing the door behind her.

Wennergren watched her thoughtfully as she walked towards the exit with a hideous bag over her shoulder. 'You're right,' he said. 'It would be very good indeed if we could organize an appeal to the Supreme Court. Hold our banner high, right to the end. What do you think? Will we have time?'

'That depends on when we close down,' Schyman said.

'Come up with some thoughts about that too, will you?' Wennergren said, and gathered his things together.

The children went to bed late, kept awake by the early-summer light outside the window and anticipation of the following day's celebrations to mark the end of the school year.

Once they had finally fallen sleep, Annika walked from room to room in the apartment, listening out for the lift and Jimmy. His flight from Brussels had been delayed because of a thunderstorm.

Contradictory images of Birgitta were gnawing at her: talented, abused, loved, alcoholic . . .

On impulse, Annika went to the wardrobe and dug out the box containing old letters and newspaper cuttings, and there it was: the shoebox of childhood photographs. She sat down in the living room with it. Her mother had always meant to put them in a nice photograph album, to paint a rosy picture of the past, but had never got round to it.

In the fading light from the window she leafed through the photos: endless summer evenings, Christmas Eves, birthdays. Birgitta always smiling at the camera, and the young Annika looking away. There was the picture from the beach at Tallsjön, the ice-creams and the blue rug, the towels, herself in profile, Birgitta smiling . . . Birgitta as a child was very like someone else. She reminded Annika of someone she had met very recently.

Destiny, of course.

She lowered the pictures to her lap and let the tears come.

What if Birgitta never came back, if something really had happened to her? What would become of her little daughter?

The lock in the front door rattled, and she wiped her cheeks.

'Hello,' Jimmy said quietly, as he put his overnight bag and briefcase on the hall floor. 'Why are you sitting here in the dark?'

She smiled at him, even though he probably couldn't see it. 'I'm glad you're home,' she said.

Jimmy walked into the room, sat down beside her on the sofa, and kissed her. 'Are all the little ones asleep?'

'Only just. They're really wound up about the last day of school.'

'I can take them – you're seeing the psychologist first thing tomorrow, aren't you?'

She sat up, pulled him towards her and kissed him hard.

'How are you?' Jimmy whispered.

'Not too great,' she said.

He held her tight, gently rocking her. She let the last of the tears fall and subside. His arms were solid; he smelt of skin and warmth.

'How did you get on?' she asked.

Jimmy sighed and loosened his grip. 'Brussels was okay, but I'm having a massive problem with Thomas.'

She looked up at him.

'I don't understand what the hell he's playing at,' Jimmy said. 'He's obstructing the conclusion of the inquiry, insisting on pushing through a change to the law that guarantees online anonymity for the very worst internet nutters for ever. I was forced to stop him presenting his proposals at tomorrow's cabinet meeting.'

'He won't have been happy about that,' Annika said.

'You're absolutely right. He looked like I'd just chopped his other hand off. Anyway, tell me, have you heard anything from your sister?'

Annika swallowed. 'It turns out she actually went missing nearly three weeks ago. The manager of the shop she worked in withdrew a promise of a permanent job, so she went to a bar and got drunk. When she got home she had a row with Steven and stormed out, and he hasn't spoken to her since, but they've exchanged texts. She's ashamed and says she wants to be left alone, but she's been trying to get hold of me.'

Jimmy whistled.

'She was in Hälleforsnäs last week,' Annika went on. 'I bumped into Roland Larsson, and he saw her in a car in Malmköping. She was looking for somewhere to rent for the summer, possibly her old art teacher's little cottage. Maybe she was thinking of moving home.' She gulped. 'And she phoned Harpsund and asked if she could rent Lyckebo.'

He blew into her hair. 'Where did you see Roland?'

'In the café of the discount store in Hälleforsnäs.'

'Was he eating something likely to raise his blood pressure?'

Annika wrapped her arms round his neck, picturing Roland's round face. 'He seemed happy with life, wants us to go swimming with him and Sylvia in Mellösa.'

Jimmy kissed her neck. 'You know you were his fantasy girl when we were teenagers?' he said.

'What about Birgitta?' she said. 'She was much prettier than me.'

'You were sexier,' Jimmy whispered.

They kissed each other again, more intensely this time . . .

FRIDAY, 5 JUNE

'Is that what it's usually like for you? When the attacks come?'

Annika folded her arms and crossed her legs. 'I suppose so.'

'Can you describe the process?'

Why? The psychologist had seen for herself how it happened.

'What you're suffering from is called panic syndrome,' the psychologist said. 'It's by no means unusual. You're not alone.'

As if that was going to make Annika feel better. 'I don't understand why I can't stop them,' she said. 'I mean, I can feel them coming, but I can't do anything about it.'

The woman seemed about to say something, but changed her mind. A moment later she said, 'Your behaviour is characterized by avoidance. The fact that you fight against and suppress your feelings is part of the problem. You can't stop a panic attack with willpower. Instead, if you can bear it, you can choose to let yourself

303

be confronted by your traumas, allow the panic to come, and then pass.'

That was easy for the psychologist to say, Annika thought. Presumably she had her own problems, like everyone else, but considering that you needed top grades to study psychology, it was safe to assume that she'd had a secure, stable childhood. Probably upper middle class, raised in a nice suburb or a big flat in the centre of the city. She had two shiny gold rings on her left finger, so she was married, and the slack skin around her stomach, visible through her tight blouse, suggested at least one child. What could *she* really know about panic syndrome?

'We were talking about your boyfriend, Sven, when the attack happened, and the way he used to—'

'I don't want to talk about it,' Annika said.

The psychologist closed her notebook. 'I can understand that,' she said. 'But if you want to get to grips with these attacks, I'm afraid you're probably going to have to.'

'I can't,' Annika said.

The psychologist smiled. 'You're capable of more than you think,' she said. 'The feelings that hit you when you talk about it are perfectly normal. Your body's reaction is being magnified, but it isn't remotely dangerous. I can help you.'

Annika felt her hands relax. 'How?'

'I'll catch you if you fall.'

A shiver of anticipation (aha! A basic emotion!) ran

down Annika's spine, and she cleared her throat. 'I don't know what to do,' she said.

'Why don't you start by telling me how you first met Sven?'

The walls grew darker and began to close in on her.

'What's happening now?' the psychologist asked. 'What are you feeling?'

'It's . . . getting darker in here. A bit harder to breathe.'

'On a scale of one to ten, how difficult does it feel?'

She paused (surprise! Another basic emotion!) and made an effort to consider how she felt. 'Not too bad,' she said. 'Maybe . . . a two.'

'Do you feel up to going on?'

'I think so.' More confident now. She rubbed her sweaty hands on her jeans. 'He was the handsomest boy in the whole school, all the girls wanted him, and I was the one he chose.' She felt herself stretching inside. 'It was like winning the lottery,' she said, 'and I hadn't even bought a ticket. I couldn't understand what he saw in me, because I was so . . .' Her throat tightened.

'What were you?' the psychologist asked.

'Worthless,' Annika said, and felt tears overflow, without any warning.

'How are you feeling now?' the psychologist asked. 'Uncomfortable? Or sad, perhaps?'

Annika nodded, reached for a tissue and wiped her mascara. So here she was, after all, fishing about in the box of tissues.

'How difficult is it, on the same scale?'

'Three, maybe.'

The psychologist waited patiently. Annika blew her nose.

'Now I'm going to ask a question that will activate your defence mechanisms,' she said. 'Try to feel what's happening in your body. Pay attention to any sounds that arise, different physical sensations, if you feel hot or cold. Is that okay?'

Annika nodded again. The psychologist narrowed her eyes slightly and looked at her.

'You said last time that Sven chased you, that he often threatened and hit you.'

Annika felt the pressure building inside her, as the darkness crackled at the edge of her field of vision.

'Can you tell me about one occasion when that happened?'

'There were so many.'

'Pick one.'

The television on, sound turned down, a warm pizza carton in her hands, the smell of dough and oregano, the blow striking her on the left temple with no warning, the coffee-table hitting her shoulder, melted cheese on her arm, you fucking bitch, I saw you, what the fuck were you talking to Roland about, have you been fucking him?

The room vanished and was replaced by a dark grey gloom where she couldn't breathe.

'What are you feeling now? Can you describe it?' The psychologist's voice cut through the depths and opened up a sliver of clarity.

306

'I'm falling,' Annika heard herself say. 'The greyness is swallowing me.'

'On a scale, how difficult?'

How bad was the darkness, really?

'A five, maybe . . .'

'So you can go on?'

She was breathing with her mouth open, could feel the air hitting her throat. She could breathe. There was oxygen.

Her on top of him, him deep inside her, the punch from out of nowhere, I'm doing this for your sake! Bare feet in the snow, bleeding from the crotch.

'Seven,' she said, 'hardly any air now. Eight.'

'Do you feel able to go on?'

Darkness. The ironworks closing around her. Rust and ash. She can hear the sound of his breathing echo off the concrete walls, this is the end, she knows that, she won't get away this time, you can't leave me like this, what am I going to do without you? Annika, for fuck's sake, I love you!

'Ten,' Annika managed.

'You're doing really well,' the psychologist said, from somewhere beyond the shadows. 'It's okay for it to feel this hard. You don't have to fight it.'

'I don't want to,' she gasped.

'Where are you? What can you see?'

Whiskas, oh, her sandy-coloured cat, no, no, no!

'My cat,' she said, unless she merely thought it.

The knife through the air, the cat's dying scream, NO

NO NO, *the pipe, the flaking rust against her hands. Swinging it through the air, the sky shaking, the world turning red* . . . She was standing there with her dead cat in her arms and let the darkness drain away.

Silence.

The blackness didn't swallow her.

The room came back. The air was light and soft, meeting her nose and throat with a hint of dust and sunlight. The psychologist's glasses sparkled.

'I didn't have a panic attack,' Annika said in surprise, sounding almost disappointed.

'It's going to take practice, and more exposure, but you've every chance of getting rid of them for good now,' the psychologist said.

Was it really that simple? She could hardly believe it. Annika looked at the window. 'He killed my cat,' she said.

The psychologist waited.

'It wasn't an accident,' she said. 'I wanted him to die. I killed him.'

She nodded.

'Not for what he'd done to me, but for what he'd done to my cat.'

Anders Schyman had heard thunder rumbling in the distance as he drove in from the coast. Chased by lightning, he had cruised through the traffic. Now he was jogging through the newsroom, the staff milling about him, sacrificial lambs on their way to slaughter, unaware of the fate that awaited them. The air was so dense that it was almost impossible to inhale, and he was panting as he sat down at the editorial meeting.

Patrik Nilsson was obviously very excited as he handed out printed versions of the preliminary edition to the editors responsible for different sections of the paper, all the colleagues Schyman had fostered and trained, nurtured and drilled. *Take responsibility, stretch the boundaries, see every issue from all sides.* Anders Schyman sat down at the end of the conference table, closed his eyes and waited until the voices around him died away and the meeting came to order.

'The trial of Ivar Berglund has been halted. The investigation is now being coordinated with the Spanish police,' Patrik said, bouncing on to his chair. 'Have we got hold of pictures of that Spanish businessman? Apparently he had five children, so there must be pictures of the kids.'

'They're in their fifties,' the picture editor said, without looking up.

'VICTIM OF THE TIMBERMAN,' Patrik said, in his headline voice.

'He hasn't actually been found guilty yet,' someone said – Schyman didn't catch who it was.

'We'll put *Police Suspect* above it,' Patrik said. 'And then we need to talk to some frightened tourists in San Sebastián. How upset are they by all this brutality?'

'He was from Bilbao . . .'

Patrik jotted something down. 'We've already covered

309

all aspects of the murder in Nacka, his background, the international suspicions. Where do we go next?'

'Maybe someone could call that police professor and ask him for a comment,' Carina, the head of entertainment, said.

'He just makes things up,' Sjölander said.

'That doesn't matter,' Patrik said. 'Get Berit to give him a call. What have we got in social news?'

'There was a new opinion poll this morning, saying the government is on its way out.'

'Any statistically supported change from the one the day before yesterday?'

'Not exactly,' Sjölander conceded.

'So what's our angle?'

'We could ask the police professor. He might say something scornful about a government minister while he's at it.'

'Excellent! Sport?'

'Zlatan's spoken out about being a father – it's a really strong story.'

They all made notes.

'Entertainment?'

'Tomorrow's Sweden's National Day, and Princess Madeleine still hasn't got on a plane to cross the Atlantic. We've got people at Newark waiting to see if she gets on the SAS flight to Stockholm this afternoon.'

'Who have we got lined up to be furious if she doesn't come?'

'Herman Lindqvist?' Entertainment Carina suggested.

'No, we called him last time. Check the list of last year's *Big Brother* participants – they'll say anything to drag out their fifteen minutes . . .'

Carina made notes. Schyman folded his hands over his stomach to stop himself punching his head with his fists.

'What else? Apart from "Fury at Madeleine"?'

'Rosa's aiming for the Eurovision Song Contest,' Carina said. 'She's already written a number of songs.'

Suddenly Schyman stood up and everyone turned to look at him. He could see them in the distance, their faces swirling before his eyes, about to be sucked down a gigantic drain. He could feel himself sweating. 'Carry on,' he said, 'I'm just going to . . .' He made his way out of the meeting room and stumbled over to his secretary. 'Announce a press conference at eleven o'clock,' he said. 'All staff to be present. And call Wennergren. Right away.'

The Costa del Sol quivered in the morning light. The coast of Africa shimmered on the horizon. Nina was already sweating in her long trousers and dark jacket. It would be extremely hot later, but that didn't bother her. She liked the corrosive light, the smell of warm soil. This was her Spain, the colours and architecture, the high sky and scorched mountains that sang of her childhood.

She walked along the cracked pavement in her hard shoes. The residential district was so anonymous that it was virtually devoid of all interest, narrow streets lined with long terraces of identical white-stuccoed two-storey houses. Tired hibiscus bushes framed the doorways, fallen bougainvillaea flowers blowing in the breeze. The winter rains had taken their toll on the façades: the whole area could do with repainting. It didn't look as if it had been constructed in the most recent building boom, or in the one before that.

The house belonging to Arne Berglund was number 137. It was in the middle of a row consisting of thirty-two houses, each one confusingly similar to the next. There were white metal shutters over the windows, both on his house and those around it. The entire terrace looked neglected and abandoned. There were piles of rotting leaves by the doorways.

Police Inspector José Rodríguez from Marbella's Policía Nacional stopped next to Nina and looked up at the building. 'So this is supposed to be the hideaway of an international killer?'

And his mirror image, Nina thought.

Inspector Rodríguez nodded to the janitor, who stepped forward with a bunch of keys in his hand. 'And what's the main thing we will be able to *observe* inside?'

The Spaniard was sticking to the formalities. He had been careful to emphasize her status as an observer ever since she had walked into the police station in Marbella at eight o'clock that morning, an hour that in Inspector Rodríguez's world appeared to be as torturous as *Fakala*. She herself had spent the night on two different trains, first the slow one from San Sebastián to Madrid, then an express from Madrid to Málaga on the Mediterranean coast.

The janitor, a young man barely out of his teens, jangled the keys. He found the right one, stuck it into the lock and turned it. The door had swollen and he had to use both hands to force it open. An alarm began to howl. The police inspector sighed. The janitor fumbled anxiously in his trouser pocket, pulled out a crumpled scrap of paper and, with trembling fingers, tapped a code into a panel on the hall wall. The alarm stopped abruptly. The silence that followed was deafening.

'After you, *Observatora*,' Inspector Rodríguez said, and politely held the door for Nina. She glanced at him as she fished a pair of latex gloves from her jacket pocket and pulled them on. She had already concluded that the inspector was of the less ambitious type: he wasn't going to insist on searching the house personally. She hoped his inclination to stick to the rules wasn't going to prevent her from showing a degree of initiative.

The closed shutters made the interior of the house gloomy. Nina pressed a light switch. Nothing happened.

'The electricity was disconnected six months ago,' the janitor said. 'That's what happens when you don't pay your bills.'

She peered into the darkness, as anonymous and featureless as the men who had lived there. People couldn't live their whole lives without leaving some sort of impression. There had to be something here, even if they had tried their utmost to remain invisible, non-existent. Even the absence of evidence meant something, if you could only understand what.

313

Nina pushed open the door to a small toilet, and the stench of sewage made her gasp. She pulled out her mobile and switched on its torch.

'You need to look after your house,' the janitor said. 'Otherwise the stench trap dries out. I don't know how many times I've had to explain that. This place has been empty for a long time. I don't think I've ever seen the owner, and I've been here almost two years now. It hasn't been rented out either, and I can't take responsibility for people who don't—'

'Señor,' Inspector Rodríguez said. 'Would you mind waiting outside?'

The janitor slipped out.

Nina positioned her mobile on the basin so it would illuminate the toilet. Using both hands, she teased off the lid of the cistern and looked inside. Dry and empty, its water had evaporated a long time ago. She replaced the lid, picked up her phone and looked into all the corners and beneath the basin.

Inspector Rodríguez shuffled restlessly behind her. He had had a long conversation with Commissioner Axier Elorza, and was aware of the cases in both Stockholm and San Sebastián. 'To be honest, the idea that anyone living in such a state should be internationally renowned in any context is rather hard to believe,' he said, from the living room.

By the light from her mobile Nina found her way into the kitchen. The furnishings were made of cheap wood-chip, stained yellow. The kitchen smelt of sewage as well, but not as strongly as the toilet. She opened the fridge and a waft of mould hit her.

'Between three hundred and fifty and four hundred murders are committed in Spain each year,' he said. 'Half get cleared up, so how many of the remainder has Señor Berglund committed?'

'At least one,' she said. 'Ernesto Jaka.'

Rodríguez sighed.

But not all the brothers' killings were defined as such, Nina thought. A lot were recorded in official statistics as disappearances: Viola Söderland was one, Nora Lerberg another. The question was, what had they done with the bodies?

The fridge was empty. She closed its door. Inspector Rodríguez came into the kitchen, leaned against the door frame and watched her as she opened all the kitchen cupboards, which contained a small amount of dusty porcelain and kitchen equipment, glasses and mugs, various packets, jars, and a few tins of olives and chopped tomatoes, the latest best-before date six months ago.

Each year there were 22,000 murders in Europe, two-thirds of them in Russia and Ukraine. The Berglund brothers weren't needed there: the Russian Mafia had their own thugs. The brothers' services were probably in demand in environments where they could blend in, where they could move about unseen with their toolbox, presumably mainly in Scandinavia, but also the rest of Europe.

'The body in San Sebastián had been sawn into small pieces,' the policeman went on. 'That strikes me as personal rather than professional. Why make things more complicated?'

Nina searched shelf after shelf, shining her phone's torch behind packets of spaghetti and jars of spice. She didn't agree with the inspector. Brutal murders like that could certainly be personal acts of desperation, but also the exact opposite: cold, professional, well planned. And everyday implements could be used as terrible tools of torture. She had seen what the brothers had managed to achieve with saws and pliers, hammers, ropes and awls.

'Down here on the Costa we've got every criminal gang in the world,' Rodríguez said. 'Four hundred and thirty, in fact.'

Nina pulled out drawers containing cutlery and aluminium foil, emptied them into the sink, then put the drawers upside down on the kitchen floor.

'Which of them employs Señor Berglund?' Rodríguez asked.

She crouched and shone her phone into the space below the bottom drawer. She found ants and some dead cockroaches. She stood up and straightened her back. 'Probably one of the Russian groups,' she said. 'One that managed to grab sufficient assets when Communism collapsed to allow them to conduct criminal activities on an international level. That's what the evidence suggests, from the first case as well the latest. Viola Söderland disappeared to Russia, and Ernesto Jaka was trading in Russian oil. Ivar Berglund's company was officially registered as trading in Russian timber.'

She left the kitchen, went into the small living room, and shone her torch towards a sagging sofa and a television as bulky as a small washing-machine. The inspector had been right in his comment about the state of the place. The question was: what did they do with all the money they must have made from their activities? Home furnishings certainly didn't appear to be a priority.

She passed her phone to Rodríguez, who took it without protest. He held it up while Nina pulled all the cushions from the sofa, to find some crushed crisps and something that looked like a butterfly pupa. She took her phone back, shone its light under the sofa, then behind the television and curtains. Nothing.

'Didn't you say the owner is in custody in Sweden? And has been for the past year?'

She went out into the hall and up the narrow marble staircase.

'Or are we looking for someone else?' Rodríguez said, following her. 'The man who's been dead for twenty years?'

Neither the dead man nor his brother had been in this house for the past year, that much was obvious. Nina looked around upstairs. There were two bedrooms with en-suite bathrooms. The smaller room had a single bed, the slightly larger one a double. Nina began her search in the larger room. The bed was made up with yellow sheets. Nina felt them: they weren't cotton. She pulled off the bedclothes and lifted the mattress, shining her phone's torch at the ribbed base. She moved on to the wardrobe, which contained a few jackets, pairs of trousers, and three shirts, and quickly checked the pockets and linings. Nothing there either. The bathroom didn't smell as bad as the toilet, but it wasn't far off. Empty.

'I'll wait outside,' Rodríguez said, and slid back down the stairs.

Nina stood where she was in the silence, her mobile in her hand, its light shining down at the floor.

Maybe they really were giants, Nina, disguised as windmills. Always try to see the truth!

Now she had searched the brothers' homes in both Täby and Marbella, so what wasn't she seeing? There was something in the gaps, behind the scenery, a lack of ambition in what was both visible and concealed. Her own family been engaged in criminal activity for the same reason as most other people, as a short cut to imagined happiness and success, but the Berglund brothers weren't like that. They were driven by something else.

The daylight from the front door stretched up the wall in the hall. The insight that slowly dawned on her was like a low-energy lamp being switched on, weak and murky at first, then icily clear and unavoidable.

The brothers hadn't chosen their path to earn money. Maybe they weren't after the rewards of violence, but acted out their brutality for the hell of it.

She could see Ingela Berglund's hunched frame in her mind's eye: what exactly had happened to the paws of Arne and Ivar's dog?

Had she been mistaken in the outline she had given to Commissioner Elorza? Did evil actually exist? Perhaps it didn't always arise as a consequence of powerlessness.

If that was true, then it was like this bedroom, dirty yellow and musty, dusty and lonely.

She shivered, in spite of the heat.

She walked slowly into the other bedroom. The sheets were the same polyester mix. She lifted the mattress and found some huge dust-balls.

In the wardrobe there was just one item: some pale green work overalls with lots of pockets. Nina looked through them, and found a folding rule, a screwdriver, a pair of work-gloves. And, at the bottom, a key.

She shone her torch at it and the metal shimmered in her latex-clad hand. It was a copy, no key-ring, no address label, no inscription.

The Berglund brothers ran timber businesses in Sweden and Spain, with yearly accounts and genuine activity, part of the stage scenery.

'Inspector Rodríguez?' she called.

The policeman's head appeared.

'Señor Berglund's Spanish timber business, does it have any registered storage facilities?'

Annika dropped her copy of the newspaper on Berit's desk with a light thud. The front page consisted of a single photograph and four words: a portrait of Ivar Berglund looking like a statue, and the headline SUSPECTED OF ANOTHER MURDER.

'Do you know when they're going to restart the trial?' Annika asked.

Berit didn't answer but glanced towards the newsdesk, where a number of television cameras had been erected and reporters from other newspapers were talking to Patrik. Bosse from the other evening paper, Annika's least favourite person, was there.

'What's going on?' Annika asked.

'Schyman's called a press conference,' Berit said. 'Do you know what it's about?'

Annika felt her knees go weak and sat down. The time had come. It was all over now. In a way it felt like a relief that everyone was going to know.

'Here he comes,' Berit said, nodding towards the glass box.

Anders Schyman walked over to the newsdesk, said hello to some of the reporters from state television – probably former colleagues from his days as a presenter. He exchanged a few words with Patrik, put a hand on his shoulder, then perched resolutely on the desk. 'Can I have your attention for a moment?' he said.

The hubbub that had built up in the newsroom died away. People got to their feet, moved closer. The television cameramen stared intently into their lenses, and a few photographers took pictures.

'Thanks for coming at such short notice,' he said.

The members of the audience held their breath. Berit stood up to see better, and Annika steeled herself to follow suit.

'I have some serious news to share with you today,' the editor-in-chief said. 'Last Friday, the twenty-ninth of May, the newspaper's board, led by chairman Albert Wennergren, took the decision that the print edition of the *Evening Post* will cease to be published.'

A uniform gasp spread round the room. Annika studied the reactions of the people around her: that must have been how she had looked when Schyman told her – suspicious, affronted, shocked.

'The exact date for the closure of the paper has yet to be decided,' the editor-in-chief went on, slowly and clearly, his feet planted firmly apart. He looked out across the sea of people, without directing his attention to anyone in particular. Annika realized that he was speaking to posterity, for the history books, as he announced the end of an era.

'The members of the board have asked me to wind down publication of the print edition of the *Evening Post*,' he said. 'I have been asked to examine various time-frames and ways of going about it, both rapid and more protracted.'

'This is completely mad,' Berit whispered, then looked hard at Annika. 'Did you know about this?'

Annika shook her head. There was no way she was going to become an accomplice. 'Mind you, I'm not surprised,' she whispered back. 'Sooner or later it had to happen.'

'As things stand, I'm unable to make any comment about what aspects of the organization will remain after the closure of the print edition,' Schyman went on emphatically. 'But what is clear, however, is that this marks the end of the sort of journalism and media coverage to which I have devoted my career. No doubt something new will come in its place, but I'm not the man to determine what that should be.'

'But why do we have to be first?' Berit said, in a stage-whisper. 'Couldn't we have waited for the other papers?'

Annika shrugged her shoulders.

'I accept that this development is unavoidable,' Schyman said, no longer talking to anyone in the room, but to future YouTube viewers. He was making history, his gaze already focused far into the digital eternity. 'I respect the decision of the board, but I am not going to carry it out. Someone else will have to do that.' He stared out across the crowd, his chin raised. Everyone was holding their breath. 'I'm not going to be the one who hammers the nails into the coffin,' he said. 'That isn't me. I'm not going to shut down Swedish journalism. That's not what I've stood for, not what I've worked for, and it isn't what I've taught my colleagues. As a result of this, half an hour ago I informed chairman of the board Albert Wennergren that I am resigning as editor-in-chief and legally responsible publisher of the *Evening Post* with immediate effect. As of today, I am a free agent, and I wish the board every success in their efforts to recruit my replacement. Thanks very much.'

He got down from the desk and the newsroom exploded into a chaos of voices. Everyone rushed towards him – Annika had to press herself against her own desk to avoid being swept along. A young reporter from Entertainment was shoved sideways and knocked over Berit's coffee.

'There's no point staying here,' Annika said. 'I'm going out for a while.'

Without waiting for Berit to reply, she picked up her bag and walked towards the office manager's office to get the keys to one of the paper's cars.

Thomas logged on to his computer, his fingers vibrating with anticipation and trepidation. His head was buzzing as the site loaded.

His post had moved down slightly – other opinion-shapers had felt the need to exercise their democratic rights – but it was still there.

> GREGORIUS
> *(posted 3 June, 16.53)*
> To me, equality means fucking a sexist feminist whore in the vagina with a large knife. The best thing you can do for equality in Sweden is go out with a baseball bat and beat a sexist feminist bitch to death.
> Comments:
>
> *fuckking*　　　Fucking bitch, hope she gets sorted out soon.
> *FührerForever*　We'll soon have queers coming here from all over the world.

323

hansaking	You fucking halfbreed apes I want to kill you. Youre fucking revolting.
blackbitch	Time to clear out all the shit.

The comments were the same as the previous day. Nothing new had appeared. He felt a stab of disappointment. To be honest, he was less than satisfied with the comments. The two most recent, in particular, hadn't kept to the subject, and merely expressed commonplace illiterate racism.

But he had to show a degree of tolerance – there was such a torrent of posts, and it took a bit of talent and application to keep coming up with gems, dedication and persistence to make a name for yourself.

He logged out and pushed the computer away. He had called the department and told them he wasn't well. Now he was sitting in his gloomy living room with a cup of instant coffee, watching the storm-clouds race across the sky. Professionally, however, he felt a degree of optimism.

All the opinion polls suggested that the government would lose power in September's election. That meant new bosses taking charge of existing work, at least to start with, for key personnel like him. All he had to do was drag out the inquiry until after the election. If the right-wing parties appointed that former hairdresser to be justice minister, he himself would be in a very favourable position indeed. He would have every chance of pushing the legislation through as he wanted it.

He heaved himself up to refill his mug as the doorbell

sounded. His whole body stiffened. Who could it be? He looked automatically at the hook to see if it was attached, and of course it was: it was the first thing he did every morning, and the last thing he saw to at night before switching out the light on his bedside table. His doctor (a large, menopausal woman) had explained that it was important to use a prosthesis continually to prevent future problems with his arm, shoulders, neck and back. Your posture was better and you avoided uneven weight distribution, as if that mattered. He had one arm. What difference would bad posture make? Like having a brain tumour and worrying about a fungal infection in a toenail.

He walked silently to the front door and the peephole that Annika had installed – maybe she'd changed her mind, wanted to move back home if he was prepared to forgive her. He wasn't sure that he could, considering the extent of her betrayal.

He held his breath and put his eye to the hole. Sophia was standing outside. His heart sank. He considered not opening the door.

She rang again.

He opened the door. 'Sophia,' he said, trying to sound pleasantly surprised. 'Come in.'

Her cheeks were a little flushed, possibly from shyness. It made him feel a bit embarrassed on her behalf. He took a step back to let her into the flat (it really wasn't a grand apartment). She kept her eyes on the floor as she walked in and took her shoes off. 'Am I disturbing you?' she asked softly.

'Oh, no.'

'I tried calling you at work, but they said you were off sick.'

She'd called him *at work*? What was she playing at?

He forced himself to smile. 'The department's very understanding when I need time to recuperate,' he said, and she nodded. She understood that too.

She took a step forward, right up to him, put her arms round his waist and laid her cheek against his chest. 'I've missed you so much,' she whispered. 'I'm so pleased you stayed with me.'

He didn't know what to do: if he put his hand on her back, what would he do with the hook? Just let it hang by his side? Or should he put that on her back too, a stiff lump of rubber?

She kissed him and, to his surprise, he found himself kissing her back.

She smiled. 'Have you a coffee for me too?'

He took a step back. She could tell he'd just had some, so embarrassing. 'Of course,' he said. 'Sit yourself down in the living room and I'll get you one.'

He boiled some water in the kettle, put two heaped teaspoons of Nescafé in a mug, added water and a little milk, then stirred it.

'Oh,' she said, as he handed it to her. 'You remembered how I like it.'

He smiled and sat down beside her. She was still blushing.

'I really enjoyed yesterday,' she said, her eyes sparkling.

'It felt lovely being able to spend the day with you, go for a walk and just cuddle on the sofa.'

He had been so hung-over that she'd ended up dragging him all the way round Östermalm to help him stop feeling so sick.

'It all felt so natural, like we'd never been apart,' she went on. 'I've been wondering if we couldn't . . .' She fell silent, as if she was trying to find the right words. 'You might think I'm being a bit forward now,' she said, putting her mug on the coffee-table. 'But I was wondering if you'd like to move out to the estate with me. To Säter.' She glanced at him.

He didn't know how he was expected to react, so he kept his face impassive.

'Like I said, Dad can't manage the estate now. There's eleven hundred hectares of forest and five hundred of arable land, and the manor house needs renovating.'

She took a breath and met his gaze. 'We could have a wonderful life,' she said. 'Hunting in the autumn, seeing in the spring in the villa on the Riviera, making candles at Christmas in the old country kitchen. Ellen could have her own horse, and we could make a go-kart track for Kalle . . .'

'But I've got a job,' he said.

She nodded. 'I respect that,' she said. 'What you're doing is important for Sweden. Of course we could keep the penthouse as an overnight flat. You can go on working for as long as you want to. I can take care of most of the estate on my own, but I'd like to share it with you.'

He looked at her and tried to hide his contempt. Did she really think she could bribe him with promises of a trouble-free future? What did she think he was? Some cheap whore?

The wind had died down, leaving behind it a suffocating vacuum. The trees rose up towards the sky, like stone statues. Not a single leaf was moving. Black clouds hung over the rooftops, erasing any sense of contrast.

Annika drove into town from Granhed, careful to look the other way when she passed the turning to Tallsjön.

Your behaviour is characterized by avoidance.

She parked outside the discount store and got out of the car on leaden legs. This was uncomfortable, but no worse than a two.

She slung her bag over her shoulder and locked the car, the electronic bleep bouncing briefly into the silence. Steven was waiting on his own in the gloom of the café terrace. A mother with two young children was sitting inside at the counter, staring at her mobile, but otherwise the café was deserted. Annika bought the same type of ciabatta roll and cappuccino as she had had the day before, then went out into the stagnant air and sat down opposite him. He had half a cup of coffee in front of him, his hand fluttering on the table.

'Was the drive okay?' she asked. She didn't know if Parkinson's affected things like driving, or if his medication might.

'Fine,' he said.

'Where's Destiny? With Mum?'

He nodded, then looked down at the table. 'I've tried explaining about Birgitta's mobile phone, and that she's been in Hälleforsnäs, but Barbro doesn't understand, and I'm not sure I know how that works either. Could you explain it to her?'

She took a sip of cappuccino, and had to swallow hard to get it down. 'Sure,' she said.

The silence was oppressive, the air sticky.

Your behaviour is characterized by avoidance.

'Shall we deal with the assault now and get it out of the way?' she asked.

Steven looked at the car park. His big hands were clutching the coffee cup. He thought for a long time. Eventually he said, 'I went for treatment in Eskilstuna. ATV, ever heard of it?'

Annika had a rough idea of what Alternative To Violence treatment was (admit your violence, take responsibility for it, and understand its consequences) but shook her head: she wanted to hear him explain.

He coughed, hard and rattling. 'It was hard work,' he said. 'Understanding what I'd done to her. I never did it again.'

She waited in silence for him to go on, but he said no more. The two children inside the café started to fight about something, and their mother yelled at them. 'How did you meet?' she asked.

'You're wondering how she ended up with someone like me? Well, it took a long time, but I didn't give up.

329

She used to come and see me sometimes when she felt lonely, and in the end she stayed. I'll never leave her, she knows that.'

Maybe she was all too aware of it, Annika thought. Maybe she'd had to run away in order to escape. 'Have you got those text messages she sent?'

Steven took his mobile out, pressed the screen a few times, then handed it to her.

The three last messages from Birgitta's phone to Steven's were sent on 19, 22 and 25 May, the same dates indicated by the trace.

The first one read:

Hello Steven, Sorry. Everything's fine, but I want to be alone for a while. Don't tell anyone I'm gone. There are some things I need to sort out with my sister.

Annika stared at the message. What had Birgitta suddenly felt a need to 'sort out'? Did it have something to do with her drinking? Did she want Annika to take part in some sort of family therapy, to sit in a big circle with loads of strangers and be a target for all Birgitta's failures, like in some American film?

'What did she text you?' Steven asked.

Annika reached for her bag and dug about for her old mobile, clicked to bring up Birgitta's texts, then handed it across the table. Then she read the second message Birgitta had sent to Steven, on 22 May:

330

Hello Steven, Everything's fine. I just need to think, re-evaluate things. Sorry for everything I've done. Don't call me again, I need some breathing space. I'm engaged in important matters that can't be interrupted.

And the last, sent on 25 May:

Hello Steven, I'm fine, but I need to get hold of my sister. Can you ask her to call me? She's got to help me.

'Do you know what she was "engaged in"?' Annika asked. 'Or what she wanted help with?'

He put her mobile on the table between them. 'No idea.'

'She didn't say anything before she left?'

He shook his head. 'How do they know the messages were sent from Hälleforsnäs?'

'They were sent via a mast in the area,' Annika said. 'Apart from the last one, which was sent from Luleå.'

Annika pushed away the ciabatta roll – there was no way she going to get that down. 'I agree with you,' she said. 'Something's wrong. She sounds so strange. Does she normally express herself like that?'

'How do you mean?'

Annika hesitated. 'Elevated language. I mean, "re-evaluate", "engaged in"?'

'That hadn't occurred to me,' Steven said.

Annika looked at her watch and sighed. 'Shall we go, then?'

The smell of cooking hit them when they entered the flat in Tattarbacken. The sound of cartoon voices filtered out from the living room. They took off their shoes, and Annika put her sandals on the shoe-rack that had been there since she was a child.

Steven went into the living room. 'Hi, Diny, what are you watching?'

Annika didn't hear Destiny's reply. She stood in the hall, looking towards the kitchen, the source of the smell. Fried Falun sausage: her mother's signature dish. Until she'd met Thomas she'd eaten it several times a week, but Thomas refused to touch it. He ate proper meat, not reconstituted rubbish.

She walked towards the kitchen, over the rag-rug, her feet remembering where to stand so that the floor didn't creak.

Barbro was standing by the kitchen window, smoking. She had got old – when had that happened? Her hair had always been blonde, like Birgitta's, but now it was silvery-white.

'Hello, Mum,' Annika said.

'Hello,' Barbro said, blowing smoke through the gap in the window. She watched the plume until it dissipated, then turned to Annika. 'Have you heard anything?' she asked.

Annika sank on to her seat at the kitchen table. She was a stranger now but her body remembered: it knew exactly how the pine chair felt. She ran her fingers over the grain of the table. 'No,' she said. 'Have you?'

Barbro took another drag on her cigarette, then reached for an almost empty wine glass on the worktop. 'You're the one married to the government,' she said. 'Shouldn't you be able to use your contacts? For our sakes, just this once?'

Her mother's anger struck her like a punch in the stomach. Annika gasped for breath. *Uncomfortable, uncomfortable, not at all dangerous, just go with it, a three at most, no more than that.* 'Birgitta was seen here in Hälleforsnäs last week, and her mobile was traced to here the week before, we know that much.'

'So Steven said. Where was she?'

'They can't see exactly where she was, only which mast her mobile phone was communicating with.'

Barbro took another deep drag. 'That's not right,' she said. 'The police can trace missing people to within ten metres – I read it in the paper.'

Annika clenched her fists so tightly that her colourful nails hurt her palms. 'If the mobile is switched on, the operator can trace it in real time, by triangulation. You measure the signals from three base-stations to get a rela- tively reliable idea of where the phone is at that precise moment. It's impossible to do that retrospectively.'

Another drag. 'I don't believe she was here at all because she'd have called in.' Barbro emptied her glass. Her eyes were already slightly unfocused.

'Do you think it's a good idea to be drinking now?'

Annika said, aware of the anger and contempt that had slipped into her voice.

Her mother slammed her glass down, and her blue eyes were black as they fixed on Annika's. 'So I'm going to be told how to behave as well now? And by you, of all people?'

Annika closed her eyes. 'Mum,' she said. 'Don't start.'

'You've got no idea what it's like for me, how things have been here.' She stubbed her cigarette out hard in the ashtray.

'Mum . . .'

'What do you think life's been like for me, all these years? All the whispering, all the nasty gossip? You just ran away and left me to deal with it.'

Her voice was low but aggressive. Annika kept her fists clenched and focused on her breathing. The cartoon voices were laughing hysterically in the living room.

'You killed a boy and got away with it. People don't forget something like that. Maj-Lis never shopped at Konsum again – did you know that? She and Birger used to drive to the ICA store in Flen, right up until she died, because they couldn't bear seeing me behind the till. Have you any idea how that made me feel?'

Anger gave way to darkness, swirling round Annika's head. *Not at all dangerous, just go with it.*

'Mum,' she said, 'I'm really sorry about what happened.'

'Are you?' Barbro lit another cigarette. 'You've never apologized to me,' she said.

Annika let the darkness come, embracing her from all

334

sides, making its way in through her mouth and nostrils. Strangely, she could still talk. 'Are you really the one I should be apologizing to?'

'Yes, because you never spoke to Sven's parents. You never had the decency to do that.'

Annika closed her eyes and let the darkness win. That was true. She hadn't apologized to Maj-Lis and Birger. She'd never dared to imagine doing so. She had been weak and evasive, taking refuge in shadows and work.

She heard Steven come into the kitchen.

'Has Diny eaten?'

She opened her eyes. She could still breathe. Steven was standing in the doorway with his daughter on his arm.

'Sausage and macaroni,' Barbro said, as she took her glass to the fridge. She filled it from a three-litre wine-box.

Annika stood up. 'I've got to go,' she said.

'Yes. Your job's more important than everything else,' Barbro said.

Infinite weariness washed over Annika. 'The newspaper's being shut down,' she said. 'It was made public this morning. I'll be out of work in a few months' time.'

Her mother took a slurp from the glass and looked at her, her eyes less harsh now. 'Life's catching up with you,' she said, 'the way it does with everyone.'

Annika pushed past Steven to escape, get out, away, but by the shoe-rack she stopped and stood there, staring at the letterbox. She put her sandals on, then went back to the kitchen. She looked at her mother, her sad eyes, tired hands. 'It doesn't matter how much I apologize to you,' she said. 'I can never make up for what I've done to you, but I'm going to try.'

A flicker of uncertainty crossed her mother's face.

'I apologize for being born,' Annika said. 'I didn't mean to be.'

Then she left, stumbling over the rag-rug towards the daylight, out of the flat.

Once she was back in the car, she wept.

She could have clenched her teeth and held it in, as she usually did, just switch off and move on, leave it all behind, but she decided not to struggle. She sat in the stuffy car and let the pain come, until it misted the windows and she had no energy left.

What would happen when her mother died? Annika had been mourning her all her life: would her death make any difference? She didn't know.

There was now lightning down to the south-west, towards Julita. She couldn't hear any thunder yet, but it would be there soon enough. There was tension in the air, and it needed release.

She started the car, wound down the window, drove to the junction, then turned left.

Slowly she drove towards Tallsjön, the beach she hadn't visited for over twenty years.

She stopped beside the turning, two wheels on the verge. She switched the engine off and listened to her heartbeat. Then she looked, eyes wide open, at the place where her father had died.

The tarmac didn't quite cover the whole of the carriageway, and was ragged and sandy at the edges. There were weeds growing right up to the road, their leaves dark and motionless in the peculiar light. There was nothing to indicate what had happened there. It was just a patch of road, a turning, like thousands of others, yet her pulse was still hammering, like a turbine, right through her body.

They said he didn't suffer.

Freezing to death was a painless way to die.

He had tried to get into the old inn, Värdshuset – it was still open in those days – but they hadn't let him in. He was too drunk.

He didn't actually drink that much. Not before the big cutbacks started, anyway. Hasse Bengtzon was the union representative at the works, the man who had led negotiations with the owners about who should lose their jobs and who should stay. He had fought like a tiger for his co-workers, was interviewed in the papers and on local television about the owners' heartless policies. They wanted to close the site down and sell the machinery to Vietnam, sucking every last drop out of it at the expense of their own decency.

He had taken off his coat and boots. A man delivering newspapers found him, sitting in a snowdrift with an almost empty vodka bottle in his hand.

Annika didn't believe there was any such thing as a

painless death. She took a deep breath, let her pain blaze in her chest. Oddly, she didn't cry. Maybe she had done all her grieving without realizing it.

The lightning was coming closer and she could hear the first rumbles of thunder.

She started the car, put it into reverse, listened to the wheels crunching on the gravel, then drove off towards the railway.

Birger Matsson still lived in the house on Källstigen where Sven and his elder brother, Albin, had grown up: a hundred-year-old wooden house that had been renovated beyond all recognition in the sixties, with big picture windows and cladding. The garden was dominated by a large garage with metal doors, while the house itself was tucked in beside a small hill at the edge of the forest.

Annika parked in front of one of the garage doors and pulled on the handbrake. She didn't know if Birger was at home, but if he was, he would already have seen her.

Slowly she got out of the car and hung her bag on her shoulder.

She used to walk past here in her tightest jeans, hoping Sven would see her. He did, as it turned out. Annika was still a teenager when they'd got together. And they'd stayed together until his death.

She walked towards the house, feeling as if she was going to her own funeral. Discomfort was gnawing at her hands and stomach, and she was finding it hard to breathe. *At least a four.*

Her index finger shook as she rang the doorbell.

Birger opened the door at once. He had seen her coming. He towered above her, tall and skinny, his shock of white hair like a sail on top of his head. 'Annika?' he said. 'Is that you?' He sounded bemused, almost perplexed.

'Sorry to turn up unannounced.'

He scratched his head with one hand, the way she remembered him doing, although in those days his hair was still steely grey. 'Don't worry, not a problem,' he said.

'I'd like . . . I'd like to talk to you,' she said.

He took a step back, at something of a loss. 'Of course. Come in.'

'Thanks,' she said.

He turned and went into the living room, his cardigan flapping around his thin frame. A commentator was babbling enthusiastically in German on the television. Annika stepped into the hall, took off her sandals, dropped her bag on to the floor and followed him.

They had bought a new sofa since she was last there. An Ektorp, from Ikea.

Birger sat on one of two new armchairs, reached to get the remote from a side-table and switched the television off, but not before Annika had caught a glimpse of a tennis match. Birger was very keen on sport, active in the indoor hockey club and the orienteering group, and he had passed on his interest to both his sons. Sven had been a star of the hockey team and, the last she'd heard, Albin was working as the assistant coach of an ice-hockey team in the Swedish Hockey League. Modo, maybe, or was it Frölunda?

A heavy silence settled over the room. Birger sat with the remote in his hand and gazed at her. He seemed to have pulled himself together: the look in his eyes was clear but watchful. 'Please, have a seat,' he said.

She sat in the armchair on the other side of the coffee-table. Her mouth felt dry as dust.

'I don't know how I managed to subscribe to German Eurosport,' he said, nodding towards the television. 'As luck would have it, I studied German at grammar school, because the contract's for two years.'

She tried to smile.

He put the remote down.

'I can understand if you'd like me to go,' Annika said. The roaring in her head was so loud that she almost couldn't hear herself speak.

The old man stared at her, and she made an effort not to look away, and to confront what she had done.

'It's okay, you can stay,' he said.

She took several deep breaths through her mouth. 'I've come to . . . to talk about what happened,' she said.

He folded his hands in his lap.

'To hear how it was for you and . . .' She could feel tears burning in her eyes.

She had never talked much to Birger when she and Sven were together. Maj-Lis was the one who had organized the family. Birger was often away at club meetings, or off training in the forest. One year he'd come third in the Swedish national veterans' tournament. She remembered him as being quiet and difficult to reach.

'I've thought about you a lot over the years,' Birger said.

She steeled herself. She wasn't going to duck the issue. Doing that would mean she hadn't moved on: she would still be stuck, trying to escape the swirling darkness. 'I never thought about you,' she said. 'Almost never, anyway. And as soon as I did, I forced myself to do something else.'

The old man turned to the window. Then he nodded. 'We thought about contacting you, but we always came up with the excuse that you probably didn't want us to. It was cowardly of us. We should have asked.'

Annika's head was howling. She clasped her hands together and forced herself to listen to what he was saying. She went on, 'I've been avoiding lots of things. I stopped off at the turning to Tallsjön on my way here. I haven't done that since . . . well, since Dad died there.'

'That was a real tragedy,' Birger said, 'what happened to Hasse. We weren't friends, exactly, but we did work together.'

Annika felt air fill her lungs. Birger had been one of the managers at the works. He'd left school with good grades. He'd stayed at the ironworks until the end, when he'd retired.

'Hasse was a good worker,' Birger said, 'one of the best. It was a shame he never wanted to be a foreman.'

She was taken aback. 'A foreman? Dad?'

'Mind you, he was doing a good job for the union, I can't deny that. He was an excellent negotiator, combative but good at formulating arguments. If the times had been different he would have gone a long way.'

'Is that true? Was he really offered the chance to be a foreman?'

'He turned it down, said it wasn't for him. He was one of the workers, that's how he saw himself.'

'But,' Annika said, 'could he have stayed on at the works? After the cutbacks?'

'Of course. We needed good people in charge. But I respected his position, choosing to remain one of the collective. It was an honourable decision.'

Her father could have gone on working, needn't have taken to drink.

A flash of lightning lit the room, and there was a distant rumble of thunder.

'So how can I help you, then?' Birger asked.

Annika tucked her hair nervously behind her ear. 'I've come to apologize,' she said.

Birger looked down. 'Thank you,' he said. 'But you don't have to.'

Calm breaths, in and out, *not dangerous*. 'I'm so sorry about what happened. I understand how badly I hurt you. I've got children of my own, a boy called Kalle. If anyone hurt him I'd never forgive them.'

342

Birger rubbed his face in a weary gesture of resignation. 'I don't think you understand,' he said. 'We didn't attend the trial, but that wasn't to distance ourselves from you.'

She waited for him to go on.

'We thought it would seem as if we were condoning what Sven had done if we went to see you sitting in the dock, and we didn't want that. It felt wrong. We had failed so horribly . . . Maybe *we* should have been the ones sitting there.' He glanced at her, as if to make sure she was listening. 'What sort of mistakes must someone have made as a parent if their son turns out to be a monster? It's difficult to accept. Sven died twice – as the person he had become, and the person I'd thought he was.' He shook his head. 'It wasn't until afterwards that we saw how our actions could be interpreted. That our not going to court was seen in town as a judgement on you, a lack of faith in the legal system, but that wasn't the case.'

'You realized *before* . . . what he was like?' Annika asked.

Birger shook his head. 'Well, the thought certainly crossed my mind. I mean, I saw the bruises. But I couldn't believe it. I might have had my suspicions, but I didn't want to see. And I did nothing. That shame is something I have to live with.'

She had to wipe her nose.

'Do you know,' Birger said, 'why he ended up like that?'

She shook her head.

'It was only when we read the verdict that we under-stood the extent of what you'd gone through. Why didn't you ever say anything?'

A five now, maybe a six. 'I thought it was all my fault,' she managed.

'It wasn't. Not the way you were treated.'

'But it was my fault he died.'

'Maybe not even that.'

'I didn't have to hit him so hard.'

'It was an accident,' Birger said.

She forced herself to look him in the eye. 'But what if it wasn't? What if I wanted him to die?'

'Wishing someone dead is one thing,' he said. 'Most of us do that at some point.'

'But if I really hit him and hoped he'd never get up again?'

The silence sucked all the oxygen from the room. Birger rubbed his eyes with one hand. She could barely breathe at all now. *A seven, maybe more.*

'Then you'll have to live with that,' he said.

An eight. Hard to breathe.

Out in the hall her mobile rang, the sound bouncing off the walls.

'Aren't you going to . . .?' Birger began.

'It'll stop in a moment,' Annika said.

The silence afterwards made the air feel even thicker.

Birger cleared his throat. 'I read everything you write,' he said. 'You've covered some terrible stories.' He nodded towards the bookcase. 'Maj-Lis saved all your articles in a scrapbook – it's in a drawer somewhere. I did plan to carry on after she died, but that never happened.'

Now he was looking at her again, his eyes tired and red-rimmed. 'Maj-Lis used to worry about you,' he said. 'She always thought you took too many risks, that you never let up on yourself. When you were stuck in that tunnel under the Olympic Stadium, or almost froze to death in that shed up in Norrbotten, or when your house burned down . . .'

'I've never looked at it like that,' Annika said.

'All the things you put yourself through, Maj-Lis sometimes wondered if that was because of Sven, if he'd done lasting damage.'

She glanced towards the hall and the flight of steps leading upstairs to the bedrooms. Sven and Albin had had separate rooms. She had lost her virginity up there one Sunday afternoon when the rest of the Matsson family were at a quarter-final of the Swedish indoor hockey championship. Hälleforsnäs had lost. 'Sven isn't the only person responsible for that,' she said.

Another flash of lightning lit the room briefly.

'Maj-Lis will have been dead four years this autumn,' he said. 'It's so lonely sometimes. I wonder how long I'll be left here without her.'

They sat in silence. Annika's legs felt as if they were made of lead. She couldn't help wondering how she would ever stand up.

'We've been here for many generations,' he said. 'Your family and ours. We've been shaped by hard work. It's left us all a bit battered.'

The first heavy raindrops hit the window.

'We've got iron in our blood,' Birger went on. 'It doesn't matter if we stay or go somewhere else, it's there inside us.'

The discomfort inside her eased.

She gazed at Sven's father, alone in an ugly house in a godforsaken industrial town, with a dead son and a dead wife, and German Eurosport as his main source of company.

He nodded to himself. 'It's happening quickly now,' he said. 'Everything keeps changing. Just look at the works – have you seen what they've done there? Shops and cafés.'

A clap of thunder made the house shake.

'Thanks,' Annika said. 'Thank you for seeing me.'

Birger heaved himself to his feet, walked over to her and took her hand. His grip was dry, but not hard.

The moment she stepped out on to the porch the heavens opened. She rushed to the garage and threw herself into the car. The house at the edge of the forest disappeared behind the torrent of rain.

She pulled her mobile from her bag: one missed call. The number was familiar but it took a few seconds to place it: the National Crime Unit. Good grief! National Crime had tried to reach her and she hadn't answered because she was busy clearing up her own mess. Fingers trembling, she pressed redial.

The man named Johansson answered, and Annika explained breathlessly who she was and why she was calling.

'It's about the mobile phone that's under surveillance,' Johansson said. 'The operator has been in touch: the phone in question was switched on half an hour ago.'

Everything went quiet around Annika. She was dazzled by flashes of lightning but didn't hear the thunder. 'Switched on? Are they sure?'

'The operator's triangulation shows that the signal is coming from an area of forest in Södermanland, a kilometre or so from Highway 686 in the council district of Katrineholm. The closest point of reference is a lake called . . . Hosjön.' He paused.

'Birgitta's at Hosjön? Now?'

'Her mobile is, and has been for half an hour. Or, to be more precise, for the past thirty-four minutes.'

'Thanks,' she said. 'Thank you!'

She heard the man sigh. 'Don't mention it,' he said.

Annika clicked to end the call, then rang Birgitta's number. The storm above her head was making the car shake.

The call was put through, one ring, two, three, four . . .

Someone answered.

'Hello?' Annika said. 'Birgitta?' The thunder was so loud that she had to stick a finger in her other ear to hear anything. 'Birgitta? Are you at Lyckebo?'

The line crackled and whistled. Someone was trying to say something.

A flash of lightning lit the buildings and there was another thunderclap. The phone crackled and went silent. She'd lost reception. The lightning must have knocked out one of the masts.

She rang Birgitta again but the call didn't go through. She tried Steven's number, but that didn't work either. She quickly typed a text message to Steven, hoping it would get through eventually: *Birgitta's at Lyckebo. I'm going there now.*

The industrial estate was huge, with endless rows of corrugated-metal warehouses. It lay on the outskirts of Algeciras, about an hour's drive from Marbella.

'He rents this entire run of buildings,' Rodríguez said, gesturing towards the warehouses on either side of number 738.

They hadn't bothered trying to get hold of a caretaker: Nina was confident that the key she had found in the miserable little house would fit. Just to be on the safe side, in case *la observatora* was wrong, Inspector Rodríguez had put a crowbar into the back of the car.

The warehouse was anonymous from the outside. No sign to show what sort of business was based there, just the number of the building on a tarnished scrap of metal above the door. The façade was made of sun-bleached corrugated metal that had once been blue. No windows, just a large entrance for trucks and a smaller door alongside.

Nina pulled on her gloves again, took the key out of an evidence bag and went to the door of the warehouse to the right of number 738. She held her breath as she inserted the key into the Assa lock. It slid in easily. She tried turning it to the left. It wouldn't go. She clenched her teeth, tried turning it to the right. The key went round, once, twice – and clicked.

She let the air out of her lungs without a sound.

The door swung open silently on well-oiled hinges.

The warehouse was pitch-black. Nina stepped over the high threshold and stood in the darkness. The air was hot and stagnant. She switched on the little torch on her mobile, shone it around her and discovered a light switch to the left of the door.

With a whooshing sound, the lights in the roof went on, one neon light after another, illuminating the warehouse with an intensity that made Nina squint. The electricity bills had evidently been paid here.

'What does this mean?' Rodríguez said, stopping beside her.

The warehouse was completely empty, a metal shell with no contents. The layer of dust on the cement floor was undisturbed. The building measured maybe ten by fifteen metres, and was approximately six metres high.

Nina walked slowly around the walls. If there had been anything to examine she would have done so, but there was no point even in looking. The powerful lighting revealed the utter absence of life and activity.

When she got back to the door, and Rodríguez, she

switched the lights off and they stepped out into the street. Nina locked the door behind them. Rodríguez walked over to the door of number 738, but Nina went towards the warehouse on the left. The same thing happened there: the key fitted and the door swung open.

Empty.

For once, Inspector Rodríguez was silent.

Nina did a circuit of the warehouse, inspecting the floor in case there were any concealed hatches, but there was nothing. She peered at the roof above the lights, but could see nothing unusual. She switched off the lights and locked up, then went back to the warehouse in the middle.

'Looks like this has seen more use,' Rodríguez said. 'Look here – the paint's been worn off.'

She unlocked the small door and sensed immediately that something was different. The air that met her inside was full of sawdust and turpentine. She switched the lights on.

The warehouse was full of planks and machinery.

'Why rent three warehouses and only use the one in the middle?' Inspector Rodríguez asked himself. 'What purpose do the others serve? Buffer zones?'

Nina planted both feet squarely on the floor and took in her surroundings.

The warehouse was the same size as the other two, ten by fifteen metres, six metres tall. Along the right-hand wall was a rack of timber containing planks sawn to various sizes, sorted by thickness, thin at the top, thick at the bottom. To the left she saw what looked like a shipping container, a sort of building within a building, approximately five metres long and two metres high, with a closed door in the middle.

In front of them was a large industrial saw, a workbench and, in the middle, a tall, stainless-steel cylinder.

Rodríguez, who had pulled on a pair of sturdy gloves, pointed at the floor. 'Looks like he normally drives his car in here.'

Nina looked down at the concrete. Beneath their feet she saw faint tyre-tracks from a small car. So, the Berglund brothers didn't park in the street.

There was a pile of offcuts beyond the end of the rack of timber; the stainless-steel machinery was attached to various pipes, and ran off into a drain.

'What's this?' the inspector asked, walking over to the cylinder.

A row of tools was arranged on the bench. Nina picked up a saw in her gloved hand. The steel blade shone under the bright lighting. She put it down and picked up a pair of pliers.

No marks whatsoever.

Inspector Rodríguez had opened the cylinder and stuck his head inside it.

'It's a dishwasher,' he said, his voice sounding tinny.

'A sterilizer,' Nina said. 'They wash their tools here, to get rid of any traces of DNA.' She tried the door of the shipping container, but it was locked. She got the key out again, but it didn't fit. 'Inspector Rodríguez,' she said. 'The crowbar.'

351

The policeman went out to the car, and Nina heard him open the boot, then close it. He came back to the sealed door, inserted the end of the crowbar, held it in place, then pushed. The lock snapped at once.

Rodríguez opened the door. A dull smell of old rubbish hit them. The Spaniard felt for a light switch. A lamp in the ceiling flickered, considerably weaker than the lighting out in the warehouse. 'It's a little den,' he said.

Nina stepped inside the container. A small kitchen, two chairs, a table and two beds. A toilet and shower cubicle faced each other at the far end. The smell was coming from a bag of rubbish that had been left beside the sink. It couldn't have been there for more than a week, two at most.

So this was where Arne Berglund had been hiding while his brother was in custody in Sweden. Unless it was the other way round. Had Ivar been here while Arne was in custody?

Rodríguez went over to the beds. 'Señor Berglund prefers blondes,' he said.

Nina joined him. On the wall above one of the beds a number of pictures of a beautiful young woman had been taped up. The quality was fairly poor – they looked as if they'd been taken with a mobile phone, then printed on an inkjet printer.

'It's the same woman in all the pictures,' Rodríguez said.

Nina looked hard at the largest, on a sheet of A3. The

woman was wearing summer clothes and was sitting on an outdoor terrace, looking into the camera. She was laughing, and her hair was blowing in the wind. There was also a map of Malmö, pictures of a shop named MatExtra, and a block of flats in what appeared to be a suburban setting.

'Do you know who she is?' Inspector Rodríguez asked.

Nina looked at the other photographs, some of which had evidently been taken by the woman herself, using her mobile. Towards the corner, the character of the pictures changed: they were clearly of the same woman, but showed her as a young girl. One had been taken on the grassy fringe of a sandy beach: the blonde girl was sitting on a blue rug with an ice-cream cone in her hand, wrapped in a large towel, and beside her sat another girl, slightly bigger, with darker hair. The blonde was smiling at the camera with her head slightly tilted; the darker girl was looking away so only her profile was visible.

Nina gasped. 'Yes,' she said. 'I know who the woman is.'

The rain stopped abruptly, as if a tap had been turned off.

Annika parked on the forest track that led to Lyckebo, and the car's wheels sank into the waterlogged ground. She hesitated, then decided to leave her bag on the front seat: no one was likely to steal it out there. Her mobile hadn't picked up a signal since the lightning strike, but she put it into her back pocket anyway.

She locked the car. The countryside around her was

dripping, the air clean and clear as glass. She passed the barrier, moving quickly through the vegetation, her feet and shins soaked almost instantly. There was still lightning off to the north-east, but she could no longer hear the thunder.

She wondered why Birgitta had gone to Lyckebo. She had never really liked being there, always moaning about the ants, wasps, stinging nettles, the lack of ice-cream and television. Maybe she had decided, like Annika, to confront her demons. Maybe her relapse and Steven's ultimatum had made her reconsider her life, sort things out and start again.

Annika hoped so.

Together they could put their sibling rivalry behind them, come together and move on. They had so much in common: their background and childhood, experiences that had made them who they were. She quickened her pace. The rocks were slippery as soap. She lost her footing and almost fell.

The cottage came into view in the clearing and Annika felt a warm glow spread through her. It looked as unremarkable and abandoned as before, the gutters dripping. Was there anyone else in the world who felt as she did about the place?

She strode across the old meadow towards the closed door. Tentatively she reached for the handle, and the door swung open on squeaking hinges.

'Birgitta?'

She stepped into the semi-darkness of the hall, and

blinked to get used to the gloom. She kicked off her muddy sandals and walked into the kitchen.

It was empty.

Surprised, she stopped in the middle of the floor. The kitchen was as bare as it had been when she was last there. And there was no trace of her sister.

'Birgitta, where are you?'

She caught sight of an old yellow suitcase in one corner. It hadn't been there earlier in the week, she was sure. Was it Birgitta's?

She began to walk towards it, but before she could reach it the front door closed with a slam. She spun round, but wasn't afraid: she knew it was just the wind.

Then she saw the man standing in the doorway.

She felt reality lurch. This was impossible. 'Ivar Berglund?' she said.

It was him: those tiny eyes, that compact frame. She had watched him walk into the custody hearing at Stockholm District Court a year ago, and his picture had adorned the front page of the newspaper as recently as that morning. He wasn't going to be released for the next forty years, yet here he was.

'Hello, Annika,' he said. 'How good of you to come.'

Surprise gave way to fear, making her throat contract. How could he know her name? She took a step back and her heel hit the suitcase.

Ivar Berglund turned round and locked the front door, then put the key into his back pocket. 'Sit down,' he said, pointing at one of the wooden chairs.

She remained standing, feeling panic build. *An easy seven, maybe an eight.* 'What have you done with Birgitta?'

He didn't answer, and sat on one of the other chairs, looking at her calmly. 'Are you aware of the Vidsel Test Site?'

His voice was surprisingly warm and melodic.

She stared at him. 'The missile-testing facility?'

'It's called the Vidsel Test Site these days. They test bombs there.'

'What . . .?'

'There aren't many people down here in southern Sweden who know about it. They think Norrbotten is full of Lapps and seagulls.'

She glanced at the window. Could she open it and jump out? No, the old-fashioned double-glazing was still there, screwed into place.

The man watched her. He couldn't be here. It was impossible. He was going to be extradited to Spain.

'My family comes from up there,' Ivar Berglund said.

Annika concentrated on breathing.

'The place you come from is important. It shapes you,' Berglund went on. 'We'd lived there for centuries, but now the land is used to develop weapons of mass destruction. That's all it's good for. That's all *we*'re good for, those of us who come from there. We were raised in the shadow of wholesale slaughter.'

She took a pace back and stepped over the suitcase.

We have iron in our blood.

'Anyway, are you familiar with Nausta?' he asked.

356

Nausta? Should she be?

'It's a village in the forest,' Ivar Berglund said. 'Father and Mother were born there. They grew up in the village, but they were moved when the bombs came. Simulated nuclear explosions were carried out there, and after that they weren't allowed to return. That made Father's mind a little peculiar.'

He nodded.

'The village is still there, or parts of it, inside the test area. It's the size of Blekinge – did you know that?'

She didn't answer.

'They measure the effect of explosions on nature and different materials, see how badly the forest is damaged. The Swiss built a big bridge over nothing, simply so they could blow it up. They've developed unmanned aircraft there, and advanced drones. More than forty different ones. They're everywhere now. Iran has them, Pakistan . . . and Tunisia, Bahrain, the United Arab Emirates, Indonesia, Singapore, Thailand, Venezuela . . .'

'Where's Birgitta?' Annika asked, her mouth dry.

He pursed his lips. 'In Nausta,' he said. 'Or, rather, in the forest outside it.'

Her mobile buzzed in her back pocket. She had reception again. If she could just reach it . . .

Then the implications of what he had said hit her.

'Birgitta? Has she . . . Why has Birgitta gone . . . there?'

He nodded again. 'You can get there – it's cordoned off but there's no fence. Just warning signs. No one goes there. It's deserted.'

Black dots started to dance in front of her eyes. Soon the panic attack would hit. 'Why?'

He folded his hands, a gesture she had seen him make during the custody hearing. 'I'm a simple person,' he said. 'I like justice. That's my guiding principle. People get what they deserve. An eye for an eye, a tooth for a tooth. A sister for a brother.'

Annika gasped. She fumbled for support and grabbed one of the chairs, ending up next to the table without its waxed cloth. 'You've abducted her?'

He put his hands on his stomach. 'A two-week-long trial,' he said. 'Like my brother. She was made to answer for her sins, and yours.'

She stared at the man: *his brother*? Arne Berglund. But he had been dead for twenty years.

'It's your fault,' he said, nodding emphatically to underline his words. 'Because of you, my brother is behind bars. So because of you, your sister had to pay.'

What did he mean? Her coverage of the murders in Nacka last year? Or her articles about Viola Söderland, which put Nina Hoffman on the right track and led to Ivar Berglund's arrest?

'Birgitta was very fond of you, but you weren't a very nice sister. She deserved better.'

She stared at the man. Why was he using the past tense? 'You're lying. She'd never have gone anywhere with you.'

His eyes were perfectly calm. 'Everyone comes with me,' he said. 'It's very easy. Chloroform, if they're being difficult. Then water containing a sedative when they come round. They all drink, once they're thirsty enough.'

She could still breathe.

'You waited until she was drunk,' Annika said. 'You took her when she was at her weakest and most vulnerable. Aren't you ashamed?'

He folded his hands. 'Not at all.'

'You drugged her. In the car, outside Konsum in Malmköping.'

'We were on our way north and stopped to get some shopping. It's over a thousand kilometres to Nausta.'

The abandoned village was evidently important. Annika nodded as though she understood. 'A two-week-long trial, you said. Why?'

'My brother's trial is due to last two weeks.'

'You kept her prisoner here in Hälleforsnäs. Where?'

He nodded towards the north. 'In a summer cottage not far from here. You were actually supposed to come earlier. To stand witness. But you didn't answer your messages.'

'I've changed my number,' Annika said.

He seemed completely normal, an ordinary, unremarkable man in his fifties. She'd never have noticed him in the street.

'So you're Ivar Berglund's brother,' she said. 'I thought you were dead.'

'Yes,' the man replied. 'Everyone thinks that. Unless I'm Ivar, and it's my brother who's dead.'

She ignored his attempt to confuse her. 'And where's Birgitta now?'

359

'That's rather difficult to say,' he said.

'What do you mean?'

'It's best to leave bodies for the animals to deal with. Then they disappear in just a few days.'

Nausea climbed to her throat.

'The forests are full of old bones,' he said. 'No one ever gives them a second glance. But the skull, hands and feet have to be dealt with separately – they're too recognizable. She's resting peacefully in a forest glade.'

Annika threw up over the table, a brown sludge of cappuccino from the discount store's café. The man watched her quietly.

'It's a shame you didn't get in touch sooner. You could have said goodbye. Well, the two of you can share your eternal rest.'

He stood up and went to the suitcase in the corner. It wasn't locked, and just had the usual catches on it. He opened it, revealing its contents.

It was full of tools. Pliers of various sizes, two large hammers, sharp awls, metal wire, a saw, a long, thin knife and a chisel.

'Do you recognize this?' he asked Annika, holding up a chrome-plated pipe, thirty centimetres long, with a red hook at one end.

Instead of waiting for an answer, he took out a round blue capsule, which he attached to one end of the pipe. 'It's a bolt gun,' he said. 'Also known as a slaughterhouse stun gun. This blue cartridge can handle a large ox. She didn't suffer. Death is instantaneous.'

She stared at the pipe. *A slaughterhouse stun gun.* A tool used to kill livestock.

'It was a miscalculation that you two sisters didn't get on,' the man said, polishing the implement.

She glanced at the window again, an old-fashioned mullion window: could she throw herself through it? Or was the wooden frame too strong?

'Up in Vidsel, people stick together. Being apart causes us pain. We can't be shut in, we're born to be free . . .'

There was a noise on the other side of the cottage wall, and Annika started. Footsteps through mud? Ivar Berglund didn't appear to have heard anything. Had she imagined it?

A moment later there was a knock at the door.

'Birgitta? Are you in there? Annika?'

It was Steven. Berglund glanced towards the hall with interest.

'Get out of here!' Annika yelled, but her voice was so hoarse that it came out as a hiss. 'Run! Get the police!'

'Annika? I got your text. Is Birgitta here?'

Ivar Berglund walked towards the door. Fury raged through Annika, like a blue flame, and she screamed so hard her voice cracked: 'Birgitta's dead! Get the hell out of here!'

'Are you okay, Annika?'

Ivar Berglund, or his brother, took the key out of his trouser pocket and opened the door.

'Welcome,' he said. 'Come in!'

'Don't come in!' Annika shouted.

Behind Berglund's head she could see Steven's worried face.

'What's going on?'

'He's mad! He's killed Birgitta!'

Steven stepped into the narrow hall, pushed Berglund aside and looked anxiously at Annika. 'Are you all right?' he said. 'Has he hurt you?'

Annika started to cry. 'Steven,' she said. 'You shouldn't have come here.'

'Of course I should,' he said, and turned to Berglund.

Berglund took a step towards them, raised the bolt gun and aimed it at Steven's neck. For a dazed moment, she was back in the blast furnace. Her cat was flying through the air, its guts unravelling from its split abdomen. The world turned red and she grabbed the rusty iron pipe. No, it wasn't an iron pipe but a hammer from the old suitcase. Ivar Berglund pressed the murder weapon hard against Steven's forehead, he screamed, then there was a bang. Berglund had fired. With both hands round the heavy shaft, Annika swung the hammer towards the back of Berglund's head. Steven sank to the floor in front of her, his eyes open, a round hole in his forehead. Berglund swung round and looked at her, and she hit him hard in the temple with the hammer. The killer's knees buckled and his eyes rolled back. She raised the hammer again. Flakes of rust scratched her palms. She wanted to hit him and hit him and hit him until all the life ran out of him.

Then you'll have to live with that.

She stopped herself mid-swing.

Berglund groaned. The cat was dead. There was no way to put his guts back into his body.

She stumbled over to the suitcase and grabbed the wire. Berglund was heavy. He had fallen on to his stomach with his hands at his sides. She bound them together behind his back with the wire, then opened the hatch to the cellar. With sweat dripping into her eyes she dragged him to the hole, pushed his feet over the edge, dropped his legs into the darkness, then shoved his unconscious body into the cellar. She heard him whimper – he had survived the fall. She closed the hatch and sank on to the floor beside Steven.

He was dead. Blood and brain tissue were seeping from the hole in his forehead.

She grabbed hold of his heavy body, and, surrounded by a cloud of tears, pulled him towards her on top of the hatch. She weighed fifty kilos, Steven almost a hundred: no matter how strong Ivar Berglund was, he couldn't lift one hundred and fifty kilos, with his hands tied behind his back and a fractured skull.

She sat with Steven in her arms, rocking him and sobbing. He hadn't needed to come in, he could have stayed outside. She sang a lullaby as she stroked his hair.

The light became sharper, the sun broke through the clouds, and a ray of light reflected off the shiny tools and on to the black iron stove.

She sang until she ran out of words and silence swirled around the lonely, sunlit dust.

Then she pulled her mobile phone from her back pocket and called the police.

EPILOGUE

SIX MONTHS LATER
WEDNESDAY, 16 DECEMBER

Thomas sat on the sofa in the living room with a glass of red wine in his hand (the right one, his only one) a few minutes before the interview started.

He didn't have any interest in watching it, but it had been a hectic day at work and he needed to unwind. Some entertainment from the state-funded television channel was all he could handle.

He took a large sip of wine, a Rioja from 2004, a fine vintage. He was the sort of person who appreciated things like that and, considering his employment situation, he was owed a reward in the middle of the working week. The new government was still more confused than was strictly permissible, and the situation for all the civil servants at Rosenbad was fluid, but that would settle down. People like him, responsible for their own inquiries, quickly found themselves in key positions within the new organization. He had already had two productive meetings with the new minister, the former hairdresser from Norrland, who knew nothing about the law but knew how to listen to her colleagues and take advantage of their insights.

The opening titles of the interview programme started and he took another large gulp of wine, then put the glass down. He stretched out on the sofa, more than happy to be on his own in the apartment. It was always wonderful when his fiancée was out at the estate and he had the overnight flat to himself.

As per the usual format of the programme, the subject of the interview was shown in her normal working environment: there she was, walking through the newsroom, into a glass room, closing the door behind her. On the wall behind her desk hung an ugly portrait in brightly coloured pastels of an old man.

His pulse-rate increased. He hadn't seen her for a long time, not since Birgitta's funeral. Had she put on weight?

'Annika Halenius, editor-in-chief of the *Evening Post* media group, welcome to the programme.'

The interviewer, a middle-aged woman who was trying to look younger, appeared on the screen and welcomed the viewers, then turned to her guest.

'Thanks very much,' his former wife said on screen. She was heavily made up, and someone had actually combed her hair.

He reached for his glass, his hand trembling slightly, and drank what was left in it. Should he get himself a top-up straight away, or wait a bit?

The presenter crossed her legs and glanced down at

her notes, then looked up at Annika again. (She hadn't taken *his* name when they'd got married. Oh, no.)

'Today is an historic day,' the woman said. 'Today sees the publication of the final print edition of the *Evening Post*, a newspaper for whose publication you've been legally responsible for four months. As I understand it, it's been something of a turbulent time.'

'I can't disagree with that,' Annika said, with a faint smile, the one that indicated she wasn't at all happy.

'But doesn't this mean the end of serious journalism, abandoning the print edition?'

He looked carefully at his ex-wife. He probably knew her better than anyone else did, and he could see that she was struggling to be polite. She really wasn't suited to this sort of interview situation.

'We've decided to focus on the content, rather than allow ourselves to be limited by the format,' Annika said. 'You don't necessarily have to kill trees to do good journalism. Quite the contrary. Once a piece of news has been printed on paper and distributed to the reader, it is no longer news. But paper is good for longer texts, in-depth analysis and reportage, so we're focusing hard on our printed weekend magazine, which . . .'

He stood up and went out into the kitchen. He could manage without hearing her boast about her job. The bottle of wine was standing on the worktop: he could see the label reflected in the black granite.

The new kitchen was a great success, modern yet

timeless, architect-designed and made to measure from stone, brushed steel and oak.

He took a deep breath to calm himself. There was no reason to be annoyed. The stone felt cold and hard under his good hand. He took the bottle back into the sitting room with him.

'A hundred *posts* had to go, not a hundred people,' Annika was saying on the screen. 'That's a crucial difference. We were able to meet the reduction partly through retirement and voluntary redundancies, but of course it was very hard for the people for whom there wasn't room in the new organization.'

Were they still talking about her tedious job?

Thomas poured more wine into his glass. It was the larger sort, the ones Sophia thought so vulgar, but he liked the big bowls: they felt generous, and could hold almost an entire bottle.

'It's been said that you went in pretty hard right from the outset . . . Starting by closing down the print edition didn't make you very popular.'

Annika smiled that crooked smile again. 'I wasn't very popular before that either,' she said, picking up the glass of water from the table in front of her. She took a sip.

'Can you understand why your predecessor in the role, Anders Schyman, chose to resign in protest at the cuts?'

Thomas drank some more of his wine and felt the warmth spread through his body. Strangely, he could feel the hook tingling as well, and wondered what that might be called: phantom intoxication?

'I worked with Anders Schyman for fifteen years, and have the greatest respect for him. His is an incredibly important voice in the debate about the future of the media, and he'll do an excellent job as professor at the Institute for Media and Communication.'

His head began to swim. The wine was almost gone. Maybe he should open another bottle.

The interviewer leaned forward in her chair, as though she wanted to get closer to her subject. 'You have young children,' she said, 'and your husband has just been appointed director general of the Council for Crime Prevention. You must have hesitated before agreeing to take on such a demanding job?'

Ah, they were getting to the good bit at last, all the juicy details. Annika looked distinctly uncomfortable, didn't she?

'On the contrary,' she said, sounding almost cheerful. 'I applied for the job, and fought to get it.'

Her hair was different – had she had it cut? Or was it just that it had been sorted out properly for once?

'You fought to get it? How do you mean?'

'I fought to make the board understand that it would be a huge mistake to bring in a high-profile candidate from outside. The challenges facing the evening papers are unique, and bringing in someone with a fancy name wouldn't help solve them.'

'So why you, specifically?'

'I had the necessary professional experience to take on this challenge, I know the organization inside out, and eventually I received the backing of the board. I was given the choice of either taking on the responsibility myself or finding someone else to do it. There was also a sense of duty. Not just towards the paper and the other staff, but . . . well, this sounds horribly clichéd, but towards myself as well.'

'You never had any doubts?'

'The decision to stop publishing the print edition had already been taken, and the cutbacks were going to be implemented regardless of what I or anyone else thought. It would have been much easier to sit on the sidelines and complain about developments in the media.'

He couldn't sit there listening to this, his ex-wife giving a pompous speech about her responsibilities and sacrifices. He drank the last of the wine and heaved himself off the sofa. He'd had more than enough experience of the way she dealt with her responsibilities, how loyal she was, and how much she cared about other people.

He hit the hook on the door frame as he went into the kitchen, hard, and felt his upper arm quiver.

They had invested in a wine fridge when they'd renovated the kitchen, an exclusive (and reassuringly expensive) affair that lent a touch of elegance to the whole kitchen. The door opened with a sigh as he heard Annika laugh on television. He spun the rack and made his selection: a cheap Shiraz from South Africa, a full-bodied wine to match the television interview.

He closed the door and checked the temperature on the thermostat: thirteen degrees, perfect.

'Did you have any particular demands when you accepted the job?' the interviewer asked, in the sitting room.

'Yes, I did, actually,' he heard Annika reply. 'I insisted on Berit Hamrin agreeing to be deputy editor, as well as acting publisher.'

Next to the wine fridge, they had mounted a corkscrew on the wall so he could remove the corks with just one hand. He hadn't quite got the knack yet, and the bottle slipped a few times before he got it into the right place. He was a bit sweaty and slightly out of breath when the cork finally popped out, and a few drops of wine landed on his shirt. He rubbed them with the hook as tears welled in his eyes.

Maybe he shouldn't drink any more: it left him unbalanced and clumsy, and that wasn't what he was like.

After a moment's hesitation, he took the bottle into the sitting room with him anyway, but he certainly wasn't going to drink it all.

'Arne and Ivar Berglund were sentenced to life imprisonment,' the interviewer was saying, as Thomas sat down on the sofa. 'Does that feel like a victory?'

'Not at all. There are no winners here.'

'Your sister's remains were found in woodland in Norrbotten this summer, together with those of eight other missing people, among them Viola Söderland. Have you really been able to be objective in your coverage of these events?'

'Responsibility for our coverage of Arne and Ivar

Berglund has rested with our head of news, Patrik Nilsson, and he's done an excellent job.'

'But the fact that the prosecutor-general has allowed appeals to be raised in four of the five convictions against Gustaf Holmerud has to be seen as a personal triumph for you?'

Annika looked thoughtful, a miracle of studied modesty. 'Not really,' she said. 'For me, personally, it was more important that the murder of Josefin Liljeberg was finally solved.'

'Why?'

'She deserved justice. I wrote about her during my first summer as a temp on the newspaper, and it was very important to me that the witnesses chose to speak out and give her some form of redress.'

'Do you know what made the witnesses change their minds? To step forward and tell the truth?'

Annika lowered her gaze. 'Perhaps their lies had been tormenting them for a long time. But that's just speculation. They didn't give any explanation during the trial, and none of them has volunteered to be interviewed by the media.' She looked up at the presenter. 'Carrying guilt and secrets doesn't necessarily get easier over the years,' she said. 'Quite the reverse, actually. It can become unbearable, and then you have to do something about it.'

His mobile buzzed, a message on Viber from Sophia: *Hello, darling, are you watching the interview?*

He put the phone down on his thigh as he replied – he had developed a technique that allowed him to send messages with just one hand. *Haven't got time, working. Might catch up online later. See you tomorrow! Big kiss!*

She wouldn't contact him again that evening: she respected his work.

The presenter tilted her head on the screen. 'Your mother agreed to be interviewed after your sister's death. She said it was your fault that Birgitta was murdered. How is your relationship now? Has there been any reconciliation?'

The set of Annika's mouth looked rather tense now, didn't it? 'Naturally everyone was incredibly shocked and upset after the murders of my sister and brother-in-law. My mother and Birgitta were extremely close to each other so, under the circumstances, perhaps it isn't strange that you say things in the heat of the moment that you don't really mean.'

Thomas snorted loudly. He didn't have much time for Annika's lush of a mother. There was the old saying, of course: *If you want to know what your wife will look like in thirty years' time, just look at her mother!*

He chuckled to himself. Maybe Jimmy Halenius should have gone to see Barbro in Tattarbacken before he proposed. He and Annika had got married on the jetty of that old cottage they'd managed to rent from the Harpsund estate. The whole thing stank of corruption and nepotism.

'What about the adoption of your niece? Has that been formalized now?'

'The case is with the Stockholm District Court. We're hoping it will be decided before the end of the year.'

'How has she settled in with you?'

Annika folded her arms. 'Very well.'

She evidently didn't want to talk about Birgitta's daughter. Ellen, on the other hand, wouldn't stop talking about Diny, how she, Serena and Diny had been given the big bedroom so all the girls could sleep together, how they had pictures of Diny's mummy and daddy on the fridge and by Diny's bed, but Diny hardly ever talked about them now, and how lovely it was that Diny had come to live with them.

He let his head fall back against the cushion and the voices from the television sank to a murmur . . . and the future? . . . the development of the media . . . Yes, I . . . We've heard that you're going to be taking six months off . . . Yes, well, I'm pregnant . . .

He sat bolt upright. Had he heard right?

'Congratulations,' the presenter said. 'When are you due?'

He stared at her on the screen. *Say it isn't true, that it was a misunderstanding.*

'In the spring.'

He reached for the remote and switched off the television. The room fell dark, and the silence was deafening. It crackled against his eardrums like rifle-fire.

I'm pregnant.

There was some frost on the skylight facing the courtyard. It would be cold later that night. Down in the street he heard a car start up and drive away; the radiators were singing, and the hand he no longer had itched.

He was *Someone.*

The new minister had the sense to appreciate the contribution he was making at work. She had listened seriously and attentively when he explained why the boundary for coercive measures regarding people who incited hatred online ought to be set at four years, the same as bugging. He had prepared her thoroughly for the protests that would arise when the proposed legislation was sent out for consultation: they would complain noisily that the law would be ineffective, that it would be impossible for the police to investigate crimes, but it was important to stick to the spirit of the inquiry and not compromise legal rectitude.

And the minister had pledged to push the legislation through, no matter what resistance it met. At ten the following morning he was due to present the results of his inquiry at a cabinet meeting. The press room at Rosenbad had been booked, and his article for *Dagens Nyheter* had been checked and passed for publication.

And that weekend he would be taking his hunting exam. He had studied the theory and learned to shoot at elk-shaped targets on the estate, with the barrel resting on the hook, his forefinger on the cold trigger.

In the spring.

He pulled his laptop towards him from the side-table and logged in.

Gregorius had a thing or two to say about the state of things.

Author's Acknowledgements

First of all, a declaration: Annika Bengtzon lives in an alternative reality, and her years don't necessarily correspond to ours.

The descriptions of Hälleforsnäs and its industrial history are based upon real places and events, but all characters and many of the incidents related in this novel are an expression of the author's artistic licence.

In order to depict the future of the media industry I have taken inspiration from, among others, a radio interview with Casten Almqvist on the *Ekot* news programme of 23 August 2014, Jan Scherman's book *Räkna med känslorna* ('Count on Emotion'), Thomas Mattsson's blog for *Expressen.se*, and Jan Hellin's Sunday columns for *Aftonbladet.se*.

The online post attributed to Gregorius and the four comments by his admirers are genuine, and were published anonymously on Swedish internet sites. The post dated 3 June, 16.53, was tried and dismissed in a Swedish court. The comments were all written by people who applied for politically sensitive posts in Sweden. Their identities were made public after a series of revelations by the *Expressen* newspaper in collaboration with Researchgruppen, a network of freelance journalists.

Berit and Annika's discussion about identity was inspired by an article by Håkan Lindgren in *Svenska Dagbladet*, published 13 June 2014.

Thank you to:

Matilda Johansson, a detective inspector at the NOA (Nationella Operativa Avdelningen, National Operational Department, formerly the National Crime Unit) in Stockholm, for help with police scenarios, regulations and interview routines.

Varg Gyllander, head of information at Stockholm Police, Christina Ullsten, a detective inspector at the NOA, and Lars Byström, a superintendent for the Stockholm Regional Crime Unit, for help with routines and facts about investigations into missing people.

Håkan Kvarnström, head of security at Telia Sonera, for technical details about tracing mobile phones.

Agneta Johansson, population registrar with the Tax Office, for help with historical information held in public databases in Sweden.

Dr Katarina Görts Öberg, psychologist, for help with descriptions of panic attacks and their treatment.

Mikael Aspeborg, Axel Aspeborg, Amanda Aspeborg for suggestions and proofreading. Annika Marklund and Ronnie Sandahl for conversations about the digital future of the media.

Everyone at my publishers in Sweden, Piratförlaget.

Thomas Bodström, lawyer, for editorial advice, fact-checking and discussions about plausible police and legal scenarios, government inquiries, and more.

And finally: Tove Alsterdal, author and dramatist, who has been my editor and mainstay throughout the entire series of novels about Annika Bengtzon. I am so incredibly pleased and grateful that you've wanted to come with me on this eighteen-year-long journey.

Any errors are entirely intentional.